Heather Gudenkauf

One Breath Away

An ordinary school day

A world torn apart

A *NEW YORK TIMES* BESTSELLER

Heather Gudenkauf is the critically acclaimed author of the *New York Times* bestselling novels *The Weight of Silence* and *These Things Hidden*. Her debut novel, *The Weight of Silence*, was picked for *The TV Bookclub*. She lives in Iowa with her family.

Read more about Heather and her novels at www.HeatherGudenkauf.com

Praise for Heather Gudenkauf

'Brilliantly constructed, this will have you gripped until the last page…'
Closer

'Deeply moving and lyrical…it will haunt you all summer.'
Company

5 stars 'Gripping and moving'
Heat

'Her technique is faultless, sparse and simple and is a master-class in how to construct a thriller… A memorable read… A technical triumph.'
Sunday Express

'It's totally gripping…'
Marie Claire

'Tension builds as family secrets tumble from the closet.'
Woman & Home

'This has all the ingredients of a Jodi Picoult novel.'
Waterstones Books Quarterly

'Set to become a book group staple'
The Guardian

'A skilfully woven thriller that will keep you hooked to the end'
Choice magazine

Heather Gudenkauf

One Breath Away

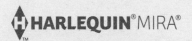
HARLEQUIN®MIRA®

Harlequin MIRA is a registered trademark of Harlequin Enterprises Limited, used under licence.

Published in Great Britain 2014
by Harlequin MIRA, an imprint of Harlequin (UK) Limited,
Eton House, 18-24 Paradise Road,
Richmond, Surrey, TW9 1SR

© Heather Gudenkauf 2012

ISBN 978 1 848 45132 2

58-0712

Harlequin's policy is to use papers that are natural, renewable and recyclable products and made from wood grown in sustainable forests. The logging and manufacturing processes conform to the legal environmental regulations of the country of origin.

Printed and bound by
CPI Group (UK) Ltd, Croydon, CR0 4YY

Also available from **Heather Gudenkauf**

THE WEIGHT OF SILENCE
THESE THINGS HIDDEN
ONE BREATH AWAY
LITTLE MERCIES
LITTLE LIES (ebook novella)

For Alex, Anna and Grace
~*My three wishes*

Holly

I'm in that lovely space between consciousness and sleep. I feel no pain thanks to the morphine pump and I can almost believe that the muscles, tendons and skin of my left arm have knitted themselves back together, leaving my skin smooth and pale. My curly brown hair once again falls softly down my back, my favorite earrings dangle from my ears and I can lift both sides of my mouth in a wide smile without much pain at the thought of my children. Yes, drugs are a wonderful thing. But the problem is that while the carefully prescribed and doled-out narcotics by the nurses wonderfully dull the edges of this nightmare, I know that soon enough this woozy, pleasant feeling will fall away and all that I will be left with is pain and the knowledge that Augie and P.J. are thousands of miles away from me. Sent away to the place where I grew up, the town I swore I would never return to, the house I swore I would never again step into, to the man I never wanted them to meet.

The tinny melody of the ringtone that Augie, my thirteen-year-old daughter, programmed into my cell phone is pulling me from my sleep. I open one eye, the one that isn't covered with a thick ointment and crusted shut, and call out for my mother, who must have stepped out of the room. I reach for the phone that is sitting on the tray table at the side of my bed and the nerve endings in my bandaged left arm scream in protest at the movement. I carefully shift my body to pick up the phone with my good hand and press the phone to my remaining ear.

"Hello." The word comes out half-formed, breathless and scratchy, as if my lungs were still filled with smoke.

"Mom?" Augie's voice is quavery, unsure. Not sounding like my daughter at all. Augie is confident, smart, a take-charge, *no one is ever going to walk all over me* kind of girl.

"Augie? What's the matter?" I try to blink the fuzziness of the morphine away; my tongue is dry and sticks to the roof of my mouth. I want to take a sip of water from the glass sitting on my tray, but my one working hand holds the phone. The other lies useless at my side. "Are you okay? Where are you?"

There are a few seconds of quiet and then Augie continues. "I love you, Mom," she says in a whisper that ends in quiet sobs.

I sit up straight in my bed, wide awake now. Pain shoots through my bandaged arm and up the side of my neck and face. "Augie, what's the matter?"

"I'm at school." She is crying in that way she has when she is doing her damnedest not to. I can picture her, head down, her long brown hair falling around her face, her eyes squeezed shut in determination to keep the tears from falling, her breath filling my ear with short, shallow puffs. "He has a gun. He has P.J. and he has a gun."

"Who has P.J.?" Terror clutches at my chest. "Tell me, Augie, where are you? Who has a gun?"

"I'm in a closet. He put me in a closet."

My mind is spinning. Who could be doing this? Who would do this to my children? "Hang up," I tell her. "Hang up and call 9-1-1 right now, Augie. Then call me back. Can you do that?" I hear her sniffles. "Augie," I say again, more sharply. "Can you do that?"

"Yeah," she finally says. "I love you, Mom," she says softly.

"I love you, too." My eyes fill with tears and I can feel the moisture pool beneath the bandages that cover my injured eye.

I wait for Augie to disconnect when I hear three quick shots, followed by two more and Augie's piercing screams.

I feel the bandages that cover the left side of my face peel away, my own screams loosening the adhesive holding them in place; I feel the fragile, newly grafted skin begin to unravel. I am scarcely aware of the nurses and my mother rushing to my side, tearing the phone from my grasp.

Augie

My pants are still damp from when Noah Plum pushed me off the shoveled sidewalk into a snow-bank after we got off the bus and were on our way into school this morning. Noah Plum is the biggest asshole in eighth grade but for some reason I'm the only one who has figured this out and I've only lived here for eight weeks and everyone else has lived here for their entire lives. Except for maybe Milana Nevara, whose dad is from Mexico and is the town veterinarian. But she moved here when she was two so she may as well have been born here, anyway.

The classroom is freezing and my fingers are numb with the cold. Mr. Ellery says it's because it is not supposed to be below zero at the end of March and the boiler has been put out to pasture. Mr. Ellery, my teacher and one of the only good things about this school, is sitting at his desk grading papers. Everyone, except Noah, of course, is writing in their note-books. Each day after lunch we start class with journal time

and we can write about anything we want to during the first
ten minutes of class. Mr. Ellery said we could even write the
same word over and over for the entire time and Noah asked,
"What if it's a bad word?"

"Knock yourself out," Mr. Ellery said, and everyone
laughed. Mr. Ellery always gives time for people to read what
they've written out loud if they'd like to. I've never shared.
No way I'm going to let these morons know what I'm thinking. I've read *Harriet the Spy* and I keep my notebook with me
all the time. Never let it out of my sight.

In my old school in Arizona, there were over two hundred
eighth graders in my grade and we had different teachers for
each subject. In Broken Branch there are only twenty-two of
us so we have Mr. Ellery for just about every subject. Mr. Ellery, besides being really cute, is the absolutely best teacher
I've ever had. He's funny, but never makes fun of anyone and
isn't sarcastic like some teachers think is so hilarious. He also
doesn't let people get away with making crap out of anyone.
All he has to do is stare at the person and they shut up. Even
Noah Plum.

Mr. Ellery always writes a journal prompt on the dry erase
board in case we can't think of what to write about. Today he
has written "During spring break I am going to…"

Even Mr. Ellery's stare doesn't work today; everyone is
whispering and smiling because they are excited about vacation. "All right, folks," Mr. Ellery says. "Get down to work
and if we have some time left over we'll play Pictionary."

"Yesss!" the kids around me hiss. Great. I open my notebook to the next clean page and begin writing.

"During spring break we're going to fly back to Arizona
to see our mother." The only sounds in the classroom are the
scratch of pencils on paper and Erika's annoying sniffles; she
always has a runny nose and gets up twenty times a day to get

a tissue. "I don't care if I ever see snow or cows ever again. I don't care if I ever see my grandfather again." I am hoping with all my might that instead of coming back to Broken Branch after spring break, my mother will be well enough for us to come home. My grandfather tells us this isn't going to happen. My mother is far from being able to come home from the hospital. My mom will be in Arizona until she is out of the hospital and well enough to get on a plane and come here so Grandma and Grandpa, who I met for the first time ever a couple months ago, can take care of all of us. But it doesn't matter what my grandpa says—after spring break, I am not coming back to Broken Branch.

A sharp crack, like a branch snapped in half during an ice storm, makes me look up from my notebook. Mr. Ellery hears it, too, and stands up from behind his desk and walks to the classroom door, steps into the hallway and comes back in shrugging his shoulders. "Looks like someone broke a window at the end of the hallway. I'm going to go check. You guys stay in your seats. I'll be right back."

Before he can even leave the classroom the shaky voice of Mrs. Lowell, the school secretary, comes on the intercom. "Teachers, this is a Code Red Lockdown. Go to your safe place."

A snort comes from Noah. "Go to your safe place," he says, mimicking Mrs. Lowell. No one else says a thing and we all stare at Mr. Ellery, waiting for him to tell us what to do next. I haven't been here long enough to know what a Code Red Lockdown is. But it can't be good.

Mrs. Oliver

The morning the man with the gun walked into Evelyn Oliver's classroom, she was wearing two items she had vowed during her forty-three-year career as a teacher never to wear. Denim and rhinestones. Mrs. Oliver was a firm believer that a teacher should look like a teacher. Well-groomed, blouses with collars, skirts and pantsuits crisply ironed, dress shoes polished. None of that nonsense younger teachers wore these days. Miniskirts, tennis shoes, plunging necklines. Tattoos, for goodness' sake. For instance, Mr. Ellery, the young eighth-grade teacher, had a tattoo on his right arm. A series of bold black slashes and swoops that Mrs. Oliver recognized as Asian in origin. "It means *teacher* in Chinese," Mr. Ellery, wearing a sleeveless T-shirt, told her after, embarrassingly, he caught her staring at his deltoid muscle one stifling-hot August afternoon during in-service week when all the teachers were preparing their classrooms for the school year. Mrs. Oliver sniffed in disapproval, but really she couldn't help but wonder how painful it must be to have someone precisely and methodically inject ink into one's skin.

Casual Fridays were the worst, with teachers, even the older ones, wearing denim and sweatshirts emblazoned with the school name and logo—the Broken Branch Consolidated School Hornets.

But on this unusually bitter March day, the last day school was in session before spring break, Mrs. Oliver had on the denim jumper she now knew she was going to die while wearing. Shameful, she thought, after all these years of razor-sharp pleats and itchy support hose.

Last week, after all the other third graders had left for the day, Mrs. Oliver had tentatively opened the crumpled striped pink-and-yellow gift bag handed to her by Charlotte, a skinny, disheveled eight-year-old with shoulder-length, burnished-black hair that chronically housed a persistent family of lice.

"What's this, Charlotte?" Mrs. Oliver asked in surprise. "My birthday isn't until this summer."

"I know," Charlotte answered with a gap-toothed grin. "But my mom and me thought you'd get more use out of it if I gave it to you now."

Mrs. Oliver expected to find an apple-scented candle or homemade cookies or a hand-painted birdhouse inside, but instead pulled out a denim stone-washed jumper with rhinestones painstakingly arranged in the shape of a rainbow twinkling up at her. Charlotte looked expectantly up at Mrs. Oliver through the veil of bangs that covered her normally mischievous gray eyes.

"I Bedazzled it myself. Mostly," Charlotte explained. "My mom helped with the rainbow." She placed a grubby finger on the colorful arch. "Roy V. Big. Red, orange, yellow, violet, blue, indigo, green. Just like you said." Charlotte smiled brightly, showing her small, even baby teeth, still all intact.

Mrs. Oliver didn't have the heart to tell Charlotte that the correct mnemonic for remembering the colors in the rainbow was Roy G. Biv, but took comfort in that fact that she at least knew all the colors of the rainbow if not the proper order. "It's lovely, Charlotte," Mrs. Oliver said, holding the dress in front of her. "I can tell you worked hard on it."

"I did," Charlotte said solemnly. "For two weeks. I was going to Bedazzle a birthday cake on the front but then my mom said you might wear it more if it wasn't so holiday-ish. I almost ran out of beads. My little brother thought they were Skittles."

"I will certainly get a lot of wear out of it. Thank you, Charlotte." Mrs. Oliver reached over to pat Charlotte on the shoulder and Charlotte immediately leaned in and wrapped her arms around Mrs. Oliver's thick middle, pressing her face into the buttons of her starched white blouse. Mrs. Oliver felt a tickle beneath her iron-gray hair and resisted the urge to scratch.

It was Mrs. Oliver's husband, Cal, who had convinced her to wear the dress. "What can it hurt?" he asked just this morning when he caught her standing in front of her open closet, looking at the jumper garishly glaring right back at her.

"I don't wear denim to school, and I'm certainly not going to start wearing it just before I retire," she said, not looking him in the eye, remembering how Charlotte had rushed eagerly into the classroom at the beginning of the week to see if she was wearing the dress.

"She worked on it for two weeks," Cal reminded her at the breakfast table.

"It's not professional," she snapped, thinking of how on each passing day this week, Charlotte's shoulders wilted more and more as she entered the room to find her teacher wearing her typical wool-blend slacks, blouse and cardigan.

"Her fingers *bled,*" Cal said through a mouthful of oatmeal.

"It's supposed to be ten below outside today. It's too cold to wear a dress," Mrs. Oliver told her husband, miserably picturing how Charlotte wouldn't even look her way yesterday, defiantly pursing her lips and refusing to answer any questions directed at her.

"Wear long johns and a turtleneck underneath," her husband said mildly, coming up behind her and kissing her on the neck in the way that even after forty-five years of marriage caused her to shiver deliciously.

Because he was right—Cal was always right—she had brushed him away in irritation and told him she was going to be late for school if she didn't get dressed right then. Wearing the jumper, she left him sitting at the kitchen table finishing his oatmeal, drinking coffee and reading the newspaper. She hadn't told him she loved him, she hadn't kissed his wrinkled cheek in goodbye. "Don't forget to plug in the Crock-Pot," she called as she stepped outside into the soft gray morning. The sun hadn't emerged yet, but it was the warmest it would be that day, the temperature tumbling with each passing hour. As she climbed into her car to make the twenty-five-minute drive from her home in Dalsing to the school in Broken Branch, she didn't realize it could be the last time she made that journey.

It was worth it, she supposed, after seeing Charlotte's face transform from jaded disappointment to pure joy when she saw that Mrs. Oliver was actually wearing the dress. Of course Cal was right. Wearing the impractical, gaudy thing wouldn't hurt anything; she'd had to suffer the raised eyebrows in the teacher's lounge, but that was nothing new. And it obviously had meant a lot to Charlotte, who was now cowering in her desk along with fifteen other third graders, gaping up at the man with the gun. At least, Mrs. Oliver thought, shocking herself with the inappropriateness of the idea, if he shot her in the chest, she couldn't be buried in the damn thing.

Meg

I'm trying to figure out what I'm going to do with all my free time for the next four days as I drive idly around Broken Branch in my squad car. This will be the first year that I won't have Maria with me for spring break. By the looks of things, spring doesn't seem like it will be appearing any time soon, even though it officially arrived two days earlier.

By rights, Tim should be able to have Maria this vacation; she's spent the past two with me. But I had it all planned out for tomorrow, my day off. We were going to bake Dutch letters, flaky almond-flavored cookies, the one family tradition I've kept from when I was young. Afterward we were going to pitch a tent and have an old-fashioned campout in the living room. Then we were going to take advantage of the freak snow-storm to go snowshoeing at the bottom of Ox-eye Bluff with hot chocolate and marshmallows and oyster chowder when we got home. I even persuaded Kevin Jarrow, the part-timer on our police force, to pick up my Saturday shift so I could spend it with Maria. But this time Tim insisted. He finally scored a full five days off from his job as an EMT in Waterloo, where we both grew up.

"Listen, Meg," he said when he called me the day before yesterday. "I don't ask for much, but I really want Maria this school break...."

"She's not an item on your grocery list," I said hotly. "I thought we had this all figured out."

"*You* had it all figured out," he said. Which was true. "I want to spend a few days with her and I don't think there's anything unreasonable about that."

"Where did this suddenly come from?" I asked.

"Hey, I'll take any minute I can get with Maria and you know it. Besides, you've had her the past two holidays." He was getting angry now. I imagined him sitting in the duplex we once shared, rubbing his forehead the way he did when he was frustrated.

"I know," I said softly. "I just had it all planned out."

"You could always come spend some of the time with us," he said cautiously. I sighed. I was too tired to have this conversation. "Meg, you know I never did the things you thought I did." Here we go, I thought. Every few months Tim insists that he didn't have the affair with his coworker, that she was an unstable liar who had wanted something more, but whom he had rebuffed. Some days I half believe him. This isn't one of those days.

"You can pick her up on Wednesday after school," I told him.

"I was hoping tomorrow, after I get done with work. Around noon."

"She'll miss her last day of school before vacation. That's when they do all the fun things." It sounded lame, I know, but it was all I had.

"Meg," he said in that way he has. "Meg, please..."

"Fine," I snapped.

So yesterday I said goodbye to my beautiful, funny, sweet, perfect seven-year-old daughter. "I'll call you every day," I promised her, feeling like I was saying goodbye forever. "Twice."

"Bye, Mom," she said, swiping a quick kiss across my cheek before climbing into Tim's car.

"If it hasn't all melted, we'll go snowshoeing when you get back," I called after her.

"So, we'll be at my folks tomorrow night for dinner and at my sister's on Sunday." His face turned serious. "I ran into your mom last week."

"Oh," I said as if I didn't care.

"Yeah, they'd really like to see Maria."

"I bet they would," I grumbled.

"Is it okay if I take her over to see them?"

I shrugged. "I guess." My parents weren't bad people, just not particularly good people. "Promise me you won't leave her at the trailer, it's a death trap. And make sure Travis isn't hanging around when you visit." My brother, Travis, is one of the main reasons I became a police officer. Growing up he made my parents' lives miserable and mine pure hell. It seemed like every week a police officer was at the door of our trailer, Travis in tow. They gave him more than enough chances to get his shit together and he blew it time and time again. It wasn't until the summer I was thirteen and Travis was sixteen, when he threatened my father with a kitchen knife, smacked my mother across the face and ripped out a chunk of my hair as I tried to pull him away from them, that the police finally got serious.

"What do you want to do?" Officer Stepanich, a frequent visitor to our home, asked wearily. His young female partner,

Officer Demelo, stood by silently, taking in the broken glass, the knocked-over chairs, the bald spot on the top of my head. Welcome to our lovely home, I wanted to say, but instead my face burned with shame.

Fully expecting my parents to finally say enough is enough and have Travis's ass arrested for assault, they once again refused to press charges.

"What do you want to do?" Officer Demelo asked, and I looked up in surprise when I realized she was talking to me and only me.

"Now, now," Officer Stepanich said, "this is really a parent decision."

"I don't think that wad of hair on the floor got there by itself and I can't imagine that Meg here pulled it out of her own head," Officer Demelo said, her eyes never leaving mine. I was surprised she remembered my name and even more impressed that she ignored the obviously senior officer's lead. "Let's see what she wants to do," Officer Demelo insisted.

Travis smirked. He was six inches taller and about eighty pounds heavier than I was, but in that moment, knowing that only an ignorant coward would beat on his family the way he did, I felt stronger, more powerful. He thought he was invincible. But in that sliver of a moment, I knew that there was a way out for our family.

"I want to press charges," I said, speaking only to Officer Demelo, who didn't look much older than I was, but carried herself with a confidence I wanted for myself.

"You sure that's what you want to do?" Officer Stepanich asked.

"Yes," I said firmly. "I do." Officer Stepanich turned to my parents, who looked bewildered but nodded their agreement. They took Travis away in handcuffs. He came back home a few days later. I expected him to exact some kind of revenge upon me, but he kept his distance, didn't lay a hand on me. It didn't keep him out of trouble, though. Over the years he's been in and out of jail, most recently for drug possession. That arrest twenty years ago didn't change Travis, but in my mind it saved my life.

"Travis will get nowhere near Maria," Tim promised. He looked as if he'd like to say more, then settled on, "Talk to you later, Meg." He drove away with Maria waving happily goodbye.

My windshield wipers can barely keep up with the thick snow that is falling. Great, I think. I'll be shoveling for hours after I end my ten-hour shift at three o'clock. I debate whether to still make the Dutch letters tomorrow and decide to ditch that idea; instead, I'll sleep in, watch TV, pick up a pizza from Casey's and feel sorry for myself.

I feel my phone vibrate in my coat pocket. I peek at the display thinking it might be Maria. Stuart. Shit. I stuff my phone back into my coat. Stuart, a newspaper reporter who wrote for the *Des Moines Observer* and lived about an hour and a half from Broken Branch, and I called it quits about a month ago when I found out he wasn't actually separated from his wife like he told me. Nope, they were still living under the same roof and, at least from her perspective, happily married. Yeah, the irony isn't lost on me. I divorced my ex for screwing around and I end up being the other woman in some poor lady's nightmare. Stuart said all the usual crap: *I love you, it's a loveless marriage, I'm leaving her, blah, blah, blah*. Then there was the little issue where Stuart used me to get the biggest story of his career. I told him if he didn't shut up I was going to shoot him with my Glock. I was only half joking.

I flip open the phone. "I'm working, Stuart," I snap.

"Wait, wait," he says. "This is a business call."

"All the better reason for me to hang up," I say shortly.

"I hear you've got an intruder at the school," Stuart says in his breezy, confident way. Asshole.

"Where'd you hear that?" I ask cautiously, trying not to give away the fact that this is news to me.

"It's all over, Meg. Our phone at the paper has been ringing off the hook. Kids are posting it on their walls and tweeting all about it. What's going on?"

"I can't comment on any ongoing investigation," I say firmly, my mind spinning. An intruder at the school? No. If there was something going on I would know about it.

"Maria. Is she okay?"

"That's none of your business," I say softly. I wasn't the only one Stuart hurt.

"Wait," he says before I can hang up. "Maybe I can help you."

"How's that?" I say suspiciously.

"I can track the media end of things, keep you informed of what we hear, give you a heads-up on anything that sounds important."

"Stuart," I say, shaking my head. "Honestly, nothing you have to say to me is important anymore."

Will

That morning, as Will Thwaite watched his grandchildren climb onto the school bus, the horizon not yet shaded with the petal-pink edging that comes before the sunrise, he realized, as he often did in the dark-cornered mornings, that he missed his wife terribly. He was so used to having Marlys there right by his side working the farm. She was the one who shook him awake at five each morning, the one who pushed a thermos of hot coffee into his hands and sent him out the door with the promise of a hot breakfast upon his return from feeding the cattle. He felt her absence the way one might miss a limb. Fifty years they would be married, this coming fall. He tried to remember the last time she had been away from the farm overnight and settled upon eleven years ago when she went to visit their fourth son, Jeffery, his wife and their newborn daughter in Omaha. She had packed a bag for four days, climbed into the Cadillac, hollered out the window that there were meals in the freezer for him to put in the microwave and drove away in a cloud of deep brown Iowa dust.

He sipped at his coffee, wincing at its bitter taste, not at all like Marlys's, understanding why Marlys had to stay away for so much longer this time. It had been two months already and still she couldn't give him a date when she would be returning home. Their youngest child and only daughter needed so much care and was having so many setbacks from the accident that it could be well into April before he would next see his wife. For many years Will thought that he might never see Holly again, she was set so hard against him. He suspected that if he tried to pin Holly down to exactly why she hated him, she wouldn't quite be able to say, though she managed to poison his grandchildren against him. At least the boy, P.J., a quiet child with brown eyes, thick round glasses and the soul of an old man, had warmed to him rather quickly. The girl, Augustine—Augie—was a different matter altogether. When Will walked into the hospital, the cool institutional air a welcome reprieve from the dry, incessant Arizona heat, he felt a quickening of his pulse as he turned the corner and entered the burn unit. Slouching in an uncomfortable-looking chair was his daughter. But of course it wasn't Holly, it couldn't be. Holly was in a hospital bed recovering from third-degree burns. Besides, the forlorn creature before him was much too young to be Holly. But she had Holly's pale skin, brown hair and plump roundness. Not fat by any means, but solid, in a healthy farm girl way, and he smiled inwardly at the thought. This was his granddaughter, and for a brief moment Will thought that this was his chance, his opportunity, to reclaim his wayward daughter, who for the past fifteen-odd years had dismissed him for reasons he couldn't quite determine.

His hopes were quickly squelched when Marlys, always

emotive and loud in the most inappropriate places, squealed in delight at seeing her grandchildren for the first time.

"Augustine? P.J.?" she asked loudly, causing the other visitors' heads to snap up. She held her arms out to the children, expecting, Will supposed, for Augie and P.J. to leap from their seats and bound into them. Instead, the two gaped up at their grandmother, who Will had to admit was quite the sight. The worry over Holly, the frantic packing, the scrambling to make sure the farm duties were covered, had exhausted Marlys even before they left Broken Branch. Then there was their flight, the first ever for Marlys, and not knowing the ins and outs left her feeling small and inept. After finally arriving in Revelation and seeing her grandchildren, Marlys could no longer hold back the emotion. She gathered the stunned children into her arms, pushed them back from her at arm's length after a moment to get a good look, then pulled them back to her.

"We're your grandparents," she cried through her tears. "Oh, aren't you beautiful?" she said to Augie, whose mouth lifted into a wisp of a smile. "You look just like your mother did at your age. And you." Marlys turned to P.J., lifting his chin with one work-worn finger. "Aren't you a handsome young thing?" Her tears dripped down her wrinkled cheeks and plopped onto P.J.'s upturned face. The boy didn't squirm away or wipe the moisture away from his forehead, but looked in awe up at his grandmother and then cast an unsure glance at his grandfather, who shrugged as if to say, *I don't know what she's doing, either.* When Will turned his gaze to Augie, hoping to share in the levity of moment, he was met with an accusing, suspicious glare. Holly had already filled his granddaughter with the tales of her childhood. The backbreaking work, the isolation of the farm, the battles over curfew, the unfairness of it all. While Marlys preened over the children, who basked in the attention, Will stepped back and busied himself with finding a nurse who could give him some information about the condition of his daughter.

Now, two months later, he was no closer to breaking down the wall that separated him from his granddaughter. God knows he had tried. He understood how hard being away from her mother must be for Augie and he tried to give her space. He waited one full week before telling her that chores were an essential part of living on the farm, that she needed to contribute. It had been easy with P.J., who followed his grandfather with rapt attention. Augie, on the other hand, would retreat to her room, Holly's old bedroom, each day after school and wouldn't emerge until the next morning. She answered any questions in monosyllabic grunts and refused to eat with them. Claimed to be a vegetarian, scowled and scoffed at the fact that he was a cattleman, that he raised animals for food. He knew better than to argue with Augie, tried to be patient. Though at times he thought he would explode with frustration, he vowed to try and educate her gradually, if not a bit gruffly. But she certainly didn't make it easy for him. She still glared at him with disdain and took every opportunity she could to argue and disagree with what he said. It was like raising Holly all over again. But the thing was, over the years, after his relationship with his daughter had disintegrated into far-flung memories of when she was little and thought he hung the moon, he swore if he had the chance to do it over again, he would do things differently. Now the opportunity had presented itself in Augie, a clone of his daughter, and damned if he still couldn't get it right.

Holly

Once again I woke up to another morning in the hospital. I'm beginning to think that I'll never be able to leave this place. I want to rip the IV from my arm and run away screaming. My entire life I've been trying to get free, first from my folks and from Broken Branch and all its small-town hokeyness. Then it was from my marriage to David and the way being tied to one person, or maybe it was just him, suffocated me. So first I severed ties with my Iowa family, leaving them behind without a hug or a kiss, just an *I've gotta get out of here or I'm going to die,* and not once did I ever look back. Ran away to Colorado with a boy who I grew up with. We got sick of each other after only a year, so off I went to Arizona where I ended up going to cosmetology school. There I met David; we got married and had Augie. That fiasco lasted an entire seven years. He tried to get me to stay, said he wanted another baby, wanted to grow old together. I told him I couldn't live this way anymore, that I would die if

I had to wake up one more morning looking at the same god-awful flocked wallpaper or listen to our next-door neighbor go on and on about how the neighborhood was going to hell.

"We'll take off the wallpaper," David had said. "We can move," he promised. So we took down the wallpaper and I got pregnant. But he knew. He understood that it wasn't the wallpaper or the neighbors. It was us. Really me, who couldn't stand being there, being married, being trapped in the suburbs, which isn't all that different from small-town Iowa. David looked so hurt, so wounded, when he watched P.J. People tended to regard me that way after they've been around me for any length of time. First my mother and father. Especially my father. How I took private glee in the look on his face when I told him that living on a farm was like hell on earth, that spending one more minute in Broken Branch was a minute wasted, thrown away, never to be retrieved. My older brothers called me selfish and ungrateful. My mother cried. I felt bad about that. But it didn't make me want to stay. My father actually helped carry my suitcase out to the old Plymouth Arrow I had saved up for by detasseling corn every summer since I was thirteen.

"You are seventeen years old, Holly," my father said. "And I know you think you've got all the answers, but what you are doing to your mother is inexcusable."

"I can't spend another day here," I told him, not able to look him in the eyes, instead staring over his shoulder out at the acres and acres of ankle-high seed corn. "I can't explain it."

My father was quiet for a minute. His green John Deere hat perched on his head, pulled low so that his eyes were shaded. But I already knew they were looking at me with disapproval. He leaned against the back hatch of the Plymouth, his tan arms folded across his chest. "You're ashamed of being the daughter of a farmer? You think you're too good enough for this life? Is that it?"

I shook my head, mortified. "No! That's not it."

"Well, from where I'm standing, it sure appears that way. I understand you wanting to travel, see the world, but there's no need to leave this way, like you've waited your whole life to get away from your mother and me."

But I have, I wanted to say to him, but didn't. "I just can't seem to stand myself in my own skin while I'm here," I tried to explain, knowing that I was failing miserably.

"You think that's going to change when you drive away from here? You think your skin is going to fit you any better?"

"Yes, in fact, I do," I said, shaken that he had pegged it exactly. I was terrified that wherever it was I ended up I would feel the exact same way. That I needed to leave.

"You'll be back," my father said with a sureness that made my chest hum with anger. "You'll come back, and when you do, you owe your mother an apology."

"I won't be back," I spat back. "I'm never coming back here, ever."

My father shook his head and laughed a little. A light chuckle. "Oh, you'll be back." He reached out to give me a hug but I stepped past him. "Well, I guess you've been through about every boy and man in the county, not much left to stay for." I just climbed into my car without even saying goodbye. As I pulled away from the farm, I looked in my rearview mirror and there was my father, already turned away from me, surrounded by the dust and gravel kicked up into the air from my tires, heading toward his cattle that never seemed to disappoint and certainly never talked back to him.

I was true to my word. I had never returned, not once, to Broken Branch in the eighteen years since I left. But I wonder if I did the next worse thing by sending my children there.

Mrs. Oliver

Mrs. Oliver hardly dared to look away from the stranger standing in front of her, but the cries of her students pulled her gaze away from the man who looked vaguely familiar.

Sixteen of the seventeen children were helplessly staring up at Mrs. Oliver, some with tears in their eyes, waiting for direction as to what to do. The monthly tornado and fire drills had done nothing to prepare them for this. Not even the Code Red Lockdown drills could have readied them for the surprisingly calm, albeit slightly manic-looking man dangling a gun from his fingers. Only one child, P. J. Thwaite, the son of one of her former students, Holly Thwaite, was peering raptly at the man, scanning his face, not as if he knew him, but as if maybe, at one time, he had seen him somewhere before. The man stared back at P.J., his expression flat and unemotional, which unnerved Mrs. Oliver even more.

As a classroom teacher Mrs. Oliver couldn't begin to count

the number of times she had needed to appear unruffled and completely in control. There was the time, her first year teaching no less, when seven-year-old Bert Gorse, on a dare, decided to climb to the top of the tall steel slide and try to jump and grab onto the branch of a nearby maple tree. Mrs. Oliver remembered watching in horror from her position across the playground as Bert leaped into the air, his eyes screwed shut, his hands reaching for the branch, fingers clawing at the rough bark. "For God's sake!" she yelled before she could stop herself. "Open your eyes!" Unable to grab the limb, Bert fell twelve feet to the hardscrabble earth below. Calmly, she told the little girl standing next to her to run as fast as she could to get help.

"You swore," the girl breathed in disbelief.

Mrs. Oliver bent down and put her face so close to the little girl's she could smell the peanut butter sandwich the child had eaten for lunch and said in the low, even tone that children for the next forty years would know to take seriously, "Run." Trying not to wobble in her new high heels, Mrs. Oliver made her way as quickly as possible over to Bert, who was sprawled out on his belly, unmoving. The knot of terrified boys who surrounded Bert began unraveling at her approach. "Go stand next to the building," she ordered, and the boys obeyed at once. Mrs. Oliver knelt down, the knees of her brand-new polyester pantsuit grinding into the dirt. Bert's eyes were open but glazed over with pain or shock. "Not dead!" Mrs. Oliver said joyfully, and behind her the children erupted with a soft whoosh of relief. "Are you okay, Bert?" she questioned, but Bert's mouth could only open and close soundlessly like a fish on dry land. "Got the wind knocked out of you?" she said in her smooth, low manner that the children found reassuring. Mrs. Oliver maneuvered herself onto her stomach and lay next to Bert so she could better see his pale, pinched face and where he could see her round, placid one.

"It's going to be just fine, Bert. Just lie still now until help comes," she said soothingly.

Bert was okay, although he ended up with two broken arms and a collapsed lung. Once Bert regained the use of his hands, he wrote his teacher a lovely letter in his messy cursive, thanking her for waiting with him until the ambulance arrived. Mrs. Oliver still had that letter, now framed and hanging in the room that her grown daughter, Georgiana, called the *Shrine to Mrs. Oliver*. Bert Gorse was now a fifty-year-old banker who lived in Des Moines with his wife and three children. Through the years, Mrs. Oliver remained steadfast in her belief that a teacher needed to be calm and in control under any circumstance. Certainly unlike Gretchen Small, the young fifth-grade teacher, who began to hyperventilate when the fire alarm accidentally went off.

Mrs. Oliver straightened her spine, cleared her throat and willed her voice to emerge strong and clear. "What do you want?" she demanded, stepping between P.J. and the man with the gun.

Meg

I'm debating whether to give Stuart's claim that there is a gunman in the school any credence and call dispatch when the squawk of my radio stops me short.

It's Randall Diehl, our dispatcher. "You need to go over to the school right now. We've got a lockdown."

Maria's school. Damn. Stuart was right.

"What's up?" I ask. Since I've lived here there have only been two lockdowns at the school, a kindergarten through twelfth-grade building. One of the last of its kind. At the end of this school year Broken Branch's only school would be closed down; too expensive and outdated to maintain, the superintendent and school board voted to consolidate with three other nearby towns. In the future, Maria's school district would be known as Dalsing-Conway-Bohr-Broken Branch Consolidated Schools.

The first lockdown I was involved with was two years ago when two inmates from the Anamosa State Penitentiary escaped and were thought to be in our area. They weren't. The second time was when two misguided high schoolers called in a fake bomb threat. They hadn't studied for their finals and thought this would cleverly get them out of the tests. It most certainly did that. And got them kicked out of school.

"We got a possible intruder in the school. Just head on over there," Randall says impatiently, which was not like him at all. "The chief will meet you and he'll fill you in. Communication is a mess. The 9-1-1 lines are jammed with calls from students, teachers, frantic parents."

"Will do," I tell him, and flip on my windshield wipers to clear away the snow. Interesting, Chief McKinney already at the scene. I check the clock. Just after noon. Probably just a misunderstanding, a prank by some kids to kick off spring vacation. Maria will be sad she missed all the excitement.

I turn the squad car around and head up Hickory Street toward the school and am grateful to have something to occupy my time besides the thought of spending four whole days without Maria, which makes me feel empty, as if my insides have been hollowed out. Tim always said he couldn't ever imagine me as a kid. The few pictures that I had of myself as a child showed me as a serious, unsmiling creature with unkempt hair, wearing a pair of my brother Travis's old jeans.

"Did you ever have any fun?" Tim teased when he first saw the photos.

"I had fun," I protested, though that was pretty much a lie. My childhood consisted of taking care of my parents, who, for reasons still unknown, were completely defeated by life, and trying to stay out of the way of my volatile brother. When Tim and I had Maria I was determined to make her childhood as carefree and joy-filled as mine wasn't. I think we did a pretty good job of this, at least until the divorce, and even then Tim and I did our best to protect Maria. We didn't argue in front of her, we didn't bad-mouth each other, but she knew. How could she not? Even if we didn't make a big spectacle out of the end of our marriage, she had to have seen my red, swollen eyes, Tim's tight, forced laughter.

In minutes I pull up to the school and find Chief McKinney already there along with Aaron Gritz—curious, because he isn't on duty today—trying to keep a small, angry-looking group away from the school's entrance. Chief McKinney's deep baritone fills the air. "Go on back to your cars or you are all going to freeze standing out here. We need to find out exactly what's going on and we can't do that if we have to concern ourselves with—"

A woman steps forward, waving her cell phone, and in a trembling voice interrupts the chief. "My son just called me from inside and he said there was a man with a gun. Can't you get them out of there?"

"Based on the information we have," Chief McKinney says patiently, "we've determined that the best response is to contain the area and not send officers into the school at this time."

"But my seventh grader called and said there were two men," another woman speaks up.

A man in a dress shirt and tie, no coat, rushes forward. "I heard there's a bomb threat. Are you evacuating?"

"This is exactly what the problem is," Chief McKinney says to me in a low voice, pointing first at the school and then the crowd, snowflakes collecting on his bristly gray mustache. "We can't begin to know what's going on in there if we're chasing rumors out here." He turns his back to the crowd and drops his voice to a whisper. "Meg, dispatch got a call from a man who says he's inside the building with a gun. Said for everyone to stay out or he'll start shooting. I want tape and barriers set up around the entire perimeter of the school." He turns to Gritz. "Aaron, escort everyone about three hundred feet back.

"Okay, folks," the chief says in a firm but nonconfrontational voice. "Please follow Officer Gritz's directions now. We need to get to work here. I promise if we have any news to share, we will let you know immediately."

I know what each of these parents is thinking of. The mass shooting at Columbine. It crossed my mind, too. Columbine changed everything in the way law enforcement responds to these situations. If we had evidence that the perpetrator in the school had started shooting, the chief would have immediately sent in a rapid deployment team to the source of the threat. Thankfully that hasn't happened in this case. Yet. Because the suspect called dispatch and threatened the students and anyone who entered the building, we were approaching this as a hostage situation, meaning we were going to try to contact the intruder, find out what he wants and attempt to calmly talk our way out of this. The second there is evidence that shooting has started, we'd be in there. But for now, we needed more information.

"Won't forcing the parents away from here cause a panic?" I ask Aaron in a quiet voice so the crowd won't hear.

"I think they are already in a panic," Aaron responds. He is wearing his rabbit-trimmed aviator hat with earflaps and his nose is red from the cold.

Just after my divorce was finalized, I got the police officer position with the Broken Branch Police Department. Aaron was on the interview team. Aaron is fortyish, divorced with two children and very handsome. At the interview Aaron asked me why I wanted to move to such a small community as Broken Branch when I was used to the larger, more urban city of Waterloo. "The fact that Broken Branch is a small, rural community is exactly why I want to settle down here. It's a

perfect place to raise a daughter." What I refrained from telling the interview team was that I needed distance from Tim
and our divorce. Waterloo wasn't such a big city. Every time I
turned a corner I ran into someone who knew my ex-husband,
my parents, had been scammed by my brother. Besides, the
hours that I worked for the Waterloo Police Force were terrible for a single mother. Broken Branch was only about an
hour from Waterloo, close enough for Tim to easily see Maria.

I fell in love with Broken Branch years earlier when Tim
and I drove through on our way to Des Moines. We stopped
to buy honey from an old man selling jars of the amber liquid
out of the back of his pickup truck.

"How did Broken Branch get its name? It's so unusual?"
I asked.

"Now, that is a great story," the man said as he placed a
large glass jar of clover honey, slim honey sticks and homemade
beeswax candles carefully into a plastic bag and handed it to
Tim. "Most people say it's because the poor people who first
settled here discovered a huge fallen tree over fifty feet long
filled with an enormous beehive in it. Thousands and thousands of bees were buzzing inside and around the tree. Wanting the honey inside, they called on the help of an old woman
who was known to have a way with bees. The story goes that
she walked down to that hollowed-out tree and began singing a strange foreign song and all the bees became silent and
followed her as she walked and sang. There were bees in her
hair and on her arms, but still she walked and sang. Not one
bee stung her. She led the bees to another felled tree down
by the creek and the bees created a new home there. The set-
tlers, who were poor and starving, gathered all that honey out
of the broken branch and lived off of it for the winter. They
were so thankful to the old woman that they offered to name
the town after her, but she said that the thanks should lie with

the bees and the tree that housed them. So they respected her wishes and named the town Broken Branch."

I was completely enchanted by the story, and as Tim and I explored the peaceful streets lined with modest homes and towering trees, I knew I would return to Broken Branch. Little did I know that it would be to stay.

Fortunately, I impressed Chief McKinney, Aaron and the rest of the interview team enough for them to offer me the job.

A few months later, I found myself sitting alone with Aaron at a local bar after Broken Branch's citywide softball tournament where I played first base. I had too much sun, not enough food and two lousy beers, and in the singular most embarrassing moment of my life, I made a halfhearted pass at Aaron. He gently pulled me off of him and told me that he wasn't interested.

"I'm boring, too serious, aren't I?" I asked. He looked at me for a very long time.

"No, Meg, you're not boring, you're great. It just wouldn't be a good idea," he said, and left me standing there. Though a few years have passed since that mortifying encounter, and Aaron has not brought it up once, I still blush bright red whenever I think of that night.

As I return to my car to retrieve a roll of crime tape, once again I feel my phone vibrate. Stuart. He just doesn't give up. A text this time. I decide to ignore it and begin unraveling the police tape.

I met Stuart last January when Maria and I were cross-country skiing in Ox-eye Bluff. Maria, a novice at skiing, fell down one too many times. The final straw was that after the umpteenth tumble Maria's skis became tangled in a thorny bramble of twigs at the side of the trail. By the time I freed her, Maria had worked herself into such a snit she refused to put her skis back on or to even walk out of the valley. We sat there for twenty minutes, Maria's tears freezing against her cheeks, until a skier came gliding down the trail. He swooshed to a stop in front of us "Everything okay?" he asked.

"We're fine," I answered. "Just an equipment malfunction. We're resting up for a few minutes."

"Your mom can't keep up with you, can she?" the man said to Maria, eliciting her first smile of the afternoon. "That's what happens when you get old." He smiled conspiratorially at her. "People can't maintain the vigorous pace of us youngsters."

"Exactly how old do you think I am?" I asked him through narrowed eyes.

"It's rude to comment on a lady's age." He sniffed and then gave me a mischievous smile. "Why don't you help me get her up," he said to Maria. "If we leave her here much longer the wolves will start circling."

I was about to tell him I was obviously fifteen years his junior and could drop a wild animal at two hundred yards with my eyes closed, but to my surprise Maria quickly scrambled to her feet and held out a hand to help me up. "Let's go, Mom," she said. "I think I hear howling."

"There are no wolves in Ox-eye Bluff," I said, reaching out my hands for the man and Maria to pull me to my feet. "I don't think there are any wolves in Iowa for that matter. Coyotes, yes. Wolves, no." The man was tall, at least six foot, fit with a lean face and closely cut brown hair flecked with gray.

He caught me looking and had the decency to blush. "It's premature."

"Yeah, right," I said, raising my eyebrows. Together, the three of us skied to the end of the trail and then hiked our way out of the valley to where my car was parked. We didn't talk much but I did learn that the man's name was Stuart Moore and that he was a writer for the *Des Moines Observer,* the larg-

est newspaper in the state. He also worked into the conversation how he had three grown children and was separated, the
divorce held up by his wife.

"You don't look old enough to have three adult children,"
I said in mock disbelief.

"Well, child marriage, you know," he answered as he
clipped my skis onto the top of my car.

"You must have been what? Like twelve?" I played along.

"Something like that." He laughed.

"What brings you here?" I asked. "Des Moines is an hour
and a half from here."

"I actually live just north of Des Moines, so it's not quite
that far. I've skied all over Iowa, Minnesota and Wisconsin.
Ox-eye has some of the best trails and no one else seems to
know about it. I almost always have the trails to myself," he
explained.

"Until now," Maria piped up.

"Until now," Stuart agreed.

Stuart and I took it slow. At first, anyway. I was still bruised
from my divorce and Aaron's mortifying rebuff and I had
Maria to think about. That winter we would run into each
other at Ox-eye and end up cross-country skiing, or snowshoeing. In the spring and summer we would, by some unspoken agreement, meet up at Ox-eye to hike the trails.
Sometimes with Maria, sometimes not.

The first time Stuart and I slept together was only about two
months ago. Maria was spending the weekend at Tim's house.
There wasn't enough snow for skiing anymore so I invited
him back to my house for the first time. Being with Stuart,
the way he touched me, the way he tucked a strand of my hair
behind my ear, made me feel safe and needed. He confided to
me how his soon-to-be ex-wife had an affair with one of his
colleagues, how it tore him apart, tore his family apart. How

the divorce was finally going through. I told him about my work as a police officer in a small town, about Tim and the slow burn of my marriage. We drank too much wine and for three hours I didn't think of DUIs or meth labs or disputes over fence lines. I didn't think of Tim or even of Maria. I led Stuart into my bedroom and shut out the rest of the world. For a while I thought that maybe, just possibly, Stuart and I would end up together. How wrong I was. Within a matter of days I learned two crucial things about Stuart: he was married and would do anything to get a story. I don't think Stuart had this grand plan of using me to get his big scoop. But the opportunity presented itself and Stuart took it.

I finish unwinding the yellow tape, bright and almost cheerful against the whiteness of the snow, if not for the bold black words declaring *Police Line Do Not Cross*.

Will

That morning Will had slipped into his warmest coveralls, his seventy-year-old joints protesting loudly. He tightly laced his brown leather work boots, pulled on the black-and-yellow winter hat that Marlys knit for him years before and wiggled his thick, rough hands into his insulated pigskin gloves. He stepped outside and made his way past the steel bins filled with corn and soybeans and past the concrete silo. It was a still, quiet morning; the sun had risen as a cold, dull orb in the gray sky, emitting a weak light. He moved toward the feed lot and the heifer paddock slightly out of breath, his heart thrumming with the exertion. Once Marlys returned home, he knew she would try and get him to the doctor and he would refuse.

The Angus had approached him in anticipation, regarding him with their large, soft eyes. And when Will bent over to check the feed bunks he saw that the cattle had licked them clean. The girls were hungry. He found the same slick bunks in the steer pen and checked his watch. He was late again. He had sluggishly gone to the barn where he methodically mixed the cattle feed, a mixture of hay, corn, cornstalks and corn gluten. Good thing he had Daniel, the hired hand, who had already cleaned out the paddocks and spread fresh hay across the frozen ground.

Being irresponsible regarding the farm chores was so unlike him, but without Marlys here everything he did was a little bit off his routine, off-kilter.

It was nearing one o'clock now and Will was making his rounds, checking on all the cows preparing for birth. This he couldn't put off; if he did, he could have some dead calves and cows on his hands.

The nightly phone calls, always at seven-thirty Iowa time, five-thirty Arizona time, were the worst. First P.J. would talk, chattering on about how much he liked the farm, the snow and sledding, his new school, until Will would gently coax the phone from his fingers and hand it to Augie, who stood by nervously chewing her fingernails.

"Hi, Mom," Augie would say, her throat dense with tears and something else, regret, guilt maybe. Then there would be a series of yeses, noes, okays. No elaboration on her new life in Broken Branch, short, curt responses. Augie would hand the phone back to Will and rush from the farmhouse, inadequately dressed in a hooded sweatshirt and tennis shoes. Will wasn't sure where she ran off to, but figured it was probably the old hayloft in the south barn. That's always where her mother had hidden when she was upset.

Then it was Will's turn to try and make conversation. "How are you?" he would ask. "Feeling better today?"

Fine, yes, Holly would answer thickly, as if her tongue was swollen or she was heavily medicated. Both were likely.

"P.J. really has taken to farm life. Who would've thought? He's a big help. Asks a lot of questions."

"Oh, well, good."

"Augie is a real city girl. Reminds me a lot of you." Will chuckled. No response. "They miss you, but I'm taking good care of them. No worries, now, you hear?"

"Okay."

"You get better fast, Hol. Love you."

"Bye."

He wasn't a particularly demonstrative man. Wasn't the hugging kind. But when his children were under his roof there was not one night that went by where he didn't tell them he loved them. He saw his share of fellow soldiers cut down in Vietnam when he served as a lieutenant. Boys who would have given anything to tell their wives, their kids, their folks, they loved them one more time. Every night Will would go to his children's bedrooms and tell them one by one that he loved them. When they were little they would throw themselves into his arms, even Holly, pressing their scrubbed faces into his neck, inhaling the complicated, earthy smells of the farm that rose from his pores. When the boys were older they would casually toss back a *Love you, too, Dad,* and Will was satisfied. Those words said, he could sleep well that night. Holly, his youngest, was another story. When she was twelve something shifted. She no longer looked at him through the eyes of a little girl who adored her father, but would look at him askance, her eyes judgmental slits. *Love you, Hol,* he would say, coming to the doorway of her bedroom but not stepping over the threshold into her realm of bottles of nail polish and piles of clothes.

"Good night," she would say without looking directly at him, snapping the pages of a fashion magazine in irritation.

"Love you, Holly," he would repeat a little more loudly.

"Uh-huh," she would answer absentmindedly, and a spark of anger would ignite low in his breastbone.

Eventually he didn't even bother opening her bedroom door to say good-night. He would knock twice on her door. "Night, Holly. Love you," he would call through the closed door and briskly walk away. He couldn't bear seeing the disdain on her face, of not hearing the sweetness of those three little words in response. Now here he was, eighteen years later, saying *I love you* to a daughter who still couldn't seem to find one reason to say it back.

After he finished feeding the cattle, he went to the big barn where he and Daniel had moved four expecting heifers earlier in the week. Over one hundred calves were due to be born by mid-May. Despite the shelter from the barn walls, the cold had still seeped in and Will worried that some of the new calves might perish in the bitter weather.

Will patted the sleek rump of the heifer. He would have to stay close and check on her throughout the day. He expected a calf by that evening. He looked up at the sound of a shout. Through the wide doorway, Daniel was waving and jogging toward him. Daniel Tucker was an equable, methodical man of around thirty, unmarried and thoroughly dedicated to the animals and the land. He was a great help to Will, had a calm, gentle way around the cattle, was dependable and a hard worker. In addition to helping Will out on his farm, Daniel was renting farmland from Will in order to raise crops, hoping to one day purchase his own slice of Iowa. As Daniel came closer, his normally placid face was creased in concern; Will realized something wasn't quite right.

"The school," Daniel said breathlessly, his cheeks red, his nose running from the biting cold. "Something is happening at the school," he said again, swiping his arm across his nose.

"What happened?" Will felt his heartbeat gathering speed

and guiltily he realized that his thoughts went immediately to P.J., Augie a beat later.

"Something about a man with a gun," Daniel said, and pulled his stocking cap from his head. "My sister just called me, my niece and nephew go to the school—she's frantic. Said there's a big crowd of parents at the school trying to find out what's going on."

"My daughter-in-law teaches fourth grade at the school," Will said, pulling his hat from his head. "I need to call my son. You want to go be with your sister?" Will asked, biting his lip.

"Thought you'd want to go check on P.J. and Augie," Daniel answered, reaching into his coat pocket for a handkerchief and blowing wetly into it. "And Todd's wife, of course."

"I'd appreciate that, Dan," Will answered gratefully. "Numbers 87 and 134 will give birth sometime today. Can you stay near?" Will asked, pointing toward a wide-shouldered black-baldie whose swollen flank and udders looked ready to burst.

"You betcha," Daniel said, patting his boss on the shoulder. "If you hear anything, let me know."

The two moved quickly but in silence back toward the house. The only sounds were the wind whistling between the outbuildings and the mild lowing of the cattle, now satiated and huddled together trying to keep warm.

"Who would do such a thing?" Daniel finally asked, stretching his stocking cap back over his ears.

Will shook his head in bewilderment. He knew just about every single person in Broken Branch, and though there were a few mean, crazy sons of bitches, he couldn't imagine anyone walking into a school with a gun. "Don't know, Daniel. I'll go see what I can find out," he assured him, and went into the house. Will didn't bother to change out of his coveralls or his dirty work boots but paused to grab the cell phone he seldom used. Then, unaware of the streaks of muck and manure he was trailing across Marlys's carpet, he made his way into his tiny office. He spun the lock on his Browning gun safe, pulled it open and retrieved his Mossberg 500 pump action shotgun and tucked a box of shells into his pocket. Just in case.

Augie

Mr. Ellery steps out of the room and Noah and Justin follow him to the doorway. "Go sit down. Now," he orders, his voice so serious that even Noah knows better than to disobey him.

"What's going on?" Beth Cragg asks nervously, chewing on her fingers. Beth is the closest thing to a friend that I have in Broken Branch. Our grandmothers are friends and had unsuccessfully tried to make our mothers into best friends when they were our age. I guess they thought this was their second chance, because ten minutes after P.J. and I arrived at the farmhouse Beth and her grandma showed up with a plate of lemon squares. But I was the one who looked like she had sucked on a lemon when I first met Beth. We seemed so different from each other. Beth is all farm girl. She wears Levi's and John Deere sweatshirts or McGee Feed Store T-shirts every single day. Beth is one of those girls who is naturally beautiful and doesn't even know it. She has freckled skin and pulls her shiny brown hair back into a ponytail or twists it into a braid that lies across her shoulder like a thick rope. Whenever I try to wear my hair in a braid it looks like an anorexic rattail. The boys in eighth grade love her because she is still interested in chasing toads and skipping stones across the creek and because she belongs to 4-H and raises calves that she shows at the county fair each summer. She can talk about crops and guns and goes pheasant and deer hunting with her father. All except this year, because of her parents' divorce. In the past two months, though, we have become friends. Beth is nice and is a good listener. Plus, she was the one person, including my grandpa and P.J., who didn't make fun of the way I dyed my hair red. Now that's a true friend. And we do have something in common. Our parents. Mine are divorced and Beth's mom and dad are getting a divorce. She listens to me while I bitch about having to leave Arizona to live with my grandfather and she complains about how sad her mom is and how her dad tries to make her feel guilty for taking her mother's side.

"What's going on?" Beth asks again, her voice shaking. I feel my stomach flip with worry and I think of P.J. Then I think of my mother back in Revelation and I want to talk to her more than anything. My cell phone is in my book bag, which is in my locker out in the hallway, and I wonder if Mr. Ellery will let me go and get it.

"We're in lockdown," Mr. Ellery says seriously when he comes back into the room. "Not a drill." He runs a hand through his black hair and pulls at his goatee. He shuts the classroom door and pushes the round button, locking us in. So much for going to get my phone.

"Hey, what are you doing?" Noah asks in surprise.

"Shhh, I'm thinking." Mr. Ellery bites his lip and looks out the small window set into the door and then turns back toward us. "Let's all move back to that corner." He points to the space behind his desk away from the door and windows.

"Is it someone with a gun?" Felicia asks, her eyes wide.

"Oh, my God," someone behind me whispers.

"We don't know that," Mr. Ellery says quickly.

"We can't stay in here and wait for someone to come in and blow us away," Noah says angrily, and I realize how much of a jerk he is all over again.

"No, we stay," Mr. Ellery says firmly. "Until we get the all clear, we stay."

Noah looks like he is going to argue, but as one by one everyone stands and goes to the back corner of the room and begins to squeeze themselves into the space between the teacher's desk and the wall, he decides to follow.

"The boys should sit on the outside," Savannah says.

"Fuck that." Noah glares at her. "I'm not going to be anyone's shield. I want to be as close to the window as I can. I'm going to get the hell out of here first chance I get."

"Hey, Noah, just cool it," Mr. Ellery says in a way that makes me think he wouldn't mind climbing out a window, too. "No one's going to be anyone's shield. Does anyone mind sitting on the edges?" Five hands go up, including Beth's and Drew's. Slowly I raise mine. "Okay, guys, thanks." Mr. Ellery nods at us. "Everyone take a seat. No talking." He flips the light switch and the room turns gray, matching the sky outside.

I settle onto the hard linoleum floor and rest my back against the side of Mr. Ellery's desk. Beth sits down on one side of me, Drew on the other. Mr. Ellery first goes to the window and lowers the blinds and then goes to the phone sitting on his desk, picks it up, puts the receiver to his ear and then eventually hangs up. He pulls himself up onto the desk, his long legs not quite touching the floor. "Phone isn't working," he says. After a minute he reaches into his pocket for his cell phone and punches in three numbers.

After several tries he finally says, "This is Jason Ellery from the school. Something seems to be going on here." He listens for a moment. "Yes, everyone in my class is safe and accounted for." He listens again and then reaches for his grade book that he keeps on his desk. One by one he reads off our names in alphabetical order. My name comes last, I suppose because I joined the class midyear. "Augustine Baker," he says, and I hear Noah snort back a laugh. "Will Thwaite's granddaughter." Again there is silence as he listens. "The classroom phones aren't working, my cell is about halfway charged." He pulls the phone from his mouth and says in a loud whisper, "Anyone have their cell phone with them?" No one says anything. We're supposed to keep our phones in our lockers and not bring them into the classroom with us. Supposedly, some kids were using their phones to look up test answers on the internet and texting during class and the principal banned phones in the classroom. "Come on," he says more loudly. "We don't have time for this. Does anyone have their cell phone with them right now?" Three hands slowly go up, including Noah Plum's. No surprise there. "Make sure they're turned off and bring them here."

"No way," Noah snorts. "It's my phone."

"Noah, I'm not kidding around here," Mr. Ellery says sharply. "We don't know how long we're going to be stuck in here. The school phones don't work and we need to conserve the batteries on the phones we do have."

"I want to call my mom," Beth calls out in a soft voice. "Can I call my mom?"

"Me, too," someone says, and there is a chorus of *me, toos* and I find my voice joining in. I want nothing more than to talk to my mother right now. I wouldn't freeze her out the way I have for the past two months, answering her questions in three words or less. *Okay, I guess. I don't know. Yeah.*

"I can't stop you, but we could be here for a long time. The 9-1-1 dispatcher knows everyone is okay and will let your folks know. Someone is going to call us back when they have more info." Mr. Ellery shrugs his shoulders and waits.

Noah immediately starts punching numbers into his phone and before I can stop myself I whisper loudly, "What an idiot."

"Shut up, *Augustine*," he snarls, but snaps the phone shut and sets it next to where Mr. Ellery is sitting. The others with phones do the same.

"Thanks, guys," Mr. Ellery says. "You can have them back at any time. For now we just wait." He pulls himself up onto his desk. He holds a long slim, wooden pointer that he uses to show us capitals of countries none of us will probably ever visit and I wonder if he really thinks that a simple stick can protect us from whatever is out there. But I'm still glad he's here. Mr. Ellery won't let anything bad happen to us.

Meg

As I move back toward the parking lot I see Dorothy Jones, the owner of Knitting and Notions, a local craft shop, and the president of the school board, walking toward me.

"Hi, Dorothy, I don't have any info. You'll have to move back behind the tape."

"Please, Meg," she begs. "I'll just take a few minutes of your time. It's important." I invite her to join me in the cruiser. She walks around to the other side of the car, opens the door and climbs in.

Dorothy is fiftyish with midnight-black hair that is cut into a severe, chin-length bob and is attractive in an eclectic, trendy way. She normally wears bright red lipstick and artfully ripped jeans and Chuck Taylor tennis shoes, but now her face is bare of any makeup and she has on sweatpants and a thin spring coat. She has resided in Broken Branch for just over two years, but has accomplished much in the short time she has lived here. A single mother of two teens who attend the school, Dorothy opened Knitting and Notions, renovated an old farmhouse south of town and managed to be elected to the local school board, ousting Clement Heitzman, who had been president for the past twelve years. Dorothy has also been instrumental in the coordination of the consolidation of several area schools, which will now lead to the closing of Broken Branch's school, sending all the high school kids to the nearby town of Conway, the middle school students to Bohr and the elementary students to Dalsing or Broken Branch, depending on where they live. The construction of Broken Branch's new elementary school is scheduled to be completed this July, ready to open at the end of August. Many folks around town are miffed with Dorothy for closing their beloved school, as most townspeople spent the entirety of their education within the walls of that building. As somewhat of an outsider, I can understand the reasoning for closing the school. It's a monstrosity, impossible to heat in the winter and sweltering in the warm months. Its water heater and furnace are ancient and I'm certain the ceilings are full of asbestos. Dorothy, along with the superintendent of schools, somehow convinced the rest of the board that by consolidating four area towns' schools, the children would be well-educated and safe.

Dorothy gathers her spring jacket more tightly around herself. "I should have never put away my winter coat. That little taste of spring we had last week fooled me." Dorothy gives me a pained smile. I try not to appear impatient, but I certainly don't have time to talk weather with the school board president. I smile back but do not respond to her small talk. Dorothy takes a deep breath and looks at me levelly. "I can't be sure about this, but I wanted to make sure you knew about a few things that had been going on in the school. Things that could possibly have some relevance to what's happening."

"What kinds of things?" I ask.

"Technically, I'm not supposed to say anything about this. The discussions we had were in a closed session of a board meeting."

Now I am beginning to become impatient. "Dorothy," I say, "if you have any information that will help us resolve what's going on in there, you need to tell me."

"I could get in big trouble for this. There are legal issues, lawyers involved."

"Dorothy," I say warningly.

"I know, I know." Dorothy bites her lip. "There was a personnel issue with a teacher last year. He was charged with assaulting a student last year."

"Yes, Rick Wilbreicht," I recall. "I remember that. I thought he moved to Sioux City, but we'll definitely have someone check it out. Thank you." I pat her on the shoulder and wait for her to exit the car. She stays put.

"Dorothy, I really need to get moving here."

"Okay." Dorothy exhales loudly. "I've become aware of a situation with one of the students here. Severe bullying. Name calling, pushing, hitting."

"Really?" I ask in surprise. Not that I'm not naive that bullying is going on in the school, but I would have thought the school administration would have reported any physical abuse to us. But still, I don't have time for this unless it directly relates to this case. "Dorothy, is this going somewhere?"

"The student did report it to his teachers, many times. But nothing changed."

"So you think this student is so angry, he would have gone into the school with a gun to get revenge? Was the bullying that bad?"

"He said it was constant. Things were posted online about his sexuality. A video making fun of him and showing kids pushing and shoving him is online also." Tears begin to pool in her blue eyes and she starts to shiver, though the interior of the car is warm, hot air blasting through the vents. An electric current runs through me. We finally might be getting a break in the case.

"Dorothy, who is this boy? Does he have access to a gun?"

She shakes her head miserably. "I can't imagine it would be too hard to get hold of one, though. Every home in the area has at least one gun safe."

"Dorothy, tell me his name," I say sharply.

She looks desperately at me, tears flowing down her cheeks. "I think it might be my son. I got a call from the school this morning. Blake didn't show up. I can't find him anywhere."

Holly

I know when it's eleven o'clock because that's when my mother shows up at the door of my hospital room for the second time each day. She comes right away in the morning at eight, and then at ten she goes for coffee in the hospital cafeteria. She always returns at eleven, and knocks on the doorjamb, pokes her head through a crack in the door and calls out in a cheerful voice, "Is this a good time to visit?" For the first week I didn't bother answering. Every movement, even forming words, was excruciating. My mother would come in, anyway, pull a chair more closely to my bedside. She brought magazines and her knitting and for the next three hours she would just sit. She didn't utter a word unless I opened my one good eye, and when I did, the familiar voice of my childhood would settle over me like a crisp, sun-warmed sheet fresh from the clothesline.

"Remember," my mother begins today, "the time when you were home alone and something spooked the cattle and they somehow got through the gate?" I try not to smile; the muscles in my face screamed with any twitch. I can feel the infection bubbling beneath my skin and wonder what new antibiotic they will try to fight this current setback.

Until just that moment I had forgotten that humid August day the cattle escaped. My parents, along with my brothers Wayne, Pete, Jeff and Todd, decided to make a day trip over to Linden Falls where there was a farm auction. I had no desire to spend my day looking at crappy old farm equipment so I pretended to be sick and stayed behind.

I had lain luxuriously in bed, long after they had left, when I heard the bellow right below my window. I was well accustomed to the mooing and lowing of cattle, but this sound was much too close. I scrambled from my bed, untangling myself from the sheets, and pushed aside my white linen curtains that hung heavily in the humid air. Below me two dozen or more white-faced black baldies wandered lazily in the front yard. I pulled on my barn boots and spent the next four hours trying to corral the cattle. I hollered and pushed and prodded and begged the beasts to return to the pen. Our six-month old blue-mottled Australian cattle dog, Roo, tried to help me, but after thirty minutes she collapsed in exhaustion beneath the lone crab apple tree in our front yard.

"Oh." My mother laughs as she also remembers that day. "When we came in the house you were sunburned, bruised and sore from your cattle wrangling, but all of the animals were back where they belonged." My mother pauses in her knitting. "I remember your father telling everyone he knew about how responsible you were that day. 'Regular cowgirl,' he said. He was so proud of you."

I remember each achy muscle, the way the heat rose from my sunburned skin, the way the ice cream that my father made a special trip into Broken Branch to get just for me felt as it slid, cold and smooth, down my throat. I feel my mother's hand against my uninjured cheek. "What would you like to order for lunch today, Holly?" she asks me. "Ice cream sounds good, doesn't it?"

I nod, my cheek absorbing the coolness of her skin against mine. I think of Augie and P.J. so far away, and even though I know it will slow the healing process, I begin to cry. I miss them terribly. Me, the person who could walk away from anyone without so much as a backward glance. "Home," I manage to grunt.

My mother looks confused for a moment and for a second I know she thinks I'm asking to go back to Broken Branch, but then her eyes clear. "Your house had too much smoke and fire damage. When you get out of here, you can stay in my hotel for a few days, then you'll come to the farm with me for a while, just until you're back on your feet. Then we'll find you a new house. I've already started looking in the newspaper." She doesn't quite understand what I mean but I'm too tired, the fever has addled my brain so that I can't explain in words what I mean. And while most of my burns are healing, I know I'm not getting better. No one is even talking about the day I'm going to get out of here anymore. Sometimes home isn't the house, I want to say, it's the people. Augie and P.J. are my home and I miss them terribly.

Mrs. Oliver

"Sit down," the man ordered. "Over there." He pointed to an empty desk in the front row. Lily Reese's desk. She was one of the students absent. The chicken pox.

"How many students are not here?" he asked.

Mrs. Oliver had felt bad that Lily and Maria Barrett were missing this last day before spring break. Now she was grateful. She wished there had been an epidemic of chicken pox, the flu, hand-foot-and-mouth disease. Anything but this. She remained silent, not wanting to reveal even the tiniest scrap of information about her students.

"How many?" he barked sharply, and Mrs. Oliver cringed.

"Now, now," she said, holding her hands up to placate the gunman. "Two. Two students are absent," she said in a rush, and the man's eyes once again swept across the room, searching. "What do you want? Certainly these children have nothing to do with—"

"I said sit down," he said sharply. Mrs. Oliver sat in Lily's chair with a plop, surprised. She thought it was only teachers and high school football coaches who had mastered that tone of voice. The one that said *I mean business.*

"If you just sit quietly and do what I tell you to, no one will get hurt."

Mrs. Oliver covered her mouth with her hand, hoping that no one could see her smile. She couldn't help it. Those were the *exact* words the bad guy on Cal's favorite police drama uttered the night before. She wondered if this man watched it, too. Maybe he sat in front of his television with a beer, a bowl of popcorn and a pad of paper, taking notes on what to say. Mrs. Oliver, despite herself, always seemed to get the giggles in the most inappropriate situations. At her cousin Bette's funeral when the pastor sneeze-tooted she had to get up and leave, covering her red face with her Kleenex to hide her amusement. Then there was the time when Cal, while making love to her, called her Love Muffin, sending her into such a fit of laughter that Cal wouldn't speak to her for two days.

Mrs. Oliver always looked back on these events with such shame and bewilderment. She prided herself on being the responsible, serious, respectful person of the group. Cal told her that she was incapable of handling the truly emotional situations and this was how she dealt with them, by masking them with laughter and mockery. She had responded by asking him if his eighth-grade diploma and fifty-two of years of working at the washing machine factory qualified him as a psychiatrist. He hadn't spoken to her for four days after that one. She hadn't meant to make fun of his educational background. In fact, Cal was one of the smartest men she had ever met. He could fix just about anything. He was good with their finances and was the one that their children went to for advice about their relationships. Not her. His job at the washing machine factory had helped pay her way through teacher's college and provided an excellent insurance and retirement package.

He was right.

For some reason, she hadn't quite figured out why, she couldn't handle the emotional moments life had to offer. Or maybe it was that she handled them too well. Cal was the one who had cried at their children's births, at their weddings, when Georgiana miscarried her first child. It wasn't that Mrs. Oliver didn't cry. She did. But in private, locked in the bathroom, with the water running and the fan on.

She glanced over at P. J. Thwaite, who was still enraptured with the stranger. The man appeared to be counting the number of people in the classroom or looking for someone in particular. Maybe he was here after one of her students? she wondered. The only domestic situation she was aware of was the divorce of Natalie Cragg's parents. She hadn't seen Mr. Cragg in years, didn't know if she would even recognize him. Mrs. Oliver looked over at Natalie Cragg, who was looking down at her desktop, crying softly. When she looked back to P.J., his eyes hadn't wavered from the man's stern face.

"P.J.," she whispered, trying to get his attention. He just continued to look at the man's face. Not at his gun or the knapsack he carried filled with God knew what. It was his face P.J. was memorizing and this more than anything scared Mrs. Oliver. The man would notice, sooner or later, P.J.'s odd fascination with him and she was afraid that he would in turn find reason to focus his attentions on P.J. "P.J.," she said more loudly, and P.J. reluctantly turned away from the man. P.J.'s black shock of hair, still mussed from his stocking cap, fell into his eyes, and he looked dazedly at his teacher. P.J. had told her once that he wouldn't let anyone but his mother cut his hair and he wasn't going to get it cut until she came to get him. "P.J., don't stare at him," she whispered fiercely.

"What are you saying? What are you telling him?" the man demanded, raised his gun and pointed it at Mrs. Oliver.

"I told him not to be scared," Mrs. Oliver lied.

"I'm not scared," P.J. piped up.

The man leveled his gaze at P.J. and Mrs. Oliver trembled. This was a cold, cruel man with dead eyes, she determined. He would kill every single one of them without a second thought. "Why aren't you scared?" the man asked P.J.

P.J. hesitated and bit his lip before answering. "Because you said you wouldn't hurt us. Not if we did what you said."

"Smart kid," he answered with a bitter smile.

Meg

I assure Dorothy that we will look into the possibility that Blake could be the one in the school and send her on her way with the order to call me if she hears anything from her son. Already I'm frustrated. We don't have enough personnel to chase down all the leads that are forming and the weather is growing worse by the minute.

My phone buzzes again. Another text message from Stuart. I read his latest text first. Come on, Meg. For old times' sake. Just one comment? I shake my head and snap my phone shut without reading the first message. I already know what it says. Stuart would do anything to get the inside scoop on a story, even resort to blackmail, and the intrusion at the school could be the biggest of his career. Up until the Merritt case, Stuart's investigative reporting in Afghanistan while covering the war a few years ago was the peacock feather in his cap and earned him the Pritchard-Say Prize for Investigative Journalism. Then there was the Merritt story, which was, besides the whole married thing, the decisive nail in the coffin that was our relationship. Now Stuart is back. He can't resist the scent of a big story and this standoff. I could see Stuart relishing the thought of a Columbine or Virginia Tech–type massacre just for the byline he would get.

By the time I've circled the school with the police line tape, the chief has called in our other off-duty officers and our reserve officers, townspeople who have gone through eighty hours of training and forty hours of supervised time with our small police force. The only time I remember our reserve officers being called in was a few years ago when a tornado ripped through the town of Parkersburg and we were asked to assist. The fact that the chief has requested them tells me this is the real thing.

A large crowd has gathered in the main parking lot. I fill in Chief McKinney on what Dorothy has told me and he digests the information silently.

"Any new info on your end?" I ask him.

"Nothing of use besides the man who phoned and said he is in the school and has a gun." He shakes his head, releasing the snowflakes that had settled in his hair. "Besides that, we have lots of information that only makes things even more confusing. I swear to God, why the hell are cell phones allowed in school? You'd think that we'd get good solid information from inside, but all they've done is jam up the phone lines and cause otherwise sane people to go crazy."

"No one has seen anything?" I ask in disbelief. "We don't know why he's in the school, what he wants?"

"From the calls we've got from within the school, here's what we know." McKinney pulls off a leather glove and ticks the points off on his fingers.

"We've got one gunman. We've got three gunmen. We've got a man with a machete, we've got someone—can't tell if it's a male or female—with a bomb. We've got shit, that's what we've got." McKinney runs his hands over his mouth and his icy mustache crunches beneath his fingers.

"We just wait it out, then? We don't go in?" I ask, already knowing the answer.

"We do just what we're doing right now, containing the scene and falling back. If we can communicate with the suspect we can get those kids and teachers out safely. It's this weather I'm worried about," McKinney says, looking up at the iron-gray sky. I do the same and instantly my vision becomes blurred as snowflakes fill my eyes. "Interstates and highways all over the state are already closed. I've called in all the off-duty and reserve officers and dispatchers, and asked Sheriff Hester to bring in his off-duty folks. I've got them covering each corner of the building."

I look to where he's pointing and see the sheriff's deputies walking around with M4s slung across their backs. "You think we're going to need a tac team?" I ask. A tactical—or tac team, as we call it—is a group of officers that comes from all over the state and are specially trained to respond to situations like this.

"Looks that way," McKinney says. "But if it keeps snowing like this, we're not getting one. We're the tac team."

I see movement through one of the main office windows and place a hand on McKinney's arm. "Look," I say, peering through the veil of snow and touching my sidearm like a talisman.

Augie

The cold from the floor is seeping through my pants and it feels as if we have been sitting here forever, but it's only been like half an hour. All I can think about is that after all that's happened, I'm not going to be able to see my mom. We're supposed to get on a plane to Arizona tomorrow and spend the week there.

I wonder what she looks like now. The last time I saw her, her hands were all bandaged up, her hair was all frizzled and her face was bright red like she'd taken a walk in the desert without her hat. Her eyelashes were gone and the nurses had rubbed a thick, shiny lotion all over her arms. P.J. and I talk to her every night, but usually for just a minute or two. She's too tired or drugged-up from pain medication to talk for very long, but mostly I think she just sounds sad. I know she feels terrible that P.J. and I had to go away, especially to Broken Branch, which she always told us she spent the first seventeen years of her life hoping to leave.

From somewhere outside the classroom we hear banging and a crashing sound and I'm sure he is coming our way. Next to me Beth covers her ears with her hands and begins rocking back and forth and I put my arm around her shoulders. I don't know what's going on with Beth. She is the tomboy of our class, the one to go four-wheeling and deer hunting, and now she's just a mess.

"I'm getting out of here," Noah says. He stands up and moves toward the windows.

"Sit down, Noah," Mr. Ellery says strictly.

"No way," Noah answers, trying to make his voice tough, like he's some sort of badass. But the words come out so squeaky that I almost feel sorry for him.

"Noah, sit down. If someone's out there he'll go right on by us if we're quiet. The door's locked. He can't get in."

"Like a fricking gun can't shoot its way through this door," Noah snaps back, and tries to open a window that leads out to the teacher's parking lot. Another crash echoes through the hallways and there's the tinkle of breaking glass and far-off shouts and Noah drops to the floor. If I wasn't just as scared as he was I would have made a crack about it. For a minute the only sound is everyone's heavy breathing and Beth's teeth chattering together.

"Who do you think it is?" Drew whispers in my ear. I shake my head. I can't speak. Beth pulls on my sleeve and I look over at her.

My dad, she mouths at me, and then covers her face with her hands.

Mrs. Oliver

Mrs. Oliver kept turning around in her seat to see how her children were doing. Most were holding it together, sitting quietly, but she was especially worried about Lucy Shelton, who had some autistic tendencies and didn't adapt well to changes in her schedule. The buses were due to arrive at one-twenty, two hours earlier than usual, marking the beginning of their spring vacation. It didn't appear as if their captor was anywhere near done with them and one-twenty was drawing closer.

She was also concerned about Wesley, who had a bladder the size of a thimble. The closest bathrooms were just outside the doorway but it was highly doubtful that he would allow the children to leave the room. Each time she twisted in her seat to check on her charges the man snapped at her to face front. *Now I know how Bobby Latham felt,* she thought wryly. Bobby had the most severe case of attention deficit disorder that she had ever encountered in her forty-three years of teaching and she had seen a lot. *Bobby, face the front,* she repeated over and over until she finally gave up and gave him a seat in the back of the room where he could stand, turn around, do cartwheels if he had to, just as long as he didn't distract the other students in class. This was long before ADHD medication such as Ritalin and Strattera were being prescribed like candy. Oh, she had come to appreciate the effect the medications had on her students with attention concerns, but she didn't like the way some teachers and parents felt as if it was the perfect panacea. Drug the kid and move on. It wasn't like that. Students like Bobby needed to learn strategies that helped them focus, tips to be more organized. The medicine just slowed down their brains long enough for their teachers to help give them those real-life skills.

Mrs. Oliver took a deep breath, trying to slow down her own brain. She often used such relaxation techniques with her students, before spelling tests or before they began the dreaded Iowa Test of Basic Skills. Now she was beginning to doubt the effectiveness of the strategy she had so emphatically pressed upon her students. She felt panic blooming in her chest, felt her heart pounding so hard that she thought the beads embroidered on her jumper were going to burst from her chest. She tried combining her deep breathing with thoughts of Cal. Cal always had a calming effect on her.

Surprisingly, Mrs. Oliver wasn't always Mrs. Oliver as most had come to believe. For the first seventeen years of her life, of course, she was Evelyn Schnickle. Then she became Mrs. George Ford.

George was just her height, was handsome and funny and had the most beautiful green eyes. He was the first boy Evelyn had ever kissed and she decided the minute that his lips touched hers that this would be the man she would marry. They were married the weekend after they graduated high school on a rainy June afternoon. At the reception George teased her that the only reason she married him was to shed her last name. And while she agreed that Evelyn Ford sounded so much better than Evelyn Schnickle, that was certainly *not* the reason she married him and she glanced daringly downward, causing poor George to blush. Two months after George and Evelyn were married, George was sent off to Vietnam and Evelyn lived with George's parents in Cedar Falls and enrolled in the teacher's college there. Three months later, two uniformed soldiers showed up on the doorstep with the message that her new husband had died at Plei Mei along with one third of his battalion. Upon hearing the terrible news, Evelyn threw up all over one of the soldier's shiny black shoes, which she tried to clean up with the elder Mrs. Ford's favorite afghan. So after a mere five months of marriage, at the tender age of eighteen, Evelyn was a widow. And pregnant.

Evelyn didn't know how to be a widow; she hadn't even had time to figure out how to be a wife. She cried, in private, of course, for the loss of George. She couldn't sleep thinking about him dying all alone in a steamy jungle. Her in-laws were touched by their new daughter-in-laws's obvious heartbreak and did their best to comfort her. They told her she was welcome to stay with them as long as she needed. That was the thing, though; she thought she would go absolutely insane if she had to stay with the Fords any longer than she had to. She felt suffocated by the sadness in the house and, if she was honest with herself, terrified at the thought of becoming a mother.

All that changed when she met Cal Oliver. Now forty-five years later, she wondered if this time it would be Cal being visited by a man in uniform, a police officer, telling him that his spouse was dead. Killed by a crazy man with a gun in the middle of March in a snowstorm in a classroom in a small town in Iowa. Who would have dreamed this was the way she would go? She assumed she would die of a stroke like her father or of breast cancer like her aunts had. Not by some murderous cretin. She wondered if Cal would cry and sniffed at the thought of him being dry-eyed at her funeral. Of course he would cry, though; he was the emotional one. She wondered how he would tell their children. He was so bad on the phone. Whenever she stuck a receiver in his hand his power of speech would disappear. The man could talk for hours to someone in the same room with him, but not through a phone. "I like to see their faces when I talk to them," he tried to explain. Evelyn just clucked her tongue at him and snatched the phone right back from him. She regretted that now, the way she could be impatient with Cal. If she got the chance she would do things differently. She would never nag at him about the way he would walk into the kitchen, reach into the cupboard and grab a box of crackers or cereal and walk away leaving the cupboard doors wide open for someone to crack their head on. She wouldn't gripe about how fastidious he could be about keeping the garage clean and orderly but couldn't throw away even one piece of paper without agonizing over it.

No, Mrs. Schnickle-Ford-Oliver was not going to die today. She was going to go home this afternoon, kiss her husband. Hard. Call her children and grandchildren, then change out of her rainbow-studded dress.

Will

Climbing into his pickup truck, Will wondered if he should call Marlys to let her know that something was happening at the kids' school. He quickly nixed the idea. He had no idea what was going on, knew that Marlys would have a load of questions that he could not answer and then she would be left with the burden of whether or not to tell Holly. No, that wouldn't be fair. There was nothing that Marlys could do way over in Revelation, Arizona, to help this situation. Her job was to take care of Holly, who just couldn't seem to catch a break. The latest setback was an infection that somehow seeped into her bloodstream even though she had been pumped full of antibiotics the minute she arrived at the hospital. No, Will wouldn't say a word about the goings-on at the school until he had solid information and even then he might not mention it. Marlys was exhausted, Holly needed to concentrate on getting better and worrying about P.J. and

Augie wouldn't be beneficial. Instead, he called his son Todd, whose wife was the fourth-grade teacher at the school.

"I'm already here," Todd said when Will mentioned he was on his way and would meet him in front of the school.

Broken Branch School was a twenty-minute drive over gravel and county roads and Will made the trip in just less than twelve. As he pulled into the school parking lot he could see that a crowd had already formed. Inaudible shouts rose from the pack and were swept away by gusts of wind. Will looked down at his Mossberg on the seat next to him, trying to decide whether or not to bring it out with him. His cell phone erupted in a mind-numbing thrum of rap music that Augie programmed in as his ringtone. She thought it was hilarious whenever a torrent of curses set to music would explode from his phone in the middle of dinner or worse in public at the café or the grocery store. "Dammit, Augie," he would say, pressing frantically at the buttons, trying to silence the phone.

"What?" Augie said innocently. "You say those words all the time."

P.J. would nod his head gravely in agreement. "You do," he would say.

"Hello," Will barked into the phone.

"Will?" came the timid reply, so unlike Marlys. "Are you okay?"

"Fine, fine. How are you? How's Holly?" Will asked, looking through the windshield at four of the Broken Branch police officers trying to manage the growing crowd.

"She still has a fever and isn't eating," Marlys explained in a trembling voice. "How're the kids?"

"Fine, fine," Will said again. "P.J. has been a big help with the calving. He's a natural cattleman."

"And Augie?"

"Augie's…" Will couldn't bring himself to say anything

negative about his granddaughter when he had no idea as to her safety at this moment. "Augie is trying," he finished. Which was true. She had even joined him and P.J. in the barn the other day where number 135, a gorgeous Hereford with a shaggy red-and-white coat, was giving birth. Augie watched in awe as the calf dropped from his mother's uterus, slick with afterbirth but undeniably beautiful.

"Ohhh," Augie breathed, getting caught up in the excitement, her eyes shining, a smile appearing from her normally glowering face.

Another truck pulled in next to his and Will recognized fellow farmers Neal and Ned Vinson. Will tipped his chin in greeting and saw that the brothers had also come heavily armed.

"Will?" Marlys said tentatively. "You sound funny. What's going on?"

"Nothing," Will said, immediately regretting the sharpness of his voice.

"Are you taking your pills?" she asked, referring to the high blood pressure medication she constantly had to remind him to take.

"Yes, yes, I'm taking my pills." Will's eyes followed the Vinson brothers as they moved purposefully toward the school, their shotguns nestled in the crooks of their arms.

"Then what's going on?" Marlys said tearfully. "I can't stand worrying about Holly and have to worry about you and the kids, too. I can't take it."

"Nothing to worry about." Will tried to make his voice sound casual, light. "Augie dyed her hair red. Her head looks like a goddamn rooster's comb. I just forgot what it's like to have a teenager in the house."

"I know something else is going on," Marlys said sternly, "but I'm too tired to fight with you about it right now and I need to get back to Holly. I'm going to call you tonight and you better be straight with me, got it?"

"Okay," Will finally answered. Any other excuses would be just lies. Marlys was going to find out what was happening at the school sooner or later. It was best if she heard it from him. Just not this minute.

"All this is so hard." Marlys sniffled.

"I know, Marlys," he answered in agreement, though they were talking about two completely different things.

Holly

"What day is it?" I ask my mother, whose capable fingers are flying over her knitting. The beginnings of a sweater maybe. Funny, since it's probably sunny and eighty-eight degrees outside, just like it is almost every day here.

"It's Thursday, March twenty-fourth." I've been in the hospital for almost exactly eight weeks now. In some ways this seems like an eternity but the days have somehow melded together, one running into the next. Pain, medication, therapy, surgery. A constant cycle of healing. My mother glances up at the clock on the wall, her hands never stopping, the clicking of the needles a comforting sound that I remember from my childhood. "I called your father just a bit ago. He said everyone is doing just fine. P.J. is looking forward to helping your father with the calving."

When my mother sat down to knit, it was her quiet, relaxing time. I had never seen a person work as hard as my mother did. In the mornings, she was up before anyone else, the smell of coffee and bacon and eggs our alarm clock. After breakfast and the dishes, my mother would go out and help our father with the cattle, feeding and watering them, checking the pasture fences for loose wires or nails that might cause injury. Then she would go back to the house to clean, do laundry, make lunch, go grocery shopping, take care of the needs of five very demanding children and one equally demanding husband, make dinner, do the dishes, help with homework and finally, finally, exhausted, she would be able to sit down for a few moments and knit. Sure, we helped our mother, but there was just so much to do, there was never enough time in the day. Watching the weariness of our mother, though she never complained, I swore that wouldn't be my life and I knew I would get out of Broken Branch as soon as I was old enough.

"One o'clock, Iowa time," I say. "I wonder what the kids are doing right this minute."

Mrs. Oliver

Mrs. Oliver looked closely at the man. Getting a clear picture of him wasn't easy. He had a gray baseball cap pulled down low over his forehead. Little tufts of curly, dark brown hair poked out around his ears. He wore a black jacket zippered up to his chin and sleek leather gloves on his fingers. By the lines that seamed the corners of his blue eyes she figured he had to be at least in his early forties. He seemed overly concerned that two of the students were absent. Lily and Maria. Was one of them his target? If so, why didn't he just leave to go in search of them instead of remaining in the classroom? Was he in too deeply now, feel that he had nothing to lose?

P.J. was still staring unabashedly at the man and Mrs. Oliver had an inkling that P.J. might know the man, maybe had seen him before.

She wondered briefly if this could actually be Bobby Latham, her former student, forcing her to sit still for an excruciating amount of time just as she had done to him all those years ago. But no. She and Bobby liked each other. Had come to an understanding. She promised to never tell him to face front ever again as long as he didn't use the pages of his math book to make soggy spitballs that he shot through the barrel of his ink pen at the back of Kitty Rawlings's head. No, this wasn't Bobby Latham. Maybe it was another former student.

In her mind she ran through the Filofax of children she had taught over the years. It couldn't have been Walter Spanksi, the only student she had ever flunked. He would be in his fifties by now. How she had fretted over holding Walter back for another year of third grade. No matter how she had tried to help him learn his multiplication facts and how to read even the most basic of sentences, he just never caught on. She couldn't very well send him on to fourth grade when he didn't know a noun from a verb and consistently missed seventeen of the twenty words on the weekly spelling test. It had been her second year of teaching and she remembered vividly sitting in front of Mr. and Mrs. Spanksi, just three months pregnant with her second child, and informing them that Walter, while a very nice boy, would not move up to the fourth grade with his classmates. Mr. Spanksi held his hat in his large, earth-worn hands and pleaded with her to at least give him a chance. A lot could happen over the summer. They could work with him every day, get him a tutor. Mrs. Spanksi didn't say a word, just cried noiselessly into her handkerchief. "I'm sorry, Mr. and Mrs. Spanksi," Mrs. Oliver said, shaking her head. "I just cannot, in good conscience, promote Walter on to the fourth grade at his current skill level. I am confident that another year in third grade will be just the ticket to get him where he needs to be," she said chirpily. Well, she had another year with Walter and, as it turned out, another year in third grade did him absolutely no good. Over the course of the additional nine months Mrs. Oliver had with Walter, she saw him transform from a nice boy to a very angry boy whose second shot at the third-grade curriculum showed no marked improvement. But the man with the gun was most definitely not Walter Spanksi, though she could clearly understand why he would be tempted to return to his old classroom where a twenty-three-year-old, second-year teacher had the gall to flunk him, and point a gun at her head. How very satisfying that might be. But Walter was too old to be this man.

Over the years she had caught students cheating, fighting, smoking, stealing and many other offenses, but no one hated her. She prided herself in being fair-minded and compassionate; she learned there was so much more to a student than his or her grades. They were human beings, young and certainly not fully formed yet, but that was where she came in. She learned after that horrible second year with Walter that she had the power, no, the *supremacy,* to make a child learn, to want to learn. And in her forty-three years of being a teacher, there was only one other student, besides Walter, for whom she felt she failed to make a positive difference. Mrs. Oliver squinted, trying to see past the hat and gloves the man was wearing, the years that had passed. It could be him, she thought. There is that possibility.

Kenny Bingley. He had been a weedy-looking child, tall with long legs and proportionally short arms. Like a sprig of big stem or turkey foot, as her mother had called the long, bland prairie grass that was abundant throughout their part of the state. It could certainly be Kenny Bingley. Right age— fortyish, brown hair, mean eyes. Kenny Bingley was perhaps the student whom she lost the most sleep over. He came to school tardy every day, if at all. A perpetual musty, wet smell clung to his pale skin as if his clothing was tossed into a corner and forgotten about until he needed to put them on. No matter the child, no matter where they came from, no matter their circumstances, Mrs. Oliver was always able to find a spark of wonder and curiosity in her students' eyes. But in eight-year-old Kenny, above the blue smudges that shadowed his eyes, there was no flicker, no interest or amazement for the world. There was nothing. Just an eerie calm. He wasn't disruptive in the classroom per se, but trouble seemed to follow him wherever he went. Recess football games ended in bloody noses, lunch money went missing, classroom pets died under suspicious circumstances. But there was nothing that she could actually pin specifically on Kenny. She suspected abuse at the hands of his mother; there were no bruises, no proof, just that air of detachment, his indifferent countenance.

Two things happened the week Kenny was expelled. A horned lark was found on the school steps with both its legs snapped. Once again, Mrs. Oliver had absolutely no tangible proof that Kenny was the one who had mortally wounded the beautiful bird. But she had been the one to find it there on the school steps, its twig legs unnaturally splayed; she was the only one there to hear the ragged, high-pitched chirps, or so she thought.

The second incident that occurred had to do with a pair of scissors and a very pretty third grader named Cornelia Patts. She had stepped into the hall for just a moment, wasn't even actually all the way out of the room. The principal, Mr. Graczyk, had a question for her about some such thing or another, and had called her to the doorway. The next thing she knew, poor Cornelia was screaming and clutching at her bleeding hand. "He stabbed me," she cried in disbelief. Mr. Graczyk ran into the classroom and yanked Kenny up out of his seat, the bloody scissors sitting on his desk in front of him. While Mrs. Oliver wrapped the wound in a clean handkerchief, the classroom was silent except for Cornelia's soft sobs.

As Kenny was led from the classroom by Mr. Graczyk he pressed his thin, pale lips together, his shoulders slumped like a bent reed, and whistled a high, distorted tune, so much like that of the lark she found languishing on the school's steps.

The man with the gun before her now could very possibly be Kenny Bingley. He had never returned to school after that day, was immediately expelled, and Mrs. Oliver never learned what became of him, though she often asked after him. She decided to test her theory and began whistling the dying lark's song. Warbling and faint at first, then louder. The man, who had been sitting on the tall stool at the front of the room, the gun on his lap, looked back at her with his cold, flat eyes. "Kenny Bingley," she said stringently. "You need to stop this nonsense right this minute."

Meg

There are shrieks from the crowd as a chair comes crashing through a window. I, along with the other officers present, unholster our firearms and we watch in amazement as a pink-clad shape tumbles out of the window. Immediately I know this is no gunman. It's Gail Lowell, the elderly secretary at the school. She is coatless, wearing a bright pink sweater and chunky metallic jewelry. Her necklace and bracelets jingle gleefully as she picks her way carefully through the snow, her purse dangling from her arm. As she comes toward us, voices from the crowd pellet her. *What's going on? Are the kids okay? Is there a man with a gun?*

"How many intruders are there?" I ask in a low voice as she approaches. She appears to have been crying, but it's hard to tell because of the snow. "Did you see someone with a gun? Any injuries?" Gail looks helplessly from me to Chief McKinney and then her face crumples.

"It's all my fault," she sobs.

"Gail, this is important. Tell us exactly what's going on in there," I say more sharply than I intend to.

"Now, now, Gail," McKinney tries to soothe her. "Are you injured?" Next to them I shuffle my feet and make soft, impatient sounds until McKinney glares at me.

Gail snuffles loudly. "No, no. I'm not hurt."

"Let's get you warmed up and then you can tell us what's going on." He leads her to a squad car with an idling engine, opens the door and gently guides her into the passenger's seat. The chief climbs into the driver's side and I settle into the backseat. For a moment the only sound is Gail's soft cries and shivers. Chief McKinney fiddles with the heat and a whoosh of warm air floods the car.

"Gail," I say through the partition that separates the front and back seats, "I know how difficult this must be for you. How terrified you must be." I look at the chief and he nods for me to continue. "We need to know just three things right now, then we can take you wherever you want to go. Okay?" She bobs her head up and down and presses her fingers to her eyelids. "First, is anyone injured inside?"

Her chin wobbles. "I don't know," she says in a small voice. "I don't know. He went off down the hallway and then he was gone."

"One intruder, Gail? Did you know him? Is that what you are saying? There was just one person? Young or old?" I ask, thinking of Dorothy Jones's son, Blake.

Gail closes her eyes and shakes her head as if trying to conjure up an image. "I didn't recognize him. It was a man, just one. Forties maybe," she says in a whisper.

Chief McKinney and I look at each other in relief. At least we can assure Dorothy that her son isn't the intruder and encourage her to get him the help he needs and fast.

"I saw him come in," Gail cries. "Oh, God, he walked right

by the office window. He had on a tool belt. I thought he was going to work on the boiler—the thing is always breaking down and it's so cold today. I didn't even give it a second thought. He just walked right on by. Gave me a little wave." A fresh round of sobs erupts and the chief pats her on the knee. "I should have noticed that he wasn't dressed like a maintenance man. He was wearing dress shoes. Not work boots." She pulls her hands from her eyes and her fingers are smudged with mascara. "Can I call my husband? Please?"

"Good, Gail. You're doing great. Just one more question for now and then we're done." I wait for her to nod before I continue. "Okay, one man. Did you recognize him?" She shakes her head. "Did he have a weapon? A gun, a knife, anything that you could see?"

"I didn't see it until he came back to the office. He locked us in and then waved like he was saying goodbye. But he had a gun," she says, letting out a long, unsteady breath. "He had a gun."

Will

Will had ended his phone conversation with Marlys without speaking with Holly. She had a fever, didn't have a good night's sleep the night before. Holly had been through so much. The burns, the excruciating physical therapy. As Marlys tearfully described the procedure one evening on the telephone, Will found himself needing to sit down.

"It's terrible," Marlys said with a trembling voice. "She has to get into a whirlpool and the water loosens the burned skin and they use this brush to *scour* it away."

"Can I talk to Mom?" P.J. had asked, impatiently tugging at his sleeve. "I want to tell her about number 63 getting out and how Daniel and I got him back in."

"Not tonight, P.J.," Will told him. "Your mom isn't feeling so good tonight."

"But I want to tell her. It would cheer her up," P.J. said, jumping up and trying to grab the phone from Will.

"I said no!" Will said more harshly than he meant to. P.J. looked at his grandfather with hurt and confusion and slunk from the room.

That night Will sat at the kitchen table, his head in hands, and wept at the thought of his daughter having to endure so much pain. He couldn't help thinking that if their relationship had been better, if he had been more patient, more understanding, Holly would have never left Broken Branch and all of this would have never happened. It was Augie who came into the room and laid a hand on his shoulder. "Is Mom okay?" she asked in a fearful voice.

The unexpected touch caused Will to flinch and Augie took two steps backward. He hurriedly brushed the tears from his face with the back of his hand. "She's going to be fine," Will told Augie brusquely, unable to meet her gaze.

"Okay," Augie answered in a small, hesitant voice. Then, as if it took great effort, spoke again. "Are you okay, Grandpa?"

"I'm fine, fine," Will brusquely answered, pushing his chair away from the table. "Got to go check on the livestock," and walked purposely toward the door.

"Sorry I asked," Augie spat at his back. "I was trying to be nice. My mistake."

"You know, Augie, not every damn thing is about you," Will said, not even bothering to turn around.

Now as he sat in his truck watching the frantic parents converging on the school, worried about their children, Will was ashamed. Augie, while stubborn and more often than not unreasonable, had reached out to him, had shown him a kindness that he didn't have the decency to acknowledge. While neither mentioned the incident again, a renewed distance came between them. Augie, while neither outright rude nor disrespectful, expended as few words as possible on Will. It was as if she decided he wasn't worth the energy and Will wondered if she wasn't right on that point.

He looked at the shotgun on the seat beside him and shook his head in shame. He was acting like a ridiculous old hothead bringing a weapon to a crime scene. Good way to get shot, he thought to himself. The police might not need his help even though he had been a marine lieutenant in Vietnam but once he had a clear vision as to what exactly was going on in the school, he would have plenty of ideas as to how the police should proceed. He wouldn't have any problem telling them just how it should be done, either.

Augie

I've never met Beth's dad. By the time P.J. and I came to Broken Branch, Beth and her mother and sisters had left their farm and had moved into a small house just a few blocks away from school. Beth didn't talk much about what happened between her mom and dad, but I knew it was pretty intense. One thing I learned very quickly about living in a small town was that the men were just as gossipy as the women, except for my grandpa. Maybe the one good thing about him is he doesn't talk bad about people. The second day P.J. and I were in Broken Branch, he took us to the gas station where the old farmers met every morning. They all stood around the potato chip display drinking coffee, talking about a man named Ray and a woman named Darlene.

"I heard she went and got a restraining order," said an old man with a wrinkled red face and a scaly patch of skin on the tip of his nose. "After all Ray Cragg's done for her."

"Won't even let him see his own girls," a man wearing

overalls added. They shook their heads like it was the saddest thing they ever heard, but I saw the smile in their eyes. They were just as bad as the eighth-grade girls in my class back in Revelation when they found out that Cleo Gavin was pregnant. And supposedly didn't know who the father was.

"Now, now," my grandpa said. "We don't know exactly what's going on. Don't go making more misery than already's out there." All the men looked guiltily down at their dirt-caked shoes and someone started talking about how wet this spring was supposed to get. That was when I knew my grandpa was someone important in Broken Branch, though that didn't make me like him any more.

"It can't be him," I whisper in Beth's ear, not knowing if it is the truth or not. "Your dad wouldn't do this."

She licks her chapped lips and looks around to see if anyone is listening. "I think he could," she says sadly. "I think it's him."

Mrs. Oliver

Mrs. Oliver awaited the man's response, leaning forward in her seat, scouring his face for any hint that she was correct.

"Who the hell is Kenny Bingley?" the man asked. "Do you think I was one of your students?" he asked incredulously. "I'm sorry to disappoint you, ma'am, but your involvement here is happenstance. This has absolutely nothing to do with you."

Mrs. Oliver slumped unhappily back in her seat, well aware that her sixty-five-year-old rear end had no business in a chair built for a third grader. But now she had two clues as to the identity of the intruder. One, he was most likely not a former student of hers; he seemed genuinely unaffected by that accusation. Two, he was definitely interested in one of the children in the classroom. Over and over he scanned their faces as if looking for someone. Yes, one of the children in this room was the key. This knowledge emboldened her. "Then tell me what you want," she urged him. "Why in the world do you need to hold a classroom full of eight-year-olds hostage? How can we possibly be a means to your end?"

The man glanced at his watch. "You'll see," he responded, "soon enough, you'll see."

"What if I guess?" Mrs. Oliver asked, suddenly inspired by an idea.

"Guess what?" the man asked as he absently examined a complicated-looking cell phone. The same model she tried to get Cal to purchase to no avail.

"If I guess why you are here, will you let the children go? You certainly don't need eighteen hostages, do you? One should be enough."

This wasn't a new game to Mrs. Oliver. For fourteen years, not one of her students ever knew that her first name was Evelyn. It was by accident really that it became a challenge with her students. Over the years they tried to guess her name like a modern game of Rumplestiltskin, but without the beautiful princess or the funny little man, unless you counted Russell Franco, who was bound and determined to figure out the mystery.

"Gertrude?" Russell would say as he entered the classroom. "Shirley, Margaret, Sally, Diana, Inger, Raquel?" Mrs. Oliver would shake her head and point Russell in the direction of his desk. One spring day, near the end of the school year, so hard to believe that was over thirty years ago, Russell strutted into the classroom before any of the other students arrived and said haughtily, "Good morning, *Evelyn*." Mrs. Oliver was ready for this day. Not that she really cared that her students knew her first name; she just didn't like to lose.

"Good morning, Russell *Hubert*," she said casually. Russell froze and looked at her as if to say, *You wouldn't*.

And Mrs. Oliver smiled, letting him know she most certainly would. For the final weeks of the school year, Russell continued on with the game as if nothing had happened. "Good morning, Delores, Lorraine, Ramona?" Mrs. Oliver would just smile mysteriously.

So Mrs. Oliver was more than willing to play this guessing game with the man, especially if it meant that she could get her students released and back with their families. She had a steel-trap memory. If she thought hard about it, she could remember every single one of her former students and their parents. Certainly, this wasn't a random invasion.

"Sure, guess away," the gunman said, looking at her with his dead eyes.

"And if I'm right you'll let the kids go?" she asked hopefully.

"Yes, and for each wrong answer I get to shoot one."

Meg

There's a rap on the squad car window and the thin layer of snow that covers the glass is swept away. A wrinkled, concerned face peers into the window and Gail begins to cry again. "Can I go now?" she asks, already reaching for the door handle. Her husband, Merle, at least fifteen years her senior, is standing outside the car, waiting for her to join him.

I look to the chief, who shakes his head no. "Not quite, Gail, but we'll get someone to take you and Merle to the station. We need to get a description of the man you saw. Then you can go on home."

"I feel so bad," Gail says with a hitch in her voice. "I should be inside with everyone else, but Mrs. Brightman told me I should run, get out while I still could."

"Mrs. Brightman told you to leave?" Chief McKinney asks. Margaret Brightman is the school principal. "What was she doing when you left?"

"She's the one who threw the chair through the window. We couldn't get out of the office area—he chained it or blocked the door." I raise my eyebrows at the chief in surprise. Margaret Brightman is definitely not the chair-throwing type. Gail continues, sniffling as she speaks. "When I climbed out she wouldn't come with me. She was still trying to get through to 9-1-1. The school phones weren't working. I guess that's what he was doing in the basement, cutting the phone lines. Margaret used her cell phone and she was cut off the first time she tried 9-1-1 and when she called back the line was busy." Gail shakes her head. "I didn't know such a thing could happen. She said she wasn't going to come out of the school until all of the students and staff were out safely."

"What about a maintenance man?"

Mrs. Lowell clutches at her necklace and sits up straight. "Harlan. Harlan Jones. He has his office downstairs next to the boiler room." She looks worriedly at the chief. "Do you suppose he did something to Harlan?"

I try to keep the conversation moving forward before the hugeness of what is happening sinks in. "Gail, was there anyone else in the office area besides you and Mrs. Brightman? Any teachers or students? Is the school nurse here?"

"No, she's over at the school in Dalsing today. It was just Margaret and me. I had just sent a kindergartner back to her classroom. She complained of a stomachache and I sent her *back*."

My cell phone vibrates, I peek at the screen in case it's Maria or Tim. Stuart again. He just doesn't stop. Two weeks ago, when I opened my mailbox and unrolled the Sunday edition of the *Des Moines Observer* and saw the front page, my stomach seized with dread. I don't know exactly how Stuart got to the rape victim, how he tied her to the most powerful man in Stark County, but I know he got the information from me, although I did it unknowingly and certainly unwillingly.

In January, late one evening, I was called to the home of Martha and Nick Crosby. Their nineteen-year-old daughter, Jamie, had come home that night near hysteria and with a suspicious-looking bruise on her face.

"We can't get her to tell us anything," a tearful Martha told me. "She's locked herself in her bedroom and won't come out." Nick Crosby, hands clenched into fists, pacing the living room, didn't know what to do with himself. The two younger Crosby children, both spitting images of their father, stood by in their pajamas and bare feet looking terrified.

"Let me try," I told them, and sent the family off to the kitchen.

I gently knocked on Jamie's bedroom door. "Jamie, it's Meg Barrett," I told her, purposely leaving off the title of officer. She knew what I did for a living, but I didn't want to freak her out any more than she already was. "Your mom and dad are worried about you." I paused, waiting for a response. Nothing, just the heavy breathing of someone trying to control her sobs. "Why don't you open the door for me, Jamie, and we can talk. I promise it will just be me, no one else. I told them all to go into the kitchen and wait."

I heard a rustle of footsteps on the other side of the door. "Please go away," came Jamie's brittle, hoarse voice.

I leaned against the doorjamb, keeping my voice low and soothing. "I just want to make sure you don't need medical attention, Jamie. You don't have to say anything if you don't want to. I promise."

After five minutes of silence, the door slowly opened and a wide, fearful brown eye looked up at me. I waited until she nodded and stepped aside before entering her room. It was a typical teenager's bedroom. Clothes strewn around, bulletin boards tacked with photos of friends, blue ribbons, ticket stubs and a campaign poster of Greta Merritt, a local business-woman and the newest and youngest wildcard in the race for governor of Iowa. When Jamie saw me eyeing the poster her face crumpled into a new wave of sobs. I knew that Jamie was the nanny for the Merritt family's two children and did some clerical work for the campaign.

I regarded her carefully, knowing that one false move might cause her to completely clam up on me. Her left eye was slightly swollen and already turning purple. She held her right arm gingerly, close to her body. I waited, my eyes scanning her bedroom for some insight. A picture of a boyfriend or something. My eyes settled on one of the bulletin boards. It was filled with Merritt campaign paraphernalia—buttons, snapshots, bumper stickers. One photo caught my eye. Greta Merritt with her thousand-watt smile and her arm wrapped around the waist of her handsome husband, Matthew. Standing between two towheaded toddlers was Jamie Crosby, smiling shyly into the camera.

"Someone hurt you," I said, my eyes not leaving the photo.

"Yes," she whispered.

"You were a big help, Gail," the chief tells her as he opens the car door, and a deluge of cold air brings me back to the present.

Gail doesn't look convinced so I lean forward in my seat. "He's right. We needed you out here to give us this information. Now we know what we're dealing with. Now we can help the people inside."

Gail nods and pushes her door open. Merle is there to pull her out of the car and into his arms. Head down, to give them some kind of privacy, I walk away quickly. One man and a gun. It isn't much, but at least we now have something more to go on.

Augie

Beth is rocking gently back and forth, her shoulder scraping against mine. She has her hands over her face and is mumbling something under her breath. It takes me a few minutes to realize that she is praying. A prayer I've heard while flipping through the channels on the television being led by a woman with too much makeup standing in front of a huge crowd, many with their eyes closed, some with tears on their cheeks, arms outstretched, bodies swaying to the rhythm of the woman's words. *Amen, Sister,* I almost say out loud, but stop myself.

The first Sunday we were in Broken Branch our grandpa made P.J. and me go to church with him. I lay in bed, buried underneath the covers in the room that used to be my mother's. He knocked on the bedroom door and I could hear it squeak open. I could feel him standing there in the doorway, tall and wide in the shadows. I tried to make my breathing regular and deep as if I was sleeping.

"Augie," he whispered, his voice as low and deep as the cows that he kept in the big barn. "Augie, time to get up. We're leaving for church in thirty minutes." I held completely still, hoping that he would give up and leave without me. No such luck. "Augie," he said again, his voice booming through the room. "We're leaving in half an hour."

I peeked out from under the covers, the cold air instantly numbing my nose. "I don't feel good," I mumbled, burying my face in the soft pillow that leaked so badly that the first morning I awoke in the cold farmhouse and looked in the mirror I thought the soft white feathers were snowflakes.

"You have twenty-five minutes," he said impatiently, turning away and shutting the door behind him.

I didn't know my grandpa well enough at that point to know just how far I could push him, so I stumbled out of bed and pulled on the same jeans I had worn the day before and a long-sleeved T-shirt. I thought for sure that when I came down the stairs in that outfit, he would send me right back upstairs to change, but he was wearing jeans himself. "Better put on a winter coat," he said, holding out a red coat that smelled mildewy and must have belonged to my mother at one time. I almost reached out to take it from him, but quickly pulled my hand back.

"I'm not cold," I said, and walked right past him and climbed into the truck next to P.J., who had on a coat that had the same moldy smell but was like four sizes too big for him.

"I know," he said at my look. "It's Uncle Todd's. At least I'm warm. You're going to freeze."

"At least I don't look like a dork," I mimicked, pulling my hands up into the sleeves of my T-shirt, trying to warm them as Grandpa climbed into the driver's seat, the entire truck leaning to the left as he sat down. We drove in silence all the way to church, which turned out to be smaller than I thought it would be, but prettier than I thought it would be, too. I expected Grandpa to march us right up the aisle to the very front of the church, but he didn't. Instead, he led us to the middle of the church and off to the right. I sat down on the hard wooden bench as he lowered the kneeler. I watched him carefully out of the corner of my eye. I expected him to be some kind of Holy Roller, but he wasn't. He sang, though, clear and loud. He sounded even better than the choir director we had at my school in Revelation.

Mom never took me and P.J. to church in Revelation. I never asked, but always wondered why. P.J. asked, though, just a week before the fire. We were sitting at the little table in our breakfast nook, eating the chicken and rice that I made for supper that night.

"Why don't we ever go to church?" he asked while he shoved an enormous piece of chicken into his mouth.

If you didn't know our mom, you'd think that she was completely ignoring us. The way she took her time eating a slice of French bread, took a long drink of water, wiped her mouth with her napkin, stood and took her plate over to the sink. This was our mother's way of carefully thinking through what she was going to say before answering us.

"My father made me go to church every Sunday for seventeen years, P.J., and it didn't do me any good." She dropped her silverware into the sink and turned back to face us. "I think a person doesn't have to be in a church to feel close to God. The desert works just as well." I sat at the table, silently saying, *Shhh, don't say things like that.* Feeling guilty for her. "God doesn't take attendance and even if a person goes to church every single day, that doesn't make him some kind of saint."

I watched her standing over the sink, scraping rice down the garbage disposal, the same sink she would stand over a week later, her burned skin sliding off her arms and swirling down the drain. Sometimes I wonder if the burn was a punishment for what she said, even though deep down I knew that didn't make sense, that God couldn't be so mean.

I look up at the clock on the wall; we've been sitting here for less than an hour, but it feels like forever. Mr. Ellery slides off his desk, reaches into his pocket, pulls out his cell phone, looks at it for a minute and then puts it back into his pocket.

"Why hasn't anyone called?" Beth asks suddenly. "Why hasn't anyone come for us?"

Mr. Ellery shakes his head. I'm wondering the same thing. I can't believe we haven't heard police sirens or heard a helicopter or something. Back in Arizona our school had lockdowns at least once every few months but nothing bad ever happened. It was always some incident somewhere in the neighborhood, no one ever came near the school. I'm also wondering about P.J. He's such a weenie. He's probably cowering underneath his desk right now.

When Mom got burned, instead of helping, P.J. ran into his room and hid underneath his blankets. Which I kind of understand. It was incredibly freaky seeing our kitchen curtains going up in flames and Mom ripping them down with her bare hands, the fire streaking up her arms until it looked like she was holding a ball of flames. It was bad enough trying to get Mom out of the house; I had to pull her away from the sink and push her through the front door as she cried, "P.J., P.J.!" But to get P.J. out was nearly impossible. He wouldn't come out from beneath his covers and I finally had to grab the ends of the blanket and drag him like he was a sack of garbage. The smoke was thick and black; my lungs felt squeezed and every breath I took felt like I was swallowing crushed chalk. My arms ached from lugging P.J. through the smoke-filled hallway, feeling my way out with my feet. When I finally found the front door and stepped out onto the front stoop blinking blindly in the hot sunshine, my mother was on her knees, a group of neighbors bent over her. Next to me on the ground, P.J. was trying to get out of the blanket, and when he finally wriggled out, his brown hair was standing up like a porcupine and his glasses were lopsided on his nose.

The sirens from the fire trucks and the ambulance drowned out his voice as he cried, "Mom?" and tripped down the front steps, but before he could get to her the firefighters were running toward us and we were scooped up and taken away from the house that was still leaking gray smoke.

I can imagine P.J. in his classroom right now, his arms and head tucked into his sweatshirt like a turtle, thinking to himself, *If I can't see it, it isn't there.* "Stupid weenie," I accidentally say out loud, and Noah elbows me in the side, hard.

Our neighbor, Mrs. Florio, called my dad for us and explained what had happened. We rode in silence in the back of Mrs. Florio's rusty station wagon to the hospital where my dad would meet us.

"Do you think she's going to be okay?" P.J. asked, his brown eyes scared and big, magnified through his glasses that were smudged with soot from the fire.

"I don't know," I answered honestly. The burns on our mother's hands looked so bad, her hair on one side was burned away, her face was bright red and one ear was blistered and oozing. Before the smoke soaked into my clothes and hair, making me smell like a campfire, I could smell her skin burning, sweet and sharp at the same time. I swallowed hard, trying not to throw up.

"Do you think she'll be able to come home tonight?" P.J. asked. "Do you think we'll be able to go back home?"

"I don't know," I said, and pinched my nose, trying to squeeze the awful smell away.

"What will we do for clothes? Where will we sleep tonight? Oh, my gosh." P.J. groaned. "My homework. Do you think my homework burned up? They make you pay for the books if you ruin them."

"P.J., shut up!" I said angrily. "I don't know any more than you do." I scooted to the far side of the car and leaned my head out the window, gulping in big breaths of fresh air.

"You could get decapitated that way," P.J. said snottily. "Not that you need your head." He waited for me to ask why in the world I wouldn't need my head, but I didn't give him the satisfaction, and pushed my face farther out the window. "Because you don't have a brain," he finished proudly.

"Ha, ha," I answered.

"Now, now, you two," Mrs. Florio said with her thick Spanish accent. "You need to take care of each other. Not fight." I loved the sound of Mrs. Florio's voice. Sometimes I would lock myself in the bathroom and stand in front of the mirror and try to copy her deep voice, which came from far inside her throat like a cat's purr. I imagined that I had her black, smooth, shiny hair instead of my own plain brown hair that just laid there. I'm not sure why we called her *Mrs.* She didn't appear to have a husband but there were dangerous-looking boyfriends who roared up in front of her house and left early in the morning before the sun came up.

"Augie," my father said, coming up to me and wrapping his big arms around me. I buried my face in his chest and breathed in. He smelled like he always did, like the thick leather belt he wore around his waist and his mediciney shaving cream. "Are you okay?" he asked, stepping back and looking me up and down. "What happened?"

"There was a fire and Mom got burned and the house smelled like smoke and Augie had to drag me out in my blanket, and the fire department came and an ambulance," P.J. said all in one breath.

I watched my dad's face carefully. He tried so hard when it came to P.J., but he couldn't always hide whatever it was he felt about him…irritation, jealousy, hate. I don't know. "Are you okay, P.J.?" my father asked in a nice voice, and I relaxed.

"I'm okay," P.J. answered, looking up at him like he was God or something. "How are you?" I had to roll my eyes. He's such a little old man. Before my dad could answer, an ancient-looking woman with short, poodle-permed gray hair and a white coat came over to us.

"I'm Dr. Ahern," she introduced herself, shaking each of our hands, even P.J.'s. "You're the family of Holly Baker?"

"Yes," my father said. "Well, I'm Holly's ex-husband, and these are her children, Augie and P.J."

Dr. Ahern nodded in understanding. "The burns on Holly's hands and arms appear to be quite severe. We've started an IV of antibiotics to prevent infection and we have her heavily sedated to keep her comfortable. The other burns, on her face and ear, appear to be less severe, but we will monitor her carefully."

"Is she coming home tonight?" P.J. asked. His lower lip quivered and his eyes filled.

The doctor shook her head. "I'm sorry, your mother will be in the hospital for several days. The burn team will assess her injuries, but I imagine that she will be with us for a while."

One fat tear rolled down P.J.'s face, leaving a dirty path down his cheek. He looked over at me. "Where will we go?" I was wondering the same thing and I looked over at my dad, who was doing his best to not look back.

"Can we go and see her?" I sniffed, trying to keep my own tears from falling. If it hadn't been for my stupidity my mother wouldn't even be in the hospital.

She shook her head no. "Not just yet. We'll get her settled and have someone check in with you periodically. If you'd like to go and get cleaned up, you can leave your number at the nurses' station and we can call you when you'll be able to see her."

P.J. and I both looked over at my dad. "I'll take you over to the house and you can shower, and we'll get you some clean clothes." He pulled me close to him and it felt so good, but I couldn't help but notice P.J. standing off on his own a bit. No hugs for him.

"P.J., too?" I asked.

"Of course," my father said, as if it was a silly question, though I knew better.

Before I can tell Mr. Ellery that I need to go find my brother he slides off his desk. "Stay here," he orders. "I'm going to look just outside the door."

"I don't think you should," Beth says, scrambling to her feet and reaching out for his sleeve.

"It's okay, Beth," he tells her. "I'm just going to take a look out into the hall." He walks over to the door and presses his face onto the window, rolling his forehead against the glass, first left, then right, trying to see down the long hallway.

He turns the knob and silently, slowly, opens the door, being careful not to let it squeak.

"Where are you going?" Beth says frantically. "You can't *leave* us."

"Shhh, Beth," Mr. Ellery orders. "Go back and sit down."

"No, don't go out there," Beth insists. I'm surprised at the panic in her voice. She is usually so calm and unbothered by anything.

I stand and go to her and pull at her elbow, trying to lead her away from Mr. Ellery. "Come on," I say softly into her ear.

"What if he comes in here?" Beth asks in a wobbly voice. "What if he's here to get me?"

"Who?" Mr. Ellery says, looking hard at Beth's pale face. "Do you know anything about this?"

"She thinks it's her dad." I whisper so no one else can hear. "She thinks he's coming to get her."

Beth glares at me; her scared eyes have become hard and angry. There went my one friendship in Broken Branch. Gone, just like that.

I hear the faintest click as Mr. Ellery closes the door. He leads Beth away from the door, away from the other students to another corner of the room. I want to go with them, hoping to make it up to Beth, but Mr. Ellery gives a short shake of his head and I go back to my spot on the cold floor.

"What the hell is that all about?" Noah asks. I shrug and feel my face get hot when my stomach growls loudly. I wish I would have eaten something for breakfast, but *in true Augie fashion,* as my mom would say, I backed myself into a corner. I was mad at my grandpa and because he told me I should eat something before I got on the bus this morning, I told him I wasn't hungry. Plus, I didn't eat anything but a bag of chips at lunchtime. Now even though I'm scared and feel sick to my stomach, I am hungry.

Beth is crying now and Mr. Ellery is trying to shush her by patting her on the shoulder. He looks uncomfortable and with a yank of his head he signals that I should come over, but I have a feeling that would just make things worse, so instead I lay my head on my jeans and turn my face away from him, pretending I don't see.

Holly

The doctor comes in, checks the skin grafts on my arms as well as the graft site, a long stretch of skin taken from my thigh. For many weeks the pain has been so overwhelming I didn't have the energy to really think about how I look. But now I can't help looking at my damaged skin and wondering what it will be like when I'm completely healed. "It will take some time for us to be sure that the surgeries are a success, but the grafts seem like they are healing nicely, Holly," she tells me. "Our bigger concern right now is your secondary infection and why it's so slow to respond to antibiotics."

I nod. Infection has always been the greatest concern. "What about my hands?" I ask. This is my biggest worry. Not the fevers or my face and arms, but my hands. They, for some reason, weren't burned quite as badly in the fire, but still received second-degree burns. Without full use of my hands I won't be able to return to my job cutting hair. To some it may not seem that great of a profession, but I love it. I love the way a client will smile shyly with satisfaction in looking at their new haircut or new hair color. I love the up-dos that I get to do on brides-to-be and for teenagers getting ready for prom, transforming them for their special day. I may not have stuck around the farm any longer than I had to, but I did learn something growing up in my parents' house. How to work hard. And I do. The money isn't fabulous, but I do well enough to take care of Augie and P.J.

"Stick with your therapy," the doctor reassures me, "and I see no reason for you to not recover full use of your hands." I sink back against my pillows, suddenly very tired but relieved. "You're from Iowa, right?" the doctor asks as she gets up to leave. My mother and I both nod. "There's something about a school in Iowa and a gunman on the news."

"Oh, my, that's terrible," my mother exclaims as a nurse peeks her head into the room.

"Ready to lotion up?" The nurse holds up the tube of lotion that she rubs on my skin grafts in order to avoid the drying and cracking of the skin.

"Bring it on," I say. I'm ready to get well and get out of here. The sooner, the better.

Mrs. Oliver

Mrs. Oliver didn't quite know what to say to the man with the gun after his declaration that he would shoot one student for every time she guessed his identity incorrectly. She didn't really think he actually would shoot a child, but how could she be sure? He was growing very distracted, checking the screen on his phone every few minutes. It was the exact phone that she had Cal buy for her. You could talk, purchase something online and send an email all at the same time.

Once again, Mrs. Oliver surveyed her students; most continued to do remarkably well. Even Austin, who couldn't go thirty seconds without getting up and out of his seat, was staying put. And Natalie's coloring was finally returning to normal, her face so wan that Mrs. Oliver was sure she was going to faint. She wished the man would let them read books or draw, something that would relax them a little bit, put them more at ease, help pass the time.

What worried Mrs. Oliver most, besides, of course, any of the children getting hurt or worse, was how the children would feel about coming back to school once this was all over. Broken Branch School, her classroom, was meant to be a place where students felt welcomed and safe. A second home to many, and if you really watched and listened, for some students it was a more nurturing, caring environment than their own homes. Take Andrew Pippin, for example. Mrs. Oliver couldn't prove it, but she was sure the boy was being pushed around by his stepfather. There were the bruises, always explained away, but there was something else. An anxiousness in Andrew's eyes as the end of the school day loomed. Andrew would fidget even more, become more disruptive, all the while his eyes flicking to the clock on the wall as three-twenty drew closer.

Andrew would lose that sense of safety now. All the children would. All the hard work she invested in creating a warm welcoming environment, destroyed by this terrible man. The more she thought about it, the more indignant she became. Would the children have nightmares about school? Would they begin to shake and sweat upon arriving on school grounds? Would their stomachs clench and churn as they walked up the stairs and down the hallway to the classroom? Post-traumatic stress syndrome they called it, now a proven psychological disorder. Her heart would break if this was all the children would one day be able to recall of their third-grade year. *"What was your third-grade teacher's name?"* people would ask and they would respond, *"I don't remember her name, but I sure remember the day a man with a gun came into our classroom!"*

"A gun?" the person would exclaim. *"What did your teacher do?"*

Her former students would shake their heads sadly, hands stuffed in their pockets and say, *"Not a damn thing."*

Mrs. Oliver knew she was getting up there in age, had responded more times than she cared to admit to the question of when she was finally going to retire and begin to enjoy life. She knew some days she struggled to keep up with her students, that more than once she caught herself dozing at her desk. There was the time during Jillie Quinn's presentation on penguins she caught herself softly snoring. Thankfully P. J. Thwaite was the only one who noticed and he discreetly whispered that his grandfather drank four cups of coffee on Sunday mornings right before church in order to avoid the same thing happening to him.

There was no way Mrs. Oliver was going out this way. She was not going to retire this June being remembered as the teacher who had done nothing. She didn't want her students' last memories of their school, before it closed down forever and they moved on to other schools in nearby towns, to be ones of terror. She would rather die first. In the rafters of her brain she could hear Cal trying to reason with her. *"Now, Evie,"* he would say soothingly, and she could almost feel his hand on her arm. *"Do you really think it would be better for the children to see their teacher getting shot?"*

He was right, of course, he nearly always was, but taking action didn't necessarily mean death. She took a mental inventory of the possible weapons she had at her disposal—scissors, stapler, thumbtacks. There must be a way she could immobilize the man, long enough, at least, to get the children to safety.

The man looked up from his phone, catching Mrs. Oliver looking at him. "What?" he asked. "You don't have a cell phone?"

She decided to play dumb. Not something she was proud of but thought perhaps her perceived dimness might help them all later on.

"My husband doesn't believe in them," she answered demurely.

"What? Like it's the Easter bunny or something?" he asked. Several heads snapped up and her students looked to her in confusion.

She glared at the man. He didn't need to puncture every last bit of their innocence in one fell swoop. The man didn't seem to notice and returned his attention to his phone. In fact, Mrs. Oliver thought of herself as very technologically savvy. She spent hours learning the newest programs and she was the one her colleagues went to for help with creating spreadsheets and PowerPoint presentations. Cal actually very much believed in cell phones and insisted that Mrs. Oliver get one for her own safety. It was sitting in the zippered pocket of her black leather purse, which was tucked inside her lower left-hand drawer of her desk. If there was some way to get to her phone she could tell the police that he was right there in her classroom waving his gun around. She would bide her time. She could be a very patient woman.

Meg

C hief McKinney and I watch as a reserve officer drives away with Gail and her husband. "What's next?" I ask.

He looks levelly at me. "What's next is I ask you if you're okay?"

"What?" I ask in confusion. "What do you mean?"

"Your daughter goes to this school."

"Yes, but she's not there now. She's with Tim...."

"Can you handle this, Meg? Will you be able to possibly deal with your daughter's classmates, her teachers, getting shot?" McKinney asks.

I don't miss a beat. "Dammit, Chief, you know better than to ask me that. I've been to the homes of half of the kids that attend the school for one reason or another and have been nothing but professional."

"Ah, Meg, I know. I just had to ask. We're really on our own on this one."

"None of the tac team can make it?" I ask.

"No, the highways are shit. I've tried to call the folks in Waterloo and Cedar Falls in hopes that they can send some officers over to help with crowd control. The roads are terrible, though. It could be hours before more help arrives. Ice storms to the south of us, blizzards to the north. We'll have to make do with the personnel we have. In the meantime, we follow the lockdown plan we have in place. We need to get a handle on exactly who's inside that building. Teachers, students, lunch ladies. I've got Donna trying to get ahold of a current enrollment list with emergency contacts, so we can check off names as students come out and make sure they get handed off to the right adult."

I nod at the crowd. "If those kids don't come out soon, I think some of them will try and go in after them."

"That can't happen." McKinney's voice is like granite. He shakes his head. "Dammit, if these people don't let us do our job and something happens to anyone… What the hell?" he says, looking at something over my shoulder that has caught his attention, his mustache drooping even lower letting me know that the sight isn't a pleasant one. A group of men. Farmers, I conclude, by their mud-brown Carhartt overalls, feed store caps and shotguns. "Jesus, Mary and Joseph," McKinney says between clenched teeth.

Will

Will watched the Vinson brothers emerge from their truck with their shotguns and trek through the snow toward the crowd of parents and he opened his door to join them.

"Hey, boys," Will said by way of greeting. The two brothers whirled around.

"Mornin', Will," Neal said, tipping his chin to the older man. "Something else, what's going on in there," he added, and yanked his neck toward the school. Neal and his brother Ned were two years apart but looked nearly identical. They both had long, horsey faces set atop narrow shoulders. They were also known for their hair-trigger tempers. Rumor had it that Ned shot his prize Angus bull for butting him to the ground. The nine-thousand-dollar bull bleeding all over the paddock. Ned's version was that the bull had bovine tuberculosis and needed to be put down before infecting the entire herd.

"What's with the shotguns?" Will asked innocently, even though he knew that the brothers had the same thing in mind that he initially had when he left home.

"Thought it best to be prepared for whatever it was we ended up finding out here," Neal answered before hawking something thick and wet into the snow behind them.

"It looks like Chief McKinney and his men have things well under control," Will responded, even though the crowd was becoming louder and more unruly.

"Well, that's why we're here," Neal added, "to see what the story is."

"I think it might be a good idea for you to put those shotguns back into your truck," Will advised. "It looks like McKinney brought in some reinforcements from other towns. I'd hate for someone to get hurt if there's no need."

"Your grandkids in there?" Ned asked Will.

"They are," Will acquiesced.

"And you're willing to just stand by and let some crazy man hold them hostage?"

Will shrugged. "I don't think we know anything for certain as of yet. Could all be a big misunderstanding, could be some nine-year-old with a cap gun."

"Come on, Ned," Neal said impatiently. "I'm getting cold. Let's go talk to McKinney. Find out what's happening." From the opposite corner of the parking lot another group of men, shotguns in hand and shoulders hunched against the wind, worked their way toward McKinney and the brothers. "Good Lord," Will said, throwing his hands up in defeat. "Hope you don't get yourselves shot," he muttered under his breath. He spied Verna Fraise in the crowd and made his way over to her side. Verna and Marlys had been best friends for years. Verna almost made the trip to Arizona with Marlys instead of Will.

"She's your daughter, Will," Marlys had said incredulously when Will had broached the idea of not accompanying her.

"I know Holly's my daughter. But she hasn't spoken to me in fifteen years. I just don't know if this would be the best time for me to show my face."

"Will, your daughter has just been in a horrible accident. Do you think she is really going to give a rat's ass whether or not she's spoken to you in the past fifteen years?" Will raised his eyebrows in surprise. Marlys rarely cursed. "No, she will not. She will just be so happy to know that her father cared enough to come to her in her time of need."

Will knew Marlys was right. In all honesty, he wanted to go and see Holly but was afraid of what he might find when he got there. Burns were terrible things. When he was stationed in Vietnam he had seen the charred remains of the Vietcong's rampages on villages. The burned homes, the smoking corpses and, worse, the townspeople who did not die in the fires, the survivors who begged to be relieved of their pain. Will didn't want to think about his only daughter enduring that kind of agony.

"You haven't seen Todd around here, have you?" Will asked Verna as he came to her side.

She shook her head no. "What in the world is going on in there?"

"Don't know, but as soon as I can get to Chief McKinney I'm going to find out," Will assured her.

"How's Holly doing?" Verna asked, not taking her eyes off the entrance of the school.

"Same," Will responded. He found this a safe answer that didn't invite further questions. He didn't have the energy to go into detail about Holly's infections and treatments this morning. He just wanted to get his grandchildren out of the school and safely back to the farm. Then this evening they could call their mother and tell her of their adventure. He could imagine P.J.'s excitement, his words tumbling out so quickly that he would be hard to understand, and Augie would try to be so cool and nonchalant. "No big deal," she would say.

"Will, have you seen Ray around here?" Verna asked casually, but there was something in her voice that caused Will to look carefully at her face.

"No, I haven't seen Ray in weeks. Why, is there something wrong?"

"You know that Darlene and Ray are separated?" Verna rubbed her gloved hands up and down her arms, trying to warm them. Darlene Cragg was Verna's daughter. Her grandchildren, Beth and Natalie, were in the same classes as Augie and P.J.

"Yeah, Jim mentioned it last time I saw him. How's Darlene doing?" Will leaned forward on his toes, trying to see over the head of a man standing in front of him.

"You'd think that she'd be doing much better now that she is out of that house." Verna made an impatient noise with her tongue and shook her head. "But Ray is just making her life miserable. Doesn't give her a moment's peace and quiet. Always is calling her. One minute begging her to come back home to him, next minute cursing her out, saying he's going get the girls from her if it's the last thing he ever does."

Will looked around to see if anyone was listening to their conversation but everyone was focused on the school and Chief McKinney, who looked like he was about ready to give the crowd a tongue lashing. He bent his head close to Verna's and whispered, "You thinking that Ray might have something to do with this?"

"I don't know. He is capable of terrible things." Verna's lower lip trembled and Will rocked back and forth on his heels in discomfort. He wished that Marlys was here to bolster her old friend. He had no words, encouraging or otherwise, to offer.

"Looks like Chief McKinney is trying to come this way," Will observed, glad for the diversion. "You really should tell him of your concerns about Ray."

Verna sniffed and passed a gloved hand over her eyes. "Looks like the chief has his hands full with the vigilantes over there." Verna nodded toward the Vinson brothers and three others who felt the need to arm themselves. "Idiots," Verna huffed under her breath. Again Will thought about the shotgun sitting on the front seat of his truck and, despite the cold wind, felt his face warm with self-reproach.

Meg

"Meg, you and Aaron get started on the lockdown procedural list and I'll take care of these yahoos." He tilts his head toward the group of five or so armed farmers who now edge the police barrier.

"Got it," I say, already heading back to retrieve the detailed lockdown manual. I probably could get by without it; after the Columbine shootings I studied it until I knew it inside and out and then relearned it after the massacre at the Nickel Mines Amish School in Pennsylvania. Number one: *assume command and control of the response*. I look over at the chief. He's giving an earful to the farmers with the shotguns and to the crowd who are all heavily dusted with snow. Check. Number two: *control access to the school and designated off-site locations*. Not quite. We need to get everyone who doesn't need to be here off school grounds and to a neutral area that we can set up as the off-site evac location. A place where family members can go and seek information about their children, a spot where their children will be delivered to once they are safely out of the school. I have a feeling that if I don't hand that job over to someone else very quickly I'll be the one sitting at Lonnie's Café, the predetermined off-site evacuation site, fielding questions from desperate parents. No way. I grab the lockdown protocol manual and make my way toward two of my fellow officers who have been called in to assist.

"Hey, guys," I say briskly. "The chief wants you, Braun, to head over to Lonnie's to set up the off-site evac locale, and he wants you—" I look at Kevin Jarrow "—to direct families who show up here to go to Lonnie's for any information." They both look at me doubtfully. "Seriously. It's in the manual." I shake it at them.

"What does Chief McKinney have you doing?" Jarrow asks.

I sigh pathetically. "Media, I think."

"Ha!" Eric Braun says, slapping me on the arm. "Have fun with that." The two leave me feeling better than they did a second ago.

I spy Aaron attempting to calm a distraught mother who is trying to get past him and to the school. It's a woman I recognize from Maria's class. The mother of a little girl named Lucy. I don't know details, but I know that Lucy is a little bit different from the other kids.

"You're Lucy's mom, aren't you?" I ask the crying woman.

"Yes, yes! Do you know something?" She clutches at my jacket. "Is she okay?"

"We don't have any reason to believe any of the children are hurt. As we get more information, we'll get the news to Lonnie's, which will be the official information center until the kids come out."

"I'm not leaving here," Lucy's mother cries. "Lucy's autistic and doesn't like her schedule to be changed. Don't you have a daughter in there?"

I'm hoping my cool behavior will calm her down. "Actually, my daughter is in Lucy's class. Third grade, Mrs. Oliver," I add conversationally as I start walking away from the police tape and toward the parking lot. Already the chief has gotten rid of the rogue farmers and Jarrow is ushering the rest of the crowd back to their cars and to Lonnie's. "See, everyone is heading over to the café. That's where all updates will be shared. If I could, that's where I would be heading to." Lucy's mom looks unsurely from me to the parking lot.

"Aren't you scared?" she asks, staring me straight in the eyes.

"No," I lie. "We've got this all under control. It will be over before you know it and Lucy will be fine." I smile convincingly enough that she takes a few more steps toward her car. "Go to Lonnie's, get some coffee and warm up." I can feel Aaron's gaze boring into me and I know that he's going to skewer me for telling Lucy's mom that all was well. Before she can leave and before Aaron can lay into me, I begin to jog away, calling out over my shoulder, "Hey, Aaron, here comes the media." Sure enough, a Channel Three news van slides into the parking lot and a cameraman and a smartly dressed reporter leap out, the woman nearly slipping on the ice and falling on her ass. "The chief specifically asked that you set up the media response center to answer any questions."

"What?" Aaron asks in confusion.

"The media. Point 3.3.4 (e) in the manual." I toss him the booklet. "Thanks, I gotta run."

Mrs. Oliver

P. J. Thwaite is still staring at the gunman. His gaze is penetrating and unwavering. Finally, the man looked up from his phone and looked expectantly at the boy. "What?"

"Have you ever been to Revelation, Arizona?" P.J. asked, his voice tentative, shaky with nerves.

"No," the man said shortly, and walked toward the window spreading the slats of the blinds apart gently so as to peek outside.

"It's right near Phoenix." The man ignored P.J. Mrs. Oliver tried to once again catch P.J.'s eye, but he was determined not to look her way. "Have you ever met a Holly Baker?"

"I've never been to that town, never met a Holly Baker. Sorry," the man said distractedly.

P.J. chewed on a fingernail thoughtfully. "You would remember if you saw her, she's really pretty—"

The man's head snapped up. "What are you going on about?" he asked impatiently.

"P.J., shush now," Mrs. Oliver said sternly. P.J. glowered down at his desk and the man returned to peering out the window.

In some ways P.J. reminded Mrs. Oliver of her own daughter, Georgiana. Sweet but headstrong. She wondered what her children were doing just then, what Cal was doing. She wondered if they knew what was happening here at school. Were her children driving through the snowstorm to get to her? She had been her children's third-grade teacher in this very school. She remembered telling them that they needed to call her Mrs. Oliver while they were at school and could call her Mom at home. "That's so weird," an eight-year-old Georgiana declared. "Whoever heard of calling their mother *Mrs.?*" Still Mrs. Oliver insisted. To this day, Georgiana still addressed her as Mrs. Oliver, albeit affectionately. Now, she wondered if that was the right thing to have done. During the funeral service would Georgiana say something like *Mrs. Oliver was a wonderful mother...?* Mrs. Oliver shuddered at the thought.

She wondered if Cal was standing outside with the students' parents, demanding that the police tell them what was going on? Or was he blissfully unaware, sitting in his favorite chair solving his crossword puzzle and snapping off squares of a Hershey's candy bar to nibble on? She hoped he didn't know. Cal worried over things far too much. If he knew, he would try and dig out their driveway, and shoveling the heavy snow was no easy feat for a seventy-three-year-old man. Plus he wasn't as sure-footed as he once was, and she feared he would slip on the ice or drive into a tree or worse. Since the first day they met, Cal was always coming to her rescue.

Cal had come to the Ford house to fix their washing machine, which had died in the middle of a load of the elder Mr. Ford's underthings. When Cal came into the house with his toolbox and his sheepish grin, she never imagined that the two of them would become fast friends and eventually husband and wife. She was just grateful for someone to talk to besides Mrs. Ford, who chattered endlessly on about her deceased son. Not that Evelyn didn't like to hear about George's childhood, she did, but it pinched at her heart. She much preferred to remember George in the privacy of her bedroom where she could pull out his high school graduation picture and lay it on her pillow next to her head. In the photo his hair was smoothed away from his forehead and he was wearing his only suit. His face was split into a huge, toothy smile and she could see the laughter in his eyes waiting to spill forward. Evelyn loved this picture of George while Mrs. Ford was partial to George's military photo where he wore his dress uniform with its shiny brass buttons. Beneath his white hat with the black brim, his hair was cut bristle-brush short and it made his ears appear to stick out like the handles on a sugar bowl. His face was closed off and serious. Not like George at all, so Evelyn never let her eyes settle for any length of time on that photo.

So when Cal Oliver came into the house and descended the creaky steps to the basement where the washing machine was located, Evelyn followed. "You can fix it, can't you?" Evelyn asked, sitting atop the deep freezer.

"Not sure just yet," Cal said distractedly.

"I hope you can," Evelyn responded, looking down at her hands, chapped and reddened from washing items by hand.

"Well, washing machines are kind of like people, they only have so much time on this earth. Some last longer than others." When Evelyn didn't laugh or comment on his little joke, Cal looked up and saw the stricken look on Evelyn's face. "You okay?" he asked with concern.

"Yes. But what if the washing machine was ambushed by a bunch of...of dirty underwear and died before its time? That just doesn't seem fair."

Evelyn was waiting for Cal to raise his eyebrows and tell her to leave him alone and let him work, he was busy. But he didn't. Instead, he said a curious thing. "I would say that the washing machine was valiant in its efforts. That it did what it was called to do, rid the world of the oppression of grime and dirt. I would say that while the washing machine expired much too soon, it did its duty so that other washing machines could safely perform their duties and live a long, long time."

"Oh," was all that Evelyn could say. But she felt better. She spent the rest of the afternoon handing Cal his tools and they talked. Evelyn told Cal all about George and living with the Fords and Cal told her how due to a heart murmur he wasn't allowed to join the military but his older brother was killed in Bihn Gia. He didn't share many details, but from what she could gather, he felt a mix of guilt and relief at not being able to serve his country.

There is the sudden sound of seventeen startled bodies jumping in their chairs at the shrill ring of the one-twenty dismissal bell. Mrs. Oliver edged toward the windows and looked through behind the blinds, out the classroom window and saw that the steely gray sky was becoming shadowed and heavy with snow. Behind her, she heard the brittle scrape of chair legs against the linoleum floor followed by the scuffling steps of one of her students.

"It's time to go," Lucy said in the mechanical tone she has, standing at her teacher's elbow. "It's time to say our goodbyes."

Mrs. Oliver dared a glance at the man. How she wished she knew his name, had something to call him. In the police shows that Cal watched, the hostage negotiator always asked for a name, as if knowing the crazy person's name would somehow prevent disaster. Usually it worked. She kept waiting for a policeman to shout out to them from behind a megaphone. *We've got you surrounded, Bill (or Larry or Alphonse), come out with your hands up.*

"Go back and sit down," the man told Lucy. "It's not time to go yet."

Lucy started wringing her hands like she did whenever her carefully constructed schedule, complete with pictures and transition cards, was disrupted. "The bell rang, the bus is coming." Lucy directed her words at Mrs. Oliver, sensing correctly that this man was no friend of hers and was definitely not a clock watcher.

"Lucy, honey," Mrs. Oliver said soothingly, "the buses are late today." She almost wished that Mrs. Telford, Lucy's paraprofessional who helped Lucy maneuver the ins and outs of classroom life, was here today, but she was on a cruise somewhere in the Caribbean.

Lucy clasped her hands together more tightly until her fingernails were white and bloodless-looking. "The bus will leave, Mrs. Oliver," she insisted.

"Get her to go sit down," the man commanded. "It shouldn't be much longer now. Tell her she will be able to go home in a little while."

By this time Lucy had retreated back to her desk, lifted the hinged wooden top and pulled out a pile of books. "Time to get on the bus," she said, like she did every day at this time, her words strangled with anxiety. "Goodbye and happy spring," she added as she headed for the door.

"Hey!" the man shouted. "Stop!" He leaped from his stool and roughly snagged Lucy by the hood of her sweatshirt.

By the time Mrs. Oliver rose from her chair, her back protesting at the quick movement, the man was dragging Lucy back to her desk. "Let her go!" Mrs. Oliver shouted as she limped over to them. "You let her go right this instant!"

"Listen," the man snapped while he struggled with a writhing and twisting Lucy. "I don't want anyone to get hurt any more than you do, but these kids need to stay still and shut up!"

"Let her go!" Mrs. Oliver said, prying his fingers from the young girl. "She doesn't like to be touched. Just let her go and let me talk to her. I can calm her down."

The man abruptly released his grip on Lucy and she collapsed in a small heap to the floor, crying. Mrs. Oliver carefully lowered herself to the ground, much like she had done forty-three years before after Bert Gorse had fallen from the tree, her joints popping and creaking with each movement. "Shhh, now, Lucy," she whispered in the girl's ear, being careful not to touch her. For reasons that were beyond Mrs. Oliver, Lucy reacted to unexpected touches like someone whose hand was held above a flame. "Shhh, it's going to be okay. Just a change in schedule, no big deal. We've talked about this before."

"But the bell rang." Lucy hiccuped. "The little hand said one and the big hand said four. Time to get on the bus." Lucy, on her back, knees raised, began to pound her feet on the floor, slow and rhythmic at first, then faster, more insistent. The drubbing echoed through the room. Mrs. Oliver heard the crying and moaning of the other students. Lucy's outbursts were disconcerting on a good day, but on a day when a man entered the classroom waving a gun, it was downright terrifying.

"Stop it now, Lucy, you're going to hurt yourself," Mrs. Oliver said gently, and placed her hand on Lucy's knees to try and stop the thrashing.

"Little hand on the one, big hand on the four. Time. To.

Go!" Lucy's teeth were clenched and her eyes were screwed tightly shut, her heels hitting the floor with each word.

"You've got to be kidding me," the man muttered. "Get her to stop."

Mrs. Oliver looked helplessly up at him. "I can't. She gets herself so worked up, she just has to wear herself out. Just give her time."

"I can't think with her crying like this," he said, looking up at the white clock with the black hands hanging on the wall above the classroom door. From her vantage point on the floor, Mrs. Oliver could see the man's shoes. Brown, polished dress shoes. Nice, but not too expensive. Not the shoes of a maniac, she thought. For a brief moment, the shoes left the floor and, with a clatter, the clock was knocked from the wall and came crashing to the floor, its glass-covered face cracked, the black hands frozen at one and five. The sudden noise caused a renewal of cries in the students still in their seats but Lucy's shrieks became tangled in her throat and she fell silent. Mrs. Oliver watched in horror as Lucy's face turned a sickly shade of blue and was preparing to flip her over and pound her on the back when she heard a gurgle of breath. Wide-eyed, Lucy inhaled deeply and began to bellow and once again pound her heels into the floor.

"Christ," the man said in defeat. "Where does that go to?" he asked, pointing to a door in the corner of the room.

"Storage closet," Mrs. Oliver answered loudly over Lucy's cries. "That door is the only way out," she said, hoping that he would at least release Lucy.

"Open it," he ordered the boy sitting closest to the storage closet. The boy sat, frozen with fear, his eyes flicking back and forth between Mrs. Oliver and the man, not sure what to do.

Mrs. Oliver nodded at the boy, who warily rose from his chair and twisted the knob of the door, pulled and quickly released it as if shocked and returned to his seat. The man reached down, scooped up Lucy, carried her to the closet, hastily deposited her onto the storage room floor, shut the door and secured it shut with a chair lodged beneath the knob.

"You can't do that," Mrs. Oliver protested. "I will not allow it." Mrs. Oliver rose creakily to her knees, swayed and struggled to her feet. The man took three long steps to meet her, grabbed the front of her jumper, sending a few jeweled beads scattering to the floor, and pulled her to the front of the room.

"Sit," he demanded, "or you'll end up in the closet with her." Lucy's cries were muffled but strong. Surely someone must hear her screams, Mrs. Oliver thought. Someone must be out there ready to help. She swallowed back tears, silently chiding herself for the uncharacteristic show of emotion. In forty-three years of teaching she hadn't, not once, cried in front of her students. Not when she came to the heartbreaking ending of *Shiloh* that she was reading out loud to the students that resulted in a classroom filled with tears, even the boys. Not when Mr. Dutcher came to her door and informed her that Shirley Ouderkirk, the eighth-grade teacher she had worked with for years, had died in a car accident on her way to school that morning. Nor did she cry on 9/11 when every other teacher in the building had the news footage playing on their classroom television sets. It wasn't that she necessarily saw weakness in tears. It wasn't that exactly. It was just that she had worked so hard to keep her emotions separate from her teaching life. She had seen too many abused children, had students die from terrible diseases, seen her students suffer through divorces and simple heartaches that to an eight-year-old meant the world. It wasn't that she didn't care; she realized right then and there, she did. Maybe too much. But what good would it do the children to see their teacher crumple to the floor in a flood of tears?

Meg

B y the time I make it over to Chief McKinney the crowd is dispersing, Aaron is wrangling with the television reporter, and my hands are officially frozen.

The muffled ring of the dismissal bell from inside the school causes everyone in the parking lot to pause. All eyes turn toward the front entrance. I find myself holding my breath hoping for a crush of students to pour from the building, whooping with excitement for spring vacation. Nothing. The doors remain shut.

"Dammit," the chief says when it's clear that no one is coming out. At least, not yet.

"The off-site evac location is being manned by Braun," I say, "Jarrow will head off any more parents who show up here, and Aaron has got the media under control."

"Aaron and the media?" he asks with a frown.

I shrug. "He was more than happy to do it."

The chief gives me a *yeah, right* look and shakes the snow from his coat.

"What's next?" I ask.

"Most of these incidents resolve themselves within twenty minutes. Good or bad. We're already at—" he checks his watch "—forty-five minutes. But we've got to prepare ourselves for the reality this might last much longer." He shakes his head. "Goddamn ancient school. Only video camera is mounted at the entrance and we can't get to it."

"This is the last year the school is going to be open. I guess the school board didn't want to dump any more money into it," I say.

"Yeah, bet they'll be regretting that decision." Chief Mc-Kinney pulls a handkerchief from his coat pocket and blows his nose. "One camera, no buzzer system to let people in, and the layout of the school…" His eyes roll heavenward. "It's going to take hours to do a sweep. It's like a goddamn monstrosity with all its wings and nooks and crannies. You got a floor plan?"

"Yeah, in the squad car," I tell him. It was part of our emergency responder training for safer schools to keep floor plans of the school in our squad cars for just these situations.

"Go get it. We need to start making sense of the 9-1-1 calls, see if we can pinpoint where the gunman is located. I've got Jay Sauter bringing his RV over for us to use as a makeshift command center. We can spread out the blueprints, compare notes with Randall at dispatch. Hopefully we can get the principal on the line and get more info out of her."

"Any word on the tac team?" I ask.

"Only one guy from Waterloo can make it. Goddamn roads are a mess. It will be hours before anyone can get here." His shoulders slump at the thought.

"I'll go get the plans, then what do you want me to do?" I ask. I feel sorry for the chief. You couldn't pay me enough to be in his position. Virtually all the children of Broken Branch between the ages of five and eighteen are in that building with a man with a gun who had unknown motives.

"Meg, I need you to find out who the hell is in there. I want you to get the principal on the line and find out what she knows. I want to know about any custody disputes, any former employee grudges, any disgruntled students."

I nod, taking in the hugeness of it all. Every scrap of information I can gather is crucial.

"And after you talk to the principal, I want you to go back and talk to the secretary. No one knows more about the inner workings of a place than the secretary."

"Got it," I say as the chief's old friend Jay Sauter slides across the school parking lot in his run-down RV and comes to an abrupt stop by plowing into a snowbank.

"Jesus," he mutters. "At least we'll be warm."

Will

The crowd in front of the school was being herded away like cattle and while Will could understand the need to get the civilians out of the way for their own safety as well as for the sake of the investigation, it still irked him. He didn't like not knowing what was going on, and though he implicitly trusted Chief McKinney, whom he had known for years, he would feel better if he knew what the game plan was or at least if there *was* a game plan.

"You have a ride over to Lonnie's?" Will asked Verna, who nodded.

"I'm going to go check on Darlene first, see how she's holding up. She's waiting in the car."

"I'll meet you over there," Will promised. "I want to have a quick chat with McKinney first." Will waited until McKinney chewed the Vinson brothers and the other men who brought shotguns onto school grounds up one side and down the other. Will couldn't help chuckling to himself. McKinney was all of five-eight and slender. The biggest thing about him was his mustache, but he emitted an air of confidence, and when the chief spoke, people listened.

When Neal and Ned sheepishly slinked away, shotguns hanging limply at their sides, Will approached McKinney, who greeted him with an exasperated shake of his head. "Can you believe the stupidity of those boys?"

"Youth can be blamed for many things," Will responded, wincing inwardly.

"Yeah, well, I don't have time for that bullshit," McKinney said, blinking snowflakes from his eyelashes. "Damn snowstorm's got I-80 and I-35 closed down."

"What's that got to do with the price of eggs?" Will asked impatiently. He was concerned about what was going on in his grandchildren's school, not the weather and its effect on travel conditions.

"What's it got to do with, is the fact that the tactical team, the officers who are trained to handle these situations, can't get here," McKinney said sharply. "All I've got is my team and a few officers from nearby towns."

"You've got a town full of sharpshooters, you know," Will reminded him. "Hunters who can drop a buck at three hundred yards."

"I don't need a sharpshooter, Will," McKinney said wearily. "I need specially trained officers who, if that man in there starts shooting, can go in there and bring him out—dead or alive, I don't care—and who can bring each one of those children and teachers out safely. Plus, I don't have anyone specifically trained in hostage negotiation."

"Why the need to negotiate? Can't you just tell him to come the hell out or you're coming in after him?" Will asked.

"You don't ever want to corner something meaner than you." McKinney scratched at his face. "Listen, Will, I need to go. I'm setting up a conference call with a tac team trainer and a state police negotiator out of Des Moines."

"I'm here if you need anything, Chief," Will assured him. "My grandkids are in that school and I'd do about anything to get them out. Holly can't take one more bad thing happening to her."

"I appreciate that, Will." McKinney clapped him on the shoulder. "You can do one favor for me—keep an ear out at Lonnie's. Listen to what people are saying, who they think might be capable of this."

"Verna Fraise thinks that her son-in-law, Ray Cragg, could be capable. Ugly divorce."

McKinney nodded. "We'll follow up on that. Thanks for letting me know." The two men shook hands and Will trudged through the now nearly empty parking lot, back to his truck, which was enveloped in a snowy cocoon. Using his sleeve, he wiped the heavy snow from the windshield and looked back toward the school; it was nearly invisible through the curtain of swirling snow.

He of all people knew the challenge of fighting an enemy you couldn't see, couldn't quite locate, from his time in Vietnam. First he'd head to Lonnie's, check in with Daniel to see if the calving was going well, maybe he'd call Marlys and give her the details of what was happening. He didn't think the going-ons in small-town Iowa would make national news, but you never knew. He'd hate for Marlys and Holly to find out by watching the television. Then maybe he'd make his own trip over to Ray Cragg's farm, pay a friendly visit. It would ease his mind knowing that his neighbor, a man who married the daughter of a good friend of the family, wasn't capable of holding a school full of innocent children hostage over a marital spat.

Augie

The dismissal bell rings as Mr. Ellery leads Beth back to her spot on the floor, next to me. She is still crying, but it's softer now, not as desperate sounding. "I'm sorry," I whisper, and she scoots as far away from me as she can. Noah gives me a nasty smirk and I resist the urge of poking him in the eye with Mr. Ellery's pointer that he left sitting on the edge of his desk.

Above us there is a thudding noise, faint at first, then louder, a thumping like someone is beating a drum. That or someone is pounding their head against the floor. Everyone's eyes fly upward. "What is it?" Beth asks. "What's going on?"

Mr. Ellery returns to the door and opens it again, slowly, carefully. The pounding continues above us, harder and faster. "I'm going up there." He looks at us as if he's sorry. "I think someone is getting hurt," he tries to explain. "Just stay put. No matter what, stay here." He steps out into the hallway and shuts the door gently behind him.

"This is insane," Noah says in a regular voice, and three people shush him. "What?" he asks like he's shocked.

"Be quiet, Noah," Amanda says, looking at the door fearfully. "He might hear you."

"This is bullshit," Noah says, ignoring Amanda and talking in an even louder voice. "I can see the police cars from the window. "Let's just climb out and run."

"What if there is more than one person?" Drew asks. "What if they have guns?"

"That's the problem," Noah insists. "We don't know *anything*. We have cell phones and Mr. Ellery won't let us use them. How are we supposed to know what is going on if we can't even talk to anyone?"

"Why hasn't Mr. Ellery come back?" Beth wonders. We all look at the door.

"He probably ditched us." Noah snorts. "Typical."

"He wouldn't just leave us here if he could help it," I say angrily. But to myself I'm asking, *Would he?* The pounding hasn't stopped and there's an exit not far from our classroom that leads out into the teacher's parking lot. He could have very easily just walked out of our classroom, out the exit, climbed into his car and driven away from all of this.

"Then where is he?" Amanda asks. "Why hasn't he come back yet?"

"Maybe he got him?" Felicia says. "Maybe he got shot."

"Did you hear a gun go off, Einstein?" Noah says sarcastically.

"Maybe they have silencers, maybe they have Tasers, or baseball bats. Maybe they took him hostage, Noah," I pipe up.

"Well, I'm not waiting around to find out." Noah stands and goes to the window, which is thick with frost and difficult to see out of. He blows his breath on the glass, making a peephole to look through. "Yep, all kinds of police out there." He looks back at us. "Anyone coming with me?" No one says anything. They look around at one another, waiting for someone else to speak up.

"Maybe we better just wait for Mr. Ellery," Drew finally says.

"It's been, like, ten minutes!" Noah explodes. "He left! He doesn't give a shit about us and left us here by ourselves!" Noah's face is pale and twisted in anger and for the first time I realize he is just as afraid as the rest of us. Above us the pounding has finally stopped and for some reason that scares me more than if it would have kept on going. Noah flips the two locks on one of the large windows and pulls the frame up until it slides open. A burst of cold air rushes into the room, but it smells new and fresh and sweeps the sweaty, scared stink of twenty-two thirteen-year-olds away. One by one everyone stands and goes to the window. Even me. Using his hands Noah pushes on the screen that separates us from freedom, but it doesn't break away from the window frame. Several hundred feet away, the police officers that have been gathered at the edge of the parking lot have noticed that something is going on in our classroom and several pull out what look like guns.

"Be careful," I say to Noah before I can stop myself, and he looks at me as if I've lost my mind. Drew comes up next to him and together they push on the screen and it tumbles a few feet to the ground below. One by one, my classmates crawl through the window and begin to run as fast as they can toward the police. There is shouting and I see Noah and Drew stop short and put their arms in the air. The others do the same. I'm debating whether or not to follow them. Now there are people wrapping blankets around Noah's and Tommy's shoulders. I want more than anything to have a blanket around my shoulders, to even see my grandpa. I pull myself up onto the window ledge and throw one leg over and look over my shoulder. Beth is the only one left in the room. "Are you coming?" I ask her. She bites her lip and shakes her head.

"I need to go see if it's my dad," she says hoarsely.

In the distance, a woman police officer is waving me toward her, her arm swinging like a windmill. "Come on," she hollers.

I think of P.J. He always has to go to the bathroom when he's nervous or scared. The last thing that kid needs is the social suicide of peeing his pants in front of his classmates. I shake my head at the police officer; she drops her arm to her side and even from so far away I can see the disbelief on her face. I turn away from the policewoman and the freedom of the parking lot. Beth is looking at me, waiting to see what I'm going to do. I reach out my hand and Beth grabs it, pulling me back into the classroom.

Holly

My mother is dozing in a chair across from my hospital bed. I tell her over and over to go back to the tiny apartment she rented that is just a few blocks away, so she can get a good sleep, but she always waves her hand and says, "There's always time for sleep later." Which is so like my mother. I don't think I ever once saw my mother asleep while I was growing up on the farm. She was always awake when I got up in the morning and I always went to bed before she did. Every Mother's Day was thwarted because none of us could drag ourselves out of bed earlier than our mother in order to serve her breakfast in bed.

My earliest memory of the farm is of standing just outside the fence where the cattle were held, watching our dog, Frisbee, wind his way in and out among the knobby-kneed heifers. My father had always warned me to stay out of the cattle pen, especially away from the new arrivals, who were skittish, scurrying to far ends of the paddock at the lightest sound or movement.

I was wearing a pale blue sundress that matched the sky, and my mud-encrusted barn boots. It was a mild summer day and every once in a while a soft breeze would lift the skirt of my dress and I would tamp it down with a giggle. I watched Frisbee as he settled himself in the middle of the pen, spine straight, holding completely still. Even my four-year-old self knew that Frisbee was up to no good. Cattle are curious creatures and slowly made their way, step by cautious step, over to where Frisbee sat, unmoving. One spoon-eared heifer, the color of the anise candy my father kept in his pocket, approached Frisbee and lowered her broad nose to his, as if leaning in to give him a kiss. Frisbee leaped into the air and nipped the unsuspecting bovine on the nose, sending her and the other startled cattle to a far corner of the pen. Frisbee would take a few joyful victory laps around the paddock, egged on by my whoops and cheers, and then return to the center of the pen where he would start the game all over again.

I remember glancing around the farmyard to see if anyone was around. I was alone. I hitched up my dress and climbed between the slats of the fence and joined Frisbee in the center of the paddock. There we waited as the curious heifers crept slowly closer, their heads swaying side to side, their wide nostrils flaring, until I couldn't see the sky above me any longer.

"Stay, Frisbee," I heard my father's voice say sternly. Frisbee stayed. "Move along there, girls," he told the heifers, and they calmly lumbered away, revealing Frisbee and me. My father came into the pen and lifted me into his arms; his face was tight and worried-looking.

"Don't worry, I'm okay, Daddy," I remember saying to him as I patted his cheek with my chubby fingers.

"Stay out of the pens, Holly," he said angrily. "You'll spook the cattle." And that was how it always seemed to go.

When I was young, the farm and the land around it was the world. When I looked north and east I could see the pastures where the cattle grazed, green with clover and slightly sloping, punctuated with fence posts at predictable intervals. To the south were the cornfields that overnight seemed to become a jungle of coarse stalks and feathery tassels. I loved roaming the fields, pushing aside the stalks that left a red rash on my arms from its raspy leaves. I never knew where I was going next, didn't know where I would end up coming out. But that was why I did it. That and to drive my parents crazy.

To the west of our farm was Broken Branch, where I went each Sunday with my family to attend church. But even way back then, the town felt too small to me, too familiar, and I couldn't wait to get away.

My mother's eyes open. "Caught me," she says guiltily. The fluorescent lighting in my hospital room is unforgiving and her skin has taken on a yellowish, unhealthy tint and I am reminded how much she has aged since I last saw her.

I smile at her. "If anyone deserves a good rest, it's you, Mom. I've never known anyone work as hard as you have your whole life."

"Your father could give me a run for my money on that one," she says modestly.

"What time does their flight arrive?" I ask for the hundredth time, even though I know the answer.

"Four o'clock tomorrow," my mother says, standing and stretching her wide arms over her head. "They're coming right from the airport."

"I can't wait to see them," I say like a child anxiously awaiting Christmas.

"I know," my mother says, "and they can't wait to see you. Your father, too. He can't wait to see you. He'll make sure he gets Augie and P.J. to you safe and sound."

Will

Verna and Will pulled chairs up to an already crowded corner table at Lonnie's. The air smelled of fried onions and coffee. Apparently an armed gunman in the only school in town wasn't enough to diminish everyone's appetites. But as Will looked around, it was easy to identify those who had loved ones in the school and those who were merely spectators in someone else's nightmare.

Three tables away, a group of strangers were mowing their way through Lonnie's appetizer platter and tenderloin sandwiches. Reporters, Lonnie guessed at the sight of a man in a trench coat. The coat, not nearly warm enough for a day like this, and the stiff, coiffed hair of the woman, were a dead giveaway. Two others at the table were attempting to lean nonchalantly toward the other customers and were writing furiously in their notebooks.

"The goddamn nerve of them," said Ed Wingo, a scarecrow-thin man with hunched shoulders and a foul mouth. Ed was also probably the richest man in town, with eight hundred acres of farmland and one of the most successful hog confinement operations in the county. "Someone should tell them to get the hell out of town," he added bitterly.

"That'd be just great, Ed," Verna said dryly. "We'll just manhandle them, throw them out into the snowstorm and see what all kinds of nice things they're going to say about our fine town."

Will choked on his coffee, trying to swallow back his laughter. No wonder Marlys liked this woman, he thought. Not too many people dared to put Ed Wingo in his place.

Ed puffed out his chest and pointed a bony finger at Verna. "Do you really think it's okay that these strangers are sitting in here, eavesdropping on our conversations, taking advantage of the suffering of this town to sell a few papers or for the ratings?"

"I imagine," Will said lightly, "that these folks would like nothing better than to be at the school finding out what is actually going on rather than being stuck here with those of us who can give them absolutely no information."

"They're probably more worried about where they're going to sleep tonight," Carl Hoover, the president of the Broken Branch First National Bank, added. "The way the snow is coming down, chances are the highways are going to be closed."

"You think they realize we don't have a hotel in town? Maybe they can stay with you, Ed, in that big old house of yours." Verna laughed and then abruptly sobered when the other customers looked their way. "How much longer do you think this can go on?" Verna asked helplessly.

"Well, if I had my say," Ed said, flagging down a waitress, "I would go right into that school and use a sharpshooter to knock the man flat and then get the kids the hell out of there."

"They can't do that," Carl scoffed. "Might cause the man to start shooting. No, they have to try and make contact with him, try to negotiate and then just sit back and wait him out."

"That's what I don't understand." Ed held out his coffee cup for the waitress to refill. "Why would some asshole want to hold a bunch of kids from Broken Branch hostage? It's bullshit." He nodded his thanks to the waitress and took a long, contemplative sip. "Maybe it's that teacher they fired last year. He had quite the temper. If I remember right, roughed up a student."

"Yeah, that was bad business," Will responded, shaking his head at the memory. "The kid filled his gas tank with sugar or some such thing. Still no excuse to get physical."

"I heard that he was managing a gas station over by Sioux City now. Probably gets paid better doing that than when he was a teacher," Verna mused. "Can't imagine why he'd want to show his face back here." She glanced surreptitiously at Will. He knew she was thinking of her son-in-law and her grandchildren.

Meg

As I make my way back to my squad car I take the time to check my cell phone for any missed calls. There are five. Four from Maria. Another one from Stuart. My heart skips a beat at the thought that something must be wrong with her but then I remember the news van and what Stuart said about the lockdown being all over the media. Maria may have seen something on the television and is scared for her classmates. Tim and Maria are just probably checking up on me. I hit Send on my phone as I climb into my car.

"Hi, Mommy." I hear Maria's breathless voice. "What happened at school?"

"You don't worry about it, okay?" I say, tucking the phone between my chin and shoulder and putting the key into the ignition.

"But the TV says..." she begins.

"We're not sure just yet, Maria Ballerina," I say, using my

pet name for her. My tires slip slightly as I make a left turn out of the school parking lot.

"Okay," she says, though she doesn't sound convinced.

"I have to get back to work, so tell your dad I'll give you a call later."

"He had to go to work," Maria says, and from the sound of her voice I can tell she's as happy about it as I am.

"Who's with you?" I ask, worried that she is going to say my parents or, worse, my brother.

"Grandma and Grandpa Barrett," she answers, and I relax.

"Let me talk to Grandma Judith, okay? I'll call you later. I love you, big hugs and smooches."

"Big hugs and smooches," she echoes, but she sounds sad and near tears.

There is silence for a second as Maria hands the phone to Tim's mother.

"Judith," I say, "I thought Tim was on vacation." I try to keep the irritation out of my voice; this isn't Judith's fault.

"I know, Meg," she says, and I can hear that she is uncomfortable. This makes me so sad because Judith and I have always had a good relationship. "He got called into work. What's going on there?"

"I can't talk now, Judith. Please just have Tim call me the minute you talk to him."

"You'll probably see him before we do," she says. "I think he was called to be an EMT backup for whatever it is you aren't talking about."

I don't mean to, but I sigh. Loudly. "If you talk to him, please have him call me. And," I add before I can stop myself, "please don't let Maria watch any more news programs about what's going on."

"Meg," Judith says in exasperation. "Maria was already watching TV when all of a sudden her show was interrupted with a special report about her classmates being taken hostage. And please don't tell me you can't get into it."

"I really don't know anything for certain or I would tell you. I'm sorry, Judith, I don't mean to snap at you. It's pretty tense here. I'll call you when I have more info, okay?"

There's a long pause and I wonder if she's hung up on me. "Maria could be in there right now," she finally says.

"I know," is all I can think of to say, and I push back the thoughts of Maria being in the school with a gunman. I wonder what I would do. Would I continue on as I am now, interviewing witnesses, helping to organize the investigation? Or would I have done what the farmers had in mind? Barge into the school with a gun in order to bring her out safely.

I hang up and for half a second consider calling Stuart to see if anything new had been uncovered by the media and then quickly discount it. Things definitely did not end well with Stuart three weeks ago. I was sitting at my desk at police headquarters typing up a report when a woman stalked into the building and stopped in front of me. I remember noticing how nice this stranger looked, dressed fashionably, makeup perfectly applied, each hair in place. I later realized that she had done that for my benefit. Her chin wobbled as she slid her wedding ring off her finger and set the gold band gently on my desk.

"You may as well have it," she said softly. "You've taken everything else that's important to me."

I looked up at her in confusion, her identity still not registering with me. "Can I help you?"

She emitted a sharp bark of laughter, causing the others in the office area to look our way. From next to the coffee machine, Chief McKinney eyed the scene warily while he poured cream into his mug. "You can *help* me by telling Stuart to never come home again. The locks are changed, the

One Breath Away   153

phone number is changed. The only way I want to communicate with him is through our lawyers." The shock on my
face must have caused her to falter because for just a moment
a flash of doubt flickered in her eyes, but she quickly recov-
ered, replacing concern with cold disdain.

"I'm s-sorry," I stammered. "I didn't know."

She shook her head balefully. "Yeah, me, neither," she said
bitterly, straightened her shoulders and left.

Two days later, I opened the Sunday paper and saw the
headline in big bold letters and Stuart's byline. My blood went
cold. Stuart got his big story and used me to get it.

Stuart can go to hell, I decide as I try to brush the memory away. I drop the phone on the seat next to me, vow to
charge him with interfering with a police investigation or at
least with something the next time he contacts me, and look
back over my shoulder and see a stream of students running
from a far corner of the school. I slam on the brakes, causing
my car to slide and fishtail for what feels like an eternity. Finally, the tires grip the road and I'm able to maneuver the car
so I'm once again facing the school. Breathing hard, I take in
the sight. Twenty-some students, teens by the look of them,
are running through the snow toward the parking lot, terror
on their faces. One student's feet slide out from beneath her
and she falls with a violent smack to the ground. McKinney
has managed to get Broken Branch's one ambulance and one
more from a neighboring town and instantly there are two
EMTs at her side. I wonder if Tim is on his way and, if so,
why he hasn't called me yet.

I throw the car into Park and make my way back toward
McKinney and the other officers. I keep moving toward their
point of exit, a window that sits low to the ground. A battered
screen lies in the snow and a young girl straddles the window

ledge, one leg dangling over a snowbank. The girl keeps looking back into the classroom as if she has forgotten something.

"Come on," I call out, waving her toward me. Startled, her eyes fly to my face and for a moment we stare at each other. Then I see it, a tightening of her mouth, the squaring of her shoulders. "No, no," I call after her as she pulls her leg back over the ledge. "Come on!" I yell loudly. "This way!" She doesn't look back and disappears into the classroom. "Dammit," I mutter as I stare through the now-empty window.

Mrs. Oliver

From her chair where the man ordered her to sit, Mrs. Oliver called out to the little girl locked in the closet. "Don't worry, Lucy! It's going to be okay!" Mrs. Oliver was furtively wiping at her eyes, trying to staunch the tears before they started, when she saw him. Jason Ellery. Standing outside the door, peeking in. At first she was hopeful, her midsection fluttering with excitement, but was quickly replaced with fear. The man was angry enough as it was, who knew what he would do if Mr. Ellery, young and naive to be sure, confronted him.

"Jesus, don't you people follow your own lockdown procedures?" the man asked in exasperation. He leveled his gun at the door and Mr. Ellery ducked. "Open the door," he said loudly. No one moved and Mr. Ellery didn't reappear. "I said, open the goddamn door." Seconds passed and with a soft click the door swung gently open. Jason Ellery stood before them, his hands raised.

"Hey, man," Jason said in an apologetic tone, "I heard some pounding and crying. Thought someone was hurt, thought I better see if I could help."

The gunman approached him slowly, almost casually. "Bad idea," he said, shaking his head. "You're not a policeman?"

"No, no," Jason assured him, taking slow steps backward. "A teacher. I'm just an eighth-grade teacher."

"Come here," the man said. Mr. Ellery continued backing up. "I said come here."

"Hey, I don't want any trouble. Just came to see if I could…" He looked up pleadingly but before Mr. Ellery could finish his sentence the man swung his hand back, striking him on the temple with the gun. Mr. Ellery fell to his knees and raised his arms to block further blows.

Mrs. Oliver considered running to Mr. Ellery's rescue. She couldn't do much, she imagined, but she could jump on the man's back and flatten him into possible submission. She scanned the faces of her children, some with their heads buried in their arms on their desks, some sitting erect with fright, some crying. What would happen to them, she wondered, if she tried to be the hero? Would he shoot her, would he shoot the children? She couldn't stand the thought of not walking out of that classroom with each and every one of her children safe and sound. No, she would sit here, she decided. Sit and see what happened. Protect her students, though she hadn't protected Lucy very well. She heard Cal's voice in her head: *Better that she's in that closet, Evie. She couldn't cope with being out in that classroom.* That is exactly what he would say if he was here, Mrs. Oliver decided, and she felt a trifle bit better.

Mr. Ellery was still on his knees, scalp bleeding, when the man reached for his arm to pull him all the way into the classroom. Mr. Ellery—quite stupid and brave, Mrs. Oliver thought, for trying to come up here and single-handedly save them all—was young and fit. With a quick thrust with the heel of his hand he caught the man's testicles and he staggered backward, dropping the gun. Mrs. Oliver cheered. A resounding, "Yay," leaped from her lips, and she rose from her seat determined to pounce on the gun. "Run, Mr. Ellery!" she shouted. "Run." She was too slow, though; the man snatched up the revolver and chased Mr. Ellery down the hallway.

"Cover your ears," she ordered the children, sure that gunshots were sure to follow. Sixteen pairs of hands clasped their ears. Seconds passed and no sound. Mrs. Oliver hesitantly moved toward the doorway, hoping to find that Mr. Ellery had overpowered the gunman, had him in a headlock or a full nelson, whatever they called that move on Cal's professional wrestling shows. As she peered around the corner down the hallway, her stomach sank. The gunman had a bloodied Mr. Ellery by the scruff of his shirt, the gun pointed at his head, and was dragging him toward the janitor's closet located in the hallway. He shoved an unconscious Mr. Ellery inside and slammed the door.

"Get back in the room," the man said coldly, pointing the gun at Evelyn, who scurried back inside. "Stupid," he said upon reentering the classroom. "You are all just making this take a hell of a lot longer than it has to." He walked purposefully around the classroom, leveling the gun at each student and finally stopping just behind Mrs. Oliver. She felt the barrel of the gun lightly skim the back of her skull. "Just stay in your seats, stay quiet and this whole thing will be finished soon enough."

Augie

Beth and I creep to the classroom door and my hand shakes as I move to twist the doorknob. I'm afraid of what we'll find out there. "Which way do you want to go?" Beth asks as her head swings right, then left as she looks down the long hallway.

"P.J. and Natalie are in Oliver's room, upstairs," I say. "Let's go up there." I nod my head toward the closest set of steps, which still seem like miles away. We have to pass two classrooms and a bathroom before we can reach the staircase. Plenty of places for a maniac with a gun to hide.

"Okay," Beth says, and takes a step out of the classroom. When she realizes I haven't started to follow her, she reaches out and takes my hand in hers. It is as cold as mine, but strong, and in an instant I feel better and I find that my feet are able to move. We hunch our shoulders and take small steps as if that might keep us from being seen by anyone. We make it past the first classroom, not even bothering to peek inside its window. We try to move soundlessly up the steps and when we reach the top I slip on something. I let go of Beth's hand and land with a thump on my butt. I put my hands to the ground, trying to push myself up quickly, but find my fingers touching something wet and oily. There isn't a lot of it, but it looks almost black in the darkened hallway. Somehow I just know it's blood.

"Are you okay?" Beth looks down at me. I try to wipe the blood from my hands on the floor tiles, but that doesn't help much so I wipe my fingers on my jeans.

"It's blood," I whisper. A low moan comes from Beth's mouth and I know she's thinking of her father and I'm thinking of Mr. Ellery.

"We would have heard a gunshot," I remind her, and she nods frantically as if agreeing with me will make it true. "Should we keep going?" I ask, and she continues nodding.

Our classmates have probably already gotten long, too-tight hugs from their parents. They are probably being driven home to their warm homes where their mothers will cry thankful tears while making them their favorite dinners. Their dads will sit next to them on the couch and make them tell, over and over, the story of how Mr. Ellery disappeared and how they knocked out the window screen, and shake their heads knowing how different this day could have been for them.

I know this because it is exactly what my dad did on the day of the fire. After he took P.J. and me back to his house and we showered and put on old T-shirts and sweatpants that belonged to my stepmom, Lori. After P.J. fell asleep and my dad carried him into the small extra bedroom and after Lori went to hide away in their bedroom, which she did a lot when I was around, my dad and I sat on the couch together. He wrapped his arm around me and I laid my head on his shoulder. It felt like years since I'd done that. I told him all about the fire and the smoke and the terrible smell. One thing I really love about my dad is that he doesn't try to fix everything; he can just sit and listen. I guess he doesn't feel like he has the right to tell me what to do. He isn't around all that much and having P.J. tagging along just complicates things.

"Augie," my dad said to me after a while, his face serious and almost scared. I felt my stomach drop. My dad was never scared. He was always the one who was smiling and laughing. *Mr. Sunshine,* my mom said, but not in a nice way. "Augie," he said again, as if buying time to find the right words. "Your mom is going to be in the hospital for a long time."

"I know," I answered. I didn't want to talk about it anymore, didn't want to think about it. I just wanted to sit on the couch with my dad and watch some dumb TV show.

"I want you to know you're welcome to stay here as long as you want to." He squeezed my shoulder and I relaxed. This was just what I was hoping he would tell me. "Lori and I have talked about it. We'll fix up the extra room however you'd like it."

I felt a quick stab of panic. "What about school?"

My dad shook his head. "It's on the way to Lori's work— she can take you and pick you up. We've got it all figured out." For the first time that day, my dad smiled big and wide.

I let out a breath of relief. "P.J. and I will help out a ton," I promised him. "I can cook and P.J. knows how to do laundry...." My dad's smile dropped off his face, just disappeared. "No way!" I said loudly, and pulled away from his hug. He looked nervously toward the room where P.J. was sleeping.

"Augie," he said, like he was exhausted, like *he* was the one whose mother was burned in a fire and had everything he owned destroyed. "Augie, look at it from our perspective." He rubbed his hand over his bald head and I folded my arms across my chest and scooted as far away from him as I could on the couch. "We like P.J., he's a great kid, but Lori and I discussed it and we feel like it would be better if P.J. stayed with family."

"*I'm* his family." I was trying with all my might to keep my voice down. I didn't want P.J. to hear and I knew that Lori was hiding around a corner or behind a door, listening, waiting to see what would happen next. She was such a coward.

"Augie," he said softly, "he's not my son." There was nothing I could say to that, so I didn't do anything but glare at him. I've got this great glare. *Menacing,* my friend Arturo tells me. It's gotten me into and out of a lot of trouble through the years. "P.J.'s a great kid, but..." He held out his hands.

"But what?" I wasn't going to let him off the hook so easily.

"But he's not my son. You are welcome to stay here with us for as long as you'd like, but we have to make other arrangements for P.J."

"Why?" I asked. "He's eight years old. He doesn't eat much. He's neater than any of us."

"You know there's so much more to this than that."

I did know. I knew that my mom and dad separated soon after P.J. was born. I knew that my brother's dark brown eyes and black hair weren't from my father's side of the family. But it shouldn't have mattered. P.J. was just a little kid. "So you're just going to throw him out into the street? Nice."

Lori finally stepped out from her hiding place. "We're not going to throw him out, Augie." I was taller than Lori and about twenty pounds heavier. I looked like her older sister. She was the complete opposite of my mother. Lori was boring oatmeal, my mom was Sugar Jingles. Lori didn't say much but I got the feeling that she made all the decisions in their house. "We've called your grandparents."

"Grandma and Grandpa Baker?" I asked in surprise. My dad's parents hated my mother and wouldn't even acknowledge my brother. I couldn't imagine them letting P.J. live with them.

"No," my dad said. "Your Grandma and Grandpa Thwaite. They are flying out tonight."

My mind was spinning. My mom didn't talk much about my grandparents and I knew that she had some big falling-out with them way before I was born. Every year they sent P.J. and me a birthday and Christmas card with one hundred dollars inside. That was it. No phone calls, no emails, no summer vacation visits. "P.J. can't go live with them. They like live in *Iowa*." I said "Iowa" like it tasted bad in my mouth.

"Like your dad said," Lori reiterated, her hands resting on her stomach. "You are welcome to stay with us or you can go stay with your grandparents."

Right then it became perfectly clear to me. Lori was going to have a baby. I knew then that this was her master plan. She wanted to get rid of us. Replace me with her new baby. If Lori had insisted, my dad would have let P.J. stay with them. With us. She knew that I would never send P.J. off to live in Craptown, Iowa, with strangers all by himself. Lori didn't want P.J. or me to intrude on her new, perfect little family. The thing was, I'm mortified to admit, it sounded so tempting. To stay in Revelation at my dad's. I couldn't imagine leaving my school, my friends. Leaving my mom. To go live with people my mother didn't even like.

"We can live with Arturo or Mrs. Florio," I said. "We can go into foster care until Mom gets out of the hospital," I said, though the idea of it made my stomach sick.

My dad sighed and Lori bit her lip like she wanted to say more but knew it wasn't a good idea. "Augie, you don't have to make a decision right this minute," he said, reaching out for me, and I leaped from the couch away from his touch. I could tell I had hurt his feelings. Good, I thought. "You've had a terrible day," he went on. "Get some sleep. Everything will look better in the morning."

"Yeah, right," I mumbled, rushing to the bedroom where P.J. was sleeping and slamming the door so hard that it shook the walls and P.J. sat up straight in the bed.

"What?" he cried out. "What happened?"

"Shut up, dork," I snarled, shoving him aside on the bed to make room, and then made sure he had the blankets tucked around him just the way he liked them.

Meg

I can't imagine why the girl didn't come out of the school with the other students unless the gunman was in the room with them. That thought moves me away from the window and back to the parking lot where McKinney and an unfamiliar officer from a nearby town are patting down each of the students, taking down their names and passing them on to the EMTs, who wrap them in blankets.

I'm out of breath by the time I reach McKinney. "How are we going to get all of them over to Lonnie's?" I ask about the shivering, shell-shocked students.

"School bus," McKinney answers as the mammoth yellow bus appears, rumbling through the snow. "We're getting all their info, names, parents' names, addresses, phone numbers."

"Did anyone see anything?" I ask while I scan the group of teens, looking for a familiar face, someone that might open up to me.

The chief shakes his head. "We're just trying to account

for everyone, make sure no one's hurt. Doesn't appear to be any injuries except for the girl who slipped on the ice. Just a lot of scared kids."

"I saw one girl just about to climb out of the window. I don't know what, but something made her change her mind. I called out to her, but she wouldn't come out."

"You think that the gunman was in that classroom? That might give us a place to start. This goddamn school is such a maze, it will take us forever to sweep when we go in." Broken Branch School originally opened its doors in the forties and had an addition put on in the eighties. The building had many odd nooks and crannies, a perfect building for someone to hide in.

"I don't know." I shake my head at the memory of the girl in the window. "She didn't exactly seem scared, more like determined."

The chief closes his eyes and inhales deeply. He has aged in a matter of just over an hour. His face is windburned from the cold and an unhealthy red. His bright blue eyes are bloodshot and watery. "Will you make sure these kids get on the bus okay? We've got the sheriff's department off-duty guys here and I need to get everyone up to speed. Hopefully the hostage negotiator from Waterloo will be on-site within the hour."

I watch as he walks away and toward the RV. He is trying to move briskly but the heaviness of the snow slows him down and I know that his arthritic knees must ache from the cold. The pressure he is feeling must be enormous. The community, the state and maybe even the nation will be talking about how he has handled everything. How this department has handled everything.

As I direct the students onto the school bus, I ask each if they had seen anything. Most just shake their heads no and silently climb aboard. From out of the corner of my eye, I see a lanky boy with hunched shoulders and shaggy brown hair. Noah Plum. A familiar face to local law enforcement. Vandalism, underage drinking, driving without a license. A boy with way too much time on his hands and not enough parental supervision.

"Hey, Noah," I say. "Are you okay?"

He looks at me with scorn. "Why do you care?"

"I care, Noah," I say in a low voice, trying not to draw attention to us. "I'm glad you're not hurt."

"Yeah, adults are so worried about us. Even the fricking teacher left us all alone in there." He snorts in disgust and tries to move past me.

"Wait," I say, grabbing his arm. "The teacher left you? Are you sure?"

"Yeah, I'm sure," he spits, shaking my hand from his sleeve. "He fucking heard a noise, left the room and never came back. I bet he's safe and sound at home right now."

I shake my head. "I don't think so, Noah. What kind of sound did you hear?" My heart is pounding again. If it was a gunshot they heard, then we'll have cause to enter the building immediately.

"A pounding sound, like someone was jumping up and down above us." Noah's mouth twists into a half smile. "Asshole left us."

I relax a bit. Not a gunshot, but still. I can't imagine a teacher purposefully leaving a classroom of students all alone when a gunman is wandering around the school. "What's your teacher's name?"

"Mr. Asshole Ellery," he responds as he steps onto the bus.

Ellery. The name is familiar but I can't produce a picture of him in my mind. The last student settles into her seat on the bus and I climb aboard to give the driver and the officer that is accompanying them some last-minute directions. The bus is eerily quiet. Not how a school bus full of teenagers should sound. No raucous laughter, no switching of seats, no games of keep away with someone's hat. Just silent, sad-looking children looking out the windows or at their own laps.

"When you get to Lonnie's, students may only be released to their parents or guardians. No one else. And make sure that each parent signs the sign-out log showing that they picked up their child."

Another sheriff's deputy, a woman from the nearby town of Bohr, nods. "This is the real thing, isn't it?" she asks in a whisper. "I've been involved in lockdowns, but nothing like this."

I'm about to agree with her when a small voice pipes up from the back of the bus. "Where's Beth?"

"What?" I ask. "What did you say?"

"Beth Cragg," a girl with glasses and curly yellow hair says worriedly. "She's not here. She was in the classroom, but she's not here."

"And Augie," someone else says. "Augie isn't here. She was right behind me when I climbed out the window. Where are they?"

Will

The sky through the restaurant windows was marbled gray and the wind shook the panes of glass. The road that ran in front of Lonnie's was deserted except for the ethereal furor of snow that rushed down the street.

Will's stomach was churning from the five cups of coffee he had downed and he knew he should get something into his stomach. He had phoned Daniel, who could only spare a few seconds to tell him about the calving; the mother was in some distress, but nothing he couldn't handle. Will wondered if he would be more useful going back to the farm and helping Daniel rather than sitting there at Lonnie's, doing nothing but waiting.

Will decided to order a sandwich to soak up the vile black coffee bubbling in his stomach when through the large plate-glass window a glowing pair of headlights suddenly appeared. The café was silent, all eyes on the approaching vehicle, which gradually emerged, large and yellow, out of the blizzard. "It's a bus!" someone exclaimed unnecessarily. The hinged door opened and a sheriff's deputy stepped down followed by shivering, dazed figures.

"Oh, my God," a woman breathed, "it's the kids." A cacophony of gasps, chairs being scraped across the floor and the scuffling of rushing feet filled the air.

"It is a bus full of kids," someone confirmed.

"I see Noah Plum and Drew Holder!" a voice shouted.

"Donna, I see your Caleb," came another.

One by one, the trembling children were swept into the café by the wind, and mothers and fathers gathered them into their arms in tearful relief. Will recognized the children as students from Augie's class and craned his neck in search of his granddaughter's now bright red mop of hair.

Just this past weekend, Augie found one of Marlys's home hair color kits and locked herself in the home's only bathroom, Will and P.J. alternately pounding on the door for her to hurry up, for what seemed like eternity. She emerged with a brightly hennaed head of hair, just like her grandmother's, except that on Marlys the color looked like an elderly woman trying to look young and on Augie it looked like a purple plum setting atop her head. He had tried not to laugh, but he made the mistake of catching P.J.'s eye and the two collapsed in a fit of giggles.

"I like it," Augie said imperiously.

"Mom's going to kill you," P.J. said, trying to keep a straight face. "Mom said coloring your hair is like drinking. Once you start, it's hard to stop."

"She's going to need a few drinks once she sets her eyes on you, Augie," Will said through his laughter, and then quickly regretted his words when he saw the flash of hurt in Augie's eyes. Holding her chin proudly skyward she left the room.

When the door to Lonnie's finally clicked shut, a few

wayward napkins set aloft by the wind drifting noiselessly to the floor, and it was clear that neither Augie nor Verna's granddaughter Beth were among the students, Will sat down heavily.

Mrs. Oliver

All eyes were on the closet door where the man had discarded Lucy and shoved a chair beneath the doorknob. It had been almost two hours since the man had entered the classroom and Mrs. Oliver knew what was going to happen next. You didn't work with children for over forty years and not get to know their patterns, their needs. Poor Leah. Mrs. Oliver could tell by the way she was crossing her legs that things were getting pretty desperate.

"Excuse me," she said loudly. The man looked up from his cell phone in irritation. "The children are going to need to use the facilities."

"They'll just have to hold it," he responded, his attention returning to his handheld.

A small whimper escaped the lips of Leah and she looked urgently at Mrs. Oliver. "No, they can't hold it. They've been holding it since you've arrived. Plus, they're nervous. Everyone has to go to the bathroom when they're nervous." The man looked around the room. "The bathrooms are just outside the door, across the hallway," she explained. "It will only take a few minutes. We've got it down to a science, don't we, boys and girls?" The students nodded fervently.

"Mrs. Oliver," Leah said miserably. "Please," she begged.

"Come on now," Mrs. Oliver chided. "What can it possibly hurt?"

The man thought for a moment and looked at Leah, who was trying to squeeze back tears and, by the way she was holding herself, other bodily fluids, as well. "You have five minutes," he told Mrs. Oliver. "Get them to the bathroom and back in five minutes. One second longer and I'll start shooting."

Mrs. Oliver nodded and stood quickly, causing a dagger of pain to shoot up her leg and into her lower back. "Line up, children." Hesitantly, the students looked to one another, rose from their seats and lined up at the door. "Boys on the left, girls on the right," she ordered. Once everyone was in line, Mrs. Oliver looked at her watch. "We only have five minutes now. No dillydallying. Don't even worry about washing your hands." Seeing the look of disgust on Ryan Latham's face, she assured him that they had gallons of antibacterial gel in the classroom for their use. "Ready, now? Four boys and girls at a time. Go!" The first eight children dashed from the classroom to the restrooms across the hallway. The man had moved to a far corner of the classroom where he could still clearly keep an eye on what Mrs. Oliver and the students were doing but was obviously more concerned about what he was looking at on his phone. Another spasm of fear went through Mrs. Oliver's belly. There was much more to this than she initially had thought. Maybe it didn't have anything to do with the school, this classroom, these students. Maybe it had nothing to do with her. If it was one man fixated on one particular student or even on her, she could see the entire episode ending peacefully. But this man seemed almost indifferent to all of them. As if this was a randomly chosen room that he decided to ensconce himself within until the real action began. For some reason this thought made her much more worried. This man didn't care about them, they were expendable. He was lying in wait. For what she didn't know. Mrs. Oliver glanced at her desk, where her cell phone was hidden away. If only she could get to her phone.

Augie

Each step toward P.J.'s classroom seems like a bigger and bigger mistake, but I can't stop myself. I'm such a crappy sister. The other night when Grandpa had fallen asleep on the couch with P.J. sitting next to him, I had switched the channel to a TV documentary about serial killers. The reporter was talking about how researchers have done all these scans on the brains of murderers and found that many had head injuries as children. I looked over at P.J., and I could tell exactly what he was thinking. When I was five and P.J. was just a few weeks old I decided to run away from home. My mom and dad were fighting, again, shouting and swearing and saying mean things to each other about P.J. I couldn't stand it anymore. I packed my book bag with clothes, diapers and a bottle for P.J. and climbed over the railing and into his crib. He looked up at me with his dark eyes that were never going to turn blue like my dad's, and waited to see what I was going to do next. He was surprisingly heavy for such a little baby and I really thought I could lean over the bars of his crib and lower him gently to the ground. I didn't mean to drop him, but I did, right on his bald head. It took him several seconds to catch his breath before he could cry, but when he did, wow. I leaped out of that crib, grabbed my book bag, flew out the door and ran and ran until I found myself ten blocks from home at Bang!—the hair salon where my mom worked. I sat out front, boiling in the sun until my dad drove up in his truck. "Get in, Augie," he said.

"No," I said stubbornly, even though I was sunburned and dying of thirst.

"Augie," he said angrily, opening the truck door and climbing out. I wondered if I ever would see him smile again. "Get in the damn car."

"No," I repeated, hooking my ankles around the leg of the bench and clutching onto the metal arm. He'd have to throw the entire bench, me included, into the back of the truck to get me to go back home. I squinched up my eyes as he came toward me and felt his strong hands reach up under my armpits trying to lift me. "Gahhhhh," I hollered, knowing from experience that would stop him in his tracks. My dad didn't like people looking at him like he was a child abuser. He let go and I peeked open one eye, hoping that he would have given up and left. No such luck. Instead, my dad was on his knees in front of me, one hand over his eyes.

"P.J. is at the hospital with your mom," he said softly, his voice strangely thick and choked. I didn't like the way it sounded and I opened both my eyes. "You dropped him on his head, Augie. What were you thinking? You know you aren't supposed to pick him up without your mother or me there." That was a laugh, my five-year-old self thought. I'd never even seen my dad pick P.J. up, just stare down at him like he was something out of one of my Ripley's *Believe It or*

Not books. "Come on now, I'm serious, Augie. You could have really hurt him. You're lucky he didn't die."

My heart swelled with worry. That wasn't what I wanted at all. I had just wanted to get P.J. and me away from the yelling and name calling. "Stop fighting," I said. "Stop fighting and I'll come home."

My dad made a little huffing sound through his noise, almost a laugh, but not quite. I wasn't trying to be funny. "Okay, Augie," he said in a quiet, sad voice. "We're done fighting. I promise." I unsnaked my feet from the bench legs and allowed myself to be lifted and carried to the truck. P.J. had to spend the night in the hospital for observation and after X-rays and CAT scans he was allowed to come home. A slight concussion, the doctors said.

My dad kept his promise. Twenty minutes after my mother arrived home from the hospital with P.J., he packed up and left. They never fought anymore. Not really, not in front of us, anyway.

Through the years it got to the point where my mom and even my dad laughed about how I tried to kidnap P.J. and how I accidentally dumped him on his head. Even P.J. would smile and shake his head as if he could remember the whole thing. To me I just remember single-handedly nearly killing my brother and ending my parents' marriage.

"What's a frontal lobe?" P.J. asked. He was on the couch leaning against Grandpa's shoulder, whispering so he didn't wake him up. Traitor, I thought.

"It's what I dropped you on," I said seriously. "Right on the serial killer soft spot."

"Shut up," P.J. said, but I could hear the worry in his voice.

"I'm just saying…" I shrugged my shoulders and stood. "Now just excuse me while I go find a hammer to hide under my pillow so I can protect myself. Good night, young Dahmer."

It was a shitty thing to do, I know. P.J. could never hurt anyone and he is probably up in that classroom right now thinking that he is going to die with the damaged brain of a serial killer. I want to get to him and tell him that he had a perfectly normal brain, that scientists were never going to dissect his brain and add it to their serial killer collection.

At the top of the steps I pull on Beth's hand to get her to stop. "Listen," I whisper. "What's that?" We both freeze, turning our ears toward the sound, the soft slap of feet coming up behind us on the steps. All I can think about was the puddle of blood I slipped on below and had visions of a crazy man with a gun or a knife creeping toward us. "Run," I yell louder than I mean to, and as Beth drags me down the hallway I glance over my shoulder to see a small shape at the top of the steps. "Wait," I say, stopping suddenly, letting go of Beth's hand. I walk cautiously back down the dark hallway toward the shape. A little girl. Five, maybe six years old. She has long blond hair held back with two barrettes topped with yellow bows. She is wearing black-and-yellow leggings and a sweatshirt that says My Brother Did It. "Are you okay?" I ask. She nods, but it looks like she is going to cry. I glance back over my shoulder toward Beth for help, but she has disappeared. "Where is your teacher?" I ask.

"I was in the bathroom and when I went back to the room the door was locked." Tears start coming down her cheeks and she begins to cry loudly.

"Shhh," I say. "Have you seen anyone at all?"

She shakes her head and sniffles. "All the doors are locked."

I'm not sure what to do. I can't leave her here all alone, but I don't want to take her with me. I think of the door at the bottom of the steps that leads to the parking lot. She'd be a lot safer outside than in here. I consider sending her down the steps by herself; it would only take her a few seconds to get to the bottom. Then I think of the puddle of blood and can only imagine what she would do if she stepped in that mess. I would successfully scar another child for life and I'm only thirteen.

"Come on, I'll get you out of here." She looks like she doesn't quite believe me. "What's your name?" I ask.

"Faith," she answers, wrinkling her nose at the blood on my clothes and hands.

"It's nothing," I tell her like it's no big deal, but I feel like I could throw up and want more than anything to get the blood off of me. "I'm Augie," I tell her. I think about going back the way we came, down the steps and to the door that leads to the teacher's parking lot, but the thought of the smeared puddle of blood at the top of the stairs puts an end to that. "Let's go." I grab her hand and together we run down the long hallway, past closed classroom doors toward another staircase that leads to the gym and to another set of doors to the outside. As we run, through the windows in the classroom doors, I catch glimpses of teachers and students huddled together in corners just like Mr. Ellery had our class do. In one of the classrooms it is different, though. In one quick look over my shoulder I could see that something else was happening in this classroom. In P.J.'s classroom. I stop and peek through the window. Instead of all the kids crowded into a far corner of the room, these students are sitting in their desks, looking straight ahead, their faces scared. P.J. is in the front row and looks like he is all right. I want to grab him and bring him with me and Faith. From where I'm standing I can't see if his teacher or the bad guy, whoever he is, is in the classroom. I can't tell. I think of Beth and wonder where she went, hoping that she got out. I stare hard at P.J., trying to send my brain waves to him, telling him to look my way.

I feel Faith tugging on my hand and I look down at her. "Come on," she whispers.

"My brother," I tell her. "He's in there."

"Please, I want to go home," she says more loudly.

"Shhh," I say more angrily than I mean to, and she begins to cry.

"Shhh, Faith, he'll hear you," I say more softly, and start to pull her down the hallway.

I'm out of breath when Faith and I reach the end of the hallway and stop. "It's okay, I'm sorry," I whisper to Faith. "I'm not mad."

When I look back toward P.J.'s classroom, I see the door slowly open and the head of a woman peeks out. P.J.'s teacher, Mrs. Oliver. Nothing in her face makes me think that she has seen us, but she makes a waving motion with her hand, as if trying to push us away from the classroom. I know then that he is in that room. Whoever *he* is. With P.J. I squeeze Faith's hand more tightly and together we tiptoe down the stairs. The closest door to the outside is just through the gymnasium, which is dark and ghostly quiet. "I don't want to go in there," Faith cries, trying to pull away from me.

I have to agree with her. It is way creepy, but now that I'm sure that the man is upstairs, I know this is the safest, quickest way to get Faith out of the school. "It's okay, I promise," I tell her. "We'll run through the gym to those doors." The lights in the gym are off, but I can see the gray sky and bright snow through the glass doors that lead to a larger parking lot, the one where everyone parks for basketball games and school programs. "See," I tell her. "It's brighter out there than in here. There are people outside waiting for you. Your mom and dad, I bet." I hope that this is true. That her mother and father are bundled up outside waiting. I wonder if my mom and dad have any idea of what's going on. But they are thousands of miles away and I'm sure that it isn't on the news. Who cares about a tiny town in Iowa? Grandpa probably knows what is going on and is worried about P.J. I know he loves P.J. Me, not so much. Not that I've made liking me easy.

Faith bites her lip and says, "I'm scared."

"I am, too," I admit. "Let's close our eyes and run." Faith takes a deep breath, nods and squinches her eyes up tight. I do the same, minus the eye-closing, and we run, our feet squeaking as we cross the wooden gym floor. Once we reach the glass doors I can see that it is snowing, big, fat flakes that P.J. would want to catch on his tongue. Through the snow, at the edge of the parking lot, I can also see a line of police cars with their headlights facing the school. Dark figures are walking back and forth, hopping up and down once in a while as if they are trying to keep warm. "Right there." I point toward the police cars. "Run that way. Someone will be there to help you find your mom and dad."

"Aren't you coming?" Faith asks, still holding my hand.

"No, I have to go find my brother. You'll be fine. That's the police out there."

"Come with me, please," she begs.

"I can't. I've got to go find my brother," I explain. Faith looks unsure. "But when we get out, I'll come find you. I promise," I add.

She shakes her head no and begins to cry. "I'm scared. They look scary." She buries her face in my stomach. I can barely see the dark shapes through the heavy snow and they do look scary. Like aliens.

"Okay," I finally say. "I'll come out with you, but once you're safe, I'm going back." She thinks about this for a second and then nods. I look around for something to block open the door, knowing that it will lock behind us once it closes. I see a basketball in the corner, probably what the gym class was playing before the Code Red came over the intercom. I wonder where they all are, if they made it outside or are hiding somewhere. I pick up the basketball, push open the door and we step outside. The cold air hits my face. Faith shivers next to me, and our feet sink into the three or four inches of new snow. "Wait a second," I say to Faith as I carefully set the basketball on the ground between the door and frame so it won't close and lock behind us. Across the parking lot I see three dark figures stop pacing and take a step toward us. One lifts something long and thin. A shotgun. The wind whips my hair around my face and I'm afraid that it will blow the door shut, locking me out here and away from P.J. I wave my arms in the air to show them that I don't have a gun. "Hey!" I yell. "We're just kids!" We take a careful step forward; the police officer doesn't lower the gun. "We're just kids!" I shout again.

One of the police officers comes slowly toward us, one hand on a hip, one hand reaching out toward us. "Keep your hands up," a voice says. A woman's voice. Faith grabs my hand again and together we raise our arms. "Walk slowly forward," she says, and we do. As she gets closer I see that it's the same officer that was trying to get me to climb out of the classroom earlier. "What's your name?" she asks as she inches toward us.

"I'm Augie Baker and this is Faith…" I suddenly realize I don't know Faith's last name.

"Garrity," she whispers.

"Garrity," I shout. "Faith Garrity."

"I'm Officer Barrett," she says. "I'm here to help you. Just keep coming forward slowly. Are you hurt at all?"

"No, we're fine," I say. By the time we reach her, my face is numb with cold and my shoes are filled with snow. The policeman with the shotgun finally lowers it and is talking into a walkie-talkie.

"Is anyone hurt in there? Have you seen the intruder?"

"I didn't see him. There was bl…" I start to tell her about the puddle of blood I slipped on when over her shoulder I see an ambulance and someone wearing a big fur-trimmed parka heading our way with a pile of blankets.

"What did you see?" Officer Barrett asks as I wiggle my hand free from Faith's.

"Nothing," I say as I take a step backward and look behind me at the gym door, still propped open with the basketball.

"Come on, let's get you warmed up," Officer Barrett says, trying to put an arm around me, but I sidestep her reach and start running back to the school, slipping a bit on the snowy ground.

"What the hell?" she shouts, reaching out to grab me, but I've caught her by surprise. Just a few more yards and I'll be back in the building.

Holly

I've always known that I was a little bit different from the
other girls from Broken Branch. I don't mean that I think
I was better than them; if anything I wished I would have
been more like them. I put them into three categories: the
girls who wanted to get married right out of high school and
start having babies, the girls who wanted to go away to college
and then come back to Broken Branch and settle down, get
married and then start having babies, and me. All I wanted to
do was get the hell out of Broken Branch. Yes, I ran away with
a boy from Broken Branch, but we both knew it wasn't going
to last. It was kind of like jumping off a bluff at the Pits, the
sand and gravel pits just south of town that were filled with
water. It's so much easier to leap off a cliff holding someone's
hand. There's the thrill of being up so high, seeing the jag-
ged, rocky walls of the quarry, of knowing that your body
could hit the sides if you didn't plan your jump just right.

The problem was I kept trying to find someone to jump off those cliffs with.

I don't know what was missing inside of me that I felt like I had to fill it up with just about every man I met. I'd like to blame my father; it's so exceptionally easy to do this. I've never felt a connection to him, always felt that he always loved the farm, my brothers, more than he loved me. But in all honesty, I can't blame my dad for this aspect of my personality. Ever since I was thirteen I was sneaking out of my house in order to meet up with boys and sometimes men. To be with a different man, to know the different ways that I could be kissed and touched and *wanted,* was intoxicating to me. Almost like jumping off a cliff.

There are names for women like me. I know. But I don't feel like a bad person, I just like the way it feels when a man touches me. For me, sex never had anything to do with love, though I've certainly been in love before. When I married David, I was in love. We had Augie and we were happy for a long time. Five years. The longest I've been faithful to anyone. You'd think that after having a little girl of my own, I would have learned my lesson, tried to be a better example for Augie. I wasn't. I remember leaving Augie and David at home while I went out with some of the other girls from Bang!—the salon I worked at. We'd go to bars, drink chocolate martinis and somehow I'd end up in a bathroom or a back room or in the back of a car with some random guy. I thought I would just get it out of my system, that one day David would be enough for me. But he wasn't.

I tell P.J. that his father is a marine, a good, kind man that I loved and who went away to war. He loves to hear this. I don't have the heart to tell him that his father, in all actuality, is one of three men. An accountant from Phoenix that I met at a wedding reception, a frat boy from Ohio who was in Arizona on spring break or the guy who ran the craps table at the casino. I told you there are names for women like me. I look at my bandaged skin and touch my grizzled hair, which is starting to grow back, and wonder if any man will ever want me now.

I don't want this for Augie. But she is so different than I am. She is determined and tough, but she is content. Something I don't think I have ever been.

I'd like to ask my mother about this. I want to ask her what it is like to be married to the same man for fifty years. Not the sex part. God, no. But day-to-day bits. Those are the things I want to know about. But she has gone off to talk to someone about my health insurance and I realize I miss her. That I've missed her for the past fifteen years.

Meg

Unbelievable. First the girl runs back into the building. Then she kicks aside the basketball that holds the door open, shutting her inside the school and locking me out. Who the hell is this girl? I'm beginning to think she has something to do with this whole thing. Is it possible that this thirteen-year-old girl is an accomplice to the gunman? I pound on the gym door, yelling at her to open it up and come on out.

"I have to get my little brother," she tells me through the glass door. "I'm sorry."

"Goddammit," I say, and look behind me where several more officers have come together. Faith has disappeared into the crowd. "Open up, Augie," I say loudly so she can hear me through the door. "I'll help you find your brother."

She shakes her head no. "I can't. I'm sorry," she says, and turns her back on me.

"Augie, please," I plead with her, trying to soften my voice.

"Open the door. I can take you somewhere safe. Do you really think that you'll be able to outmaneuver a man with a gun? Do you know where he's at?"

She is walking backward away from me now, fighting back tears. She says something but I don't catch her words; they are deflected by the glass door.

"Get out here, now!" I shout.

She doesn't turn around, but moves quickly out of my line of sight. For an instant I actually consider shooting my way into the building, but instead I pick up the basketball and throw it as hard as I can toward the cornfield.

I was so close, but I scared her away. That has always been my biggest challenge as a police officer. Balancing toughness and tenderness. I learned very early on in my career that I needed to be tough, show no signs of weakness. I got enough crap about being a woman from a small but vocal group of asshole cadets while at the police academy, there was no way I was going to let someone accuse me of being a pushover. And I've done a pretty good job of it. I've cuffed violent, toothless tweakers, stood toe to toe with armed poachers and even ended up with a broken nose and twenty-six stitches in my arm after I was stabbed trying to break up a drunken bar fight. I've worked so hard at appearing strong sometimes I forget there are times, many times, as a police officer when a more gentle approach is necessary. Now this little girl, maybe the one person who can tell us what is going on in the school, is gone and I'm the one who let her get away. I let that little girl down just like I had with Jamie Crosby.

Her Own Words, the headline had read. Alleged Rape Victim Speaks about Her Terrifying Encounter with Candidate's Husband by Stuart Moore. My blood went cold.

The night I was called to the Crosby home, after an hour of pleading with her, I finally convinced Jamie to go to a rape crisis center in Waterloo—Jamie insisted that she not be taken to an area hospital—where she was examined and evidence was collected. It wasn't until three days later that Jamie named her attacker: Matthew Merritt, the husband of gubernatorial candidate Greta Merritt. Jamie was terrified. She was convinced that no one would believe that the well-liked future first husband of Iowa could be capable of overpowering and raping a plain, slightly overweight nineteen-year-old nanny in his beautiful wife's home while she was on the campaign trail. It broke my heart. I knew these weren't Jamie's words, but most likely Matthew Merritt's poisonous threats to the poor girl after the attack. I promised Jamie that her identity would be protected, that the evidence the nurses collected— the swabs, the nail scrapings, the photos of her bruises—was all the proof anyone would need.

Somehow Stuart got to Jamie. Somehow he learned that she was the rape victim. Everyone in the state, hell, in the Midwest, knew that Matthew Merritt was under investigation for sexual assault, but it wasn't public knowledge that Jamie was his victim. But Stuart figured it out and the only way he could have done that was through me and now he has the balls to try and get a quote from me for his next big story. Not going to happen.

Mrs. Oliver

"Hey, get the hell away from there!" the man barked at Mrs. Oliver, who had lingered in the doorway after all of the students had returned from the bathroom and to their seats. She saw the two girls, one a teenager, one much younger, creeping toward her down the corridor and she franticallly waved them away before shutting the door. She hoped they would disappear from sight quickly. The man was becoming tenser, like a trapped bird nervously flitting from one corner of the room to another. His gun slapping more and more erratically against his leg. She hoped he had the safety on. She returned to her spot in the front of the room, well aware that the more on edge the man became, the more likely something bad was going to happen.

It was nearing two o'clock. Not so late that Cal would begin worrying about her whereabouts. He probably wouldn't even remember that it was an early dismissal day. Besides, Mrs. Oliver would often spend an extra few hours after school making lesson plans, grading papers, putting up a new bulletin board. He was probably deciding whether or not to go ahead and eat the beef stew that had been simmering in the Crock-Pot all day. He would be getting hungry but hated to eat alone. No, he would probably turn the temperature on the slow cooker to low and slice off a hunk of cheddar cheese to tide him over until she arrived.

It was providence, Evelyn thought, that forty-six years ago, Mrs. Ford invited Cal to join them for a snack of her banana bread, warm and moist from the oven, and cold lemonade when he finished fixing their washing machine. Together with Mrs. Ford, they sat in the sunny breakfast nook, taking small bites of the fragrant bread and slow sips of the lemonade. Cal listened attentively as Mrs. Ford went through her litany of stories about George. Evelyn thought it would be intolerable hearing, yet again, Mrs. Ford's account of how George had scarlet fever as a youngster and how they thought he would never survive or the story of how George was valedictorian of his high school class. It plucked at her heart, but she found it wasn't quite so bad as usual. Hearing Mrs. Ford talk about George to someone else was quite pleasant. Cal seemed genuinely interested and asked questions in all the right places.

Mrs. Ford called Cal three more times in the following two months to come and fix something or other on the washing machine. Each time, Evelyn would join him in the basement, handing him tools and chatting about politics and books. Then Mrs. Ford would holler down to them that the cookies were just out of the oven and to come on up while they were still hot and the three of them would sit at the table. Mrs. Ford would reminisce about George, and by the end of the visit, Evelyn saw a lightness return to Mrs. Ford's face.

One cold, wintry afternoon, a few weeks after Cal declared the washing machine deceased and admitted that any more attempts to revive the appliance would only serve to lighten Mrs. Ford's pocketbook, and that he couldn't, in good conscience, keep trying, Mrs. Ford invited Cal to dinner. Evelyn had taken the bus home after spending the day signing up for classes at the college. She had used the life insurance money from George to pay her tuition. She had offered the money to Mr. and Mrs. Ford. After all, they had more of a claim on George than she did. But they told her no, that George would have wanted her to get her education. She was already half a year behind the other students, having dropped out after hearing the news of George's death, but she was determined to graduate with a degree in education right along with her classmates. She was exhausted by the time she trudged from the bus stop to the Ford home. While her pregnancy wasn't obvious to others, she could actually feel the child sucking the nutrients from her body, from the very marrow of her bones. All she wanted to do was take off her rubber boots, peel off her winter coat and climb into her bed.

The Fords had collapsed into grateful tears upon hearing the news that she was going to have George's baby. Perhaps even a son to carry their son's name, someone to not exactly replace George, but someone to whom they could shift their love to.

So while Evelyn wasn't unhappy to see Cal, whose cheerful, unassuming presence always seemed to take the pressure off of her, she was surprised to find him sitting in the living room wearing chinos and a button-down white shirt rather than the gray work shirt with his name embroidered in red thread.

Cal stood when she stepped into the house, looking as uncomfortable as she felt, as if the realization that coming to the Ford house in the evening breached some unwritten machine repairman etiquette was dawning over him. It was an odd dinner, even though Mrs. Ford and Cal tried to keep the conversation moving along. Evelyn couldn't imagine what they were thinking, bringing Cal there for supper; and Mr. Ford was so bewildered that he just kept looking to Evelyn as if asking for an explanation. While the conversation was not at all unpleasant, Evelyn was so bone tired that she could barely keep her eyes open. She tried to smile in the appropriate places but halfway through the beef Stroganoff, when her fork clanked to the floor, she had to leave the table. "I'm sorry," she said as she stood abruptly. "I'm not feeling well. Please excuse me." She fled to her room and sat on her bed holding George's graduation picture, tracing the outline of his face with her index finger until she heard a gentle knocking at her bedroom door. Thinking it was Mrs. Ford, she reluctantly got to her feet and mentally prepared an apology. She opened the door to find Cal standing there, holding a plate of apple pie and a fork.

"Here," he said, offering it to her. "I thought you might want a piece." She took the plate and stepped aside so he could enter the room. It was strange, having a man who wasn't George in her bedroom.

"Do Mr. and Mrs. Ford know you're up here?" she asked, peering through the doorway.

"Mrs. Ford is the one who told me to bring you the pie. Are you okay, Evelyn?" he asked with concern, his brown eyes crinkled in worry.

"Just tired," she responded.

Cal shoved his hands into his pockets and lowered his voice. "I don't want to upset you by coming here," he said hesitantly. "I thought you knew. I thought maybe it was your idea."

"My idea?" She was suddenly indignant. "Why would you think that?"

"I don't know." Cal shrugged. "I thought maybe you liked my company."

"I do, but...the timing isn't exactly the best now, is it?"

she whispered, hoping Mrs. Ford wasn't lurking around the corner. Evelyn looked around the room she had shared with George. "I live in the same house with my dead husband's parents." Tears started rolling down her cheeks, and she brushed them angrily away. "I'm nearly six months pregnant with their grandchild and now they are trying to set me up with the washing machine repairman." Upon seeing Cal's affronted look she sighed. "I didn't mean to say it that way, Cal. It's just that this isn't the way it's supposed to be."

Cal sat down next to her on the bed, leaving a respectful distance between the two of them. "Maybe," he said, "this is just the way it's supposed to be."

Mrs. Oliver sniffed back tears at the memory, clutched at her chest and made a groaning sound. The gunman, who had been leaning against the wall, straightened and came quickly to her side. "What?" he asked. "What is it?"

"My medicine," she croaked, indistinctly aware of the renewed cries of some of her students. "I need my medicine." She pointed a shaky finger toward her desk. "In my purse. Over there."

Will

Will watched as each child was reunited with a family member. There were long hugs, tears, relief. He and Verna looked at each other in disbelief. Where were *their* grandchildren? In all of his seventy years he had never felt as helpless as he had in the past eight weeks. He and Marlys had endured drought, floods, financial woes. Even their troubles with Holly as a youngster paled in comparison to Holly's accident and now this.

P.J. had asked Will to let him stay home that day in order to help with the calving.

"Please, Grandpa," he begged. "It's the last day before spring vacation. It won't hurt to miss just this once."

Even Augie tried to plead P.J.'s case. "You should let us stay home. He'd learn more watching you than sitting in a dumb classroom all day." This was the closest thing to a compliment that Augie had ever given him. "I can stay here, too, then," Augie went on. "I can help pack for our trip."

"You two will go to school. There will be plenty of time to watch calves being born and for packing." If only he had given in, just this once, and let the kids stay home. But no, he had to be the one in charge, needed to let them know who was boss.

He shook his head at his own stubbornness. Will fingered the phone in his pocket and knew it was time to call his wife and daughter. He just didn't know how he was going to tell them that there could be a chance that tomorrow morning Augie and P.J. might not be getting on that airplane to Arizona.

Augie

I wonder if they'll arrest me for not following a police officer's orders or resisting or whatever they call it.

I wanted to trust Officer Barrett, but I figured if I went with her she'd just haul me off to my grandpa, who would be disappointed because I wasn't looking after P.J.

My clothes are soaking wet from my wrestling match with Officer Barrett and my shoes make squelching noises as I walk across the gym floor. I kick them off, knowing that I need to be quiet when I try to get into P.J.'s classroom. Suddenly the pounding on the door stops and I turn around to see that Officer Barrett is gone. Good, I think. Maybe she'll get busy with something else and forget all about me. I wish I wouldn't have told her my name. That was stupid. I'm freezing in my wet clothes and my teeth won't stop chattering. I see a sweatshirt that is lying on the bleachers and pull off my bloodstained, soggy T-shirt and replace it with the sweatshirt. It's not really stealing; I'll return it when this is all over. I could get hypothermia or something. My pants are still wet, but the sweat-shirt is better than nothing.

I sit down on the bleachers—just for a minute, I tell myself. I need to catch my breath, make a plan before I head back up the steps and to P.J.'s classroom. I hate Broken Branch right now, hate Iowa. I can't believe I ever thought anything about Iowa was pretty. I miss Arizona and Revelation. I don't care if I see snow ever again. I want to stand out in the sunshine and feel its rays on my face and my feet burning on the ce-ment. I close my eyes and imagine the warm blue skies and the orange and purple sunsets, and all the other shades in be-tween that I have no color names for, and the Joshua trees and the spiky yuccas. I miss my dad, even though I hate him, too. P.J. and I would never be in this mess if he would have just let both of us stay with him. It's hard to take when you realize that your dad is selfish and is married to someone who doesn't care much about his own daughter.

I think of my mom and my chest aches with missing her. Ever since my dad left, I've always known that it was my mom I was going to be able to depend on. She does stupid things sometimes. She isn't great with money and sometimes we end up eating mac and cheese and ramen noodles for a week in between paychecks because she had to have a new shirt or P.J. had to have the same video game all the other kids were playing. She would buy things for me, too. A new pair of ear-rings or trendy pair of shoes. But I could never enjoy them. But one thing my mom was good at, *is* good at, is knowing when I'm feeling bad. She also knows when to try and get me to talk about things or when to leave me alone. My friends' mothers suck at that. They nag and push until they just want to scream. Though I talk to my mom every night and she goes on and on about what's happening in Arizona and with her physical therapy and how Grandma Thwaite is wonderful but can be annoying, I still feel like things will never be the same between us again.

She has every reason to hate me, but at the end of each phone call she says the same thing. *I love you, Augie.* I picture her holding the phone in her scarred hands that were once so beautiful. I remember watching her file her nails into perfectly pink-tipped ovals and try to hide my own ragged, bitten-down fingers behind my back. *I love you, Augie,* my mother would say again. I just can't say it back to her. I want to, but the words get stuck in my throat. *Goodbye, Mom,* I answer, and then quickly pass the phone to P.J. or my grandpa.

Then I run out of the house, flinging open the door extra hard, knowing that Grandpa Thwaite hates it when I let the screen door slam. I run to the barn where I can hide and where I can whisper, *I love you, too, Mom,* and only the cows with their wide, sad eyes can hear me.

I force myself to stand. I can't sit here forever dreaming about being warm and being back in Revelation. I need to go get P.J., tell him he's not some serial killer and hopefully get out of this school alive. Then we'll get on the plane to Revelation tomorrow and never come back here again.

Meg

I make my way back to the RV and the ambulances and ask around until I find little Faith Garrity. She is sitting in the back of an ambulance being checked over by an EMT.

"How are you doing, Faith?" I ask her.

"Okay," she says shyly.

"She's just fine," the EMT assures me. "She can be taken over to Lonnie's whenever you're ready."

"What do you think, Faith? Are you ready to go and see your mom and dad?"

She nods and the EMT lifts her gently out of the ambulance and sets her on the ground. "Have you ever been in a police car?" I ask her, and she shakes her head no.

"Well, today is your lucky day," I say, reaching for her hand, and she gives me a shaky smile.

"Where's Augie?" Faith asks once I buckle her into the backseat of my cruiser.

"Augie wanted to check on her little brother, but when I

see her I'll make sure to tell her that you were looking for her." I'm itching to ask Faith questions about what went on inside the school, although I know I should wait until I reunite her with her parents and get their permission for her to talk with me.

We are barely out of the parking lot when Faith decides to speak all on her own. "I bet she went back to Mrs. Oliver's room."

Immediately I become alert. "Oh?" I ask, trying to keep my tone light, conversational.

"She's the third-grade teacher. She's *really* old, but nice, I think."

"Hmm," I murmur, hoping she'll add more.

"Her brother is in Mrs. Oliver's room. She said she wanted to get him."

"Faith," I say, "did you see a man in the school? Maybe a man who shouldn't have been there?"

She is very quiet for a moment. We pull into Lonnie's, to where Faith's parents are undoubtedly waiting for her. I know the minute she walks through that door I will lose her as a witness. Through the brightly lit windows I see tables filled with frightened-looking parents. I only have a few minutes now. I put the car into Park and turn around in my seat to look at her. "Faith, did you see anything at all that might help Augie?"

Faith looks around the car nervously.

"Don't worry," I tell her. "No one can hear you but me." Some of the parents inside Lonnie's have noticed that a car has pulled into the parking lot and are approaching the front window, cupping their hands around their eyes and pressing their faces close to the glass to get a better look. There is a shout coming from inside Lonnie's. We've been spotted.

"I saw him," she whispers, brushing her snow-damp hair

from her eyes. "I was coming out of the bathroom and I saw him."

The door to Lonnie's opens and a couple steps out into the parking lot, sending a rush of snow swirling around their knees.

"What did you see?" I ask, trying to keep the urgency out of my voice.

The couple, most assuredly Faith's parents, move toward the squad car, clinging to each other as they step across the icy pavement.

"He had a gun." Her brown eyes widen. "He held it like this." She pointed her index finger at me and lifted her thumb upward. "Then he dropped his phones."

They are almost to the car. Faith hasn't seen them yet.

"His phones?" I asked in confusion. "He had more than one?"

She nodded and spread her fingers out wide. "He had like five."

"Five phones?" I ask just to make sure. Faith nods. "Anything else, Faith? Anything at all special about him that you remember? Have you seen him before?" I work hard to keep my voice neutral.

I don't want to spook her. She thinks for a second and nods again. "You know him?"

She shakes her head no. "You've seen him before, but you don't know who he is?" She nods. Now Faith spies the man and woman through the car window and is scrambling to unbuckle her seat belt. "Think, Faith," I urge. "Where did you see him before?"

Faith presses against the window. "Mommy! Daddy!" she calls, and then they are upon us.

Faith's hand pushes against the door handle and nothing

happens. She jiggles it impatiently and looks desperately to me for help.

I release the door locks and Faith's father wrenches open the door and she leaps into his arms. The woman wraps her arms around Faith and her husband and the three of them rock back and forth while I stand by, trying to patiently wait for the right time to interrupt their reunion.

"Mr. and Mrs. Garrity," I finally say, knowing that each minute that passes could mean the life of one of the remaining students or teachers in the building. The Garritys look up at me with wet eyes. "I'm Officer Barrett. I'd like your permission to speak with Faith for a few minutes."

Mr. Garrity pulls Faith more tightly into his chest and his eyes narrow in wariness. "I don't think so," the woman says, stroking Faith's hair. "Thank you for bringing her to us." Her voice breaks with emotion. "But we just want to get Faith home."

"I understand," I say. "My daughter is a third grader at the school." They lower their eyes in sympathy, thinking that Maria is still back at the school. I don't correct this misunderstanding. "Faith is a witness. Anything she can share could help a lot of kids."

Mr. Garrity shakes his head. "Tomorrow. You can talk with her tomorrow. She needs a good night's sleep." Faith is laying her head on her father's shoulder, her eyes heavy with fatigue.

"Just one minute. I promise," I plead.

A look passes between Mr. and Mrs. Garrity and for a second I think they are going to let me talk to Faith.

"I'm sorry, no," Mr. Garrity says with a finality I know I can't argue with. "Tomorrow. If she isn't too upset."

I nod, unable to keep the disappointment from my face. "Okay. Tomorrow, then." I turn my attention to Faith. "Nice to meet you, Faith. You are a very brave girl."

"You, too," she murmurs, her eyelids fluttering.

"Please call the police department if Faith says anything that you think might be helpful. Ask for Officer Barrett and they'll get a hold of me."

"She's five," Mrs. Garrity says as if apologizing.

"I understand, have a good night," I say to the family, meaning it. I stare up at the snowy sky, snowflakes dancing maniacally, causing me to teeter dizzily on my heels. I place my hand on the hood of the squad car to steady myself and review the information I was able to get from Faith: the gun, the multiple phones, the fact that she had seen him before. It wasn't much, but it was something. I spend a moment watching the Garritys shuffle across the restaurant parking lot as one seamless entity. I think of my own little family, at one time just like the Garritys. I blinked once and it all unraveled.

But at least, one by one, the children were being reunited with their families. I needed to get back to the school. But first I had to talk to Will Thwaite and find out what was going on with his granddaughter.

Mrs. Oliver

When Mrs. Oliver had time to watch television she preferred medical dramas and she tried to remember what the heart attack victims on television looked like. They always clutched at their left arm. Or was it their right? She gasped for air, her hand clawing at the air in front of her, the other at her left arm and then at her right just in case. "My medicine," she wheezed. The man look startled. *Maybe he isn't a complete monster,* Mrs. Oliver thought. He looked frantically around the room at the frightened children, some who were openly sobbing now at seeing their teacher in distress, and then back at Mrs. Oliver. Seeing the irritation on his face, Mrs. Oliver realized that this man didn't care a hill of beans about her. He was just worried that she would die and leave him in charge of seventeen hysterical third graders. Served him right, she thought, if she died. But she couldn't go and do that. Her students needed her. She tried, telepathically, to let them know that she was just acting, but it didn't seem to be working. Julia was wailing loudly, her mouth an open cavern, and poor Colin just sat there, with his eyes tightly screwed shut, shaking. Only P.J. seemed to be looking at her curiously but without alarm.

"Please, my purse." She gurgled. "In my desk." The man only hesitated for a moment and then turned to P.J.

"Go get the purse," he ordered. P.J. stood and moved quickly behind Mrs. Oliver's desk.

He rummaged around through the drawers and in triumph lifted the leather purse in the air. "Got it," he said.

"Grab the medicine and bring it over here," the man directed.

Mrs. Oliver moaned loudly and slid from her chair to the floor in what she hoped was a realistic but graceful collapse onto her stomach.

The man kneeled down beside her. "Come on," he snapped. "Bring me the medicine." P.J. dug around in the black purse until his hand found the pill bottle. He tossed it to the man and it clattered across the floor where both Mrs. Oliver and the man reached for it.

"I got it," Mrs. Oliver said more robustly than she intended and grabbed the orange bottle.

"Hey, what's going on?" came Lucy's muffled voice from the closet as she pounded on the door. "Let me out of here!"

"Quiet!" the man shouted, and Mrs. Oliver twisted the childproof lid and shook two pills into her open palm and tossed them into her mouth.

"Just give me a second," she said, lying prostrate on the floor, the bitterness of the pills prescribed to her for her arthritis pain filled her mouth. She was aware that all sound had ceased. The children had stopped crying, Lucy had stopped pounding on the closet door. Everyone was waiting to see what was going to happen next.

Augie

I tiptoe through the gymnasium, wondering what could have happened to Beth. I wonder if she is hiding in a corner somewhere, like I am, trying to get up the courage to go back to the classroom. Only she wants to find out if her dad could possibly be the one upstairs in her sister and P.J.'s classroom with a gun. I imagine for a minute what it would be like to have a dad who would do *anything* to be able to see his kids, spend time with them. My dad would rather pass up spending time with me so he can avoid spending time with a super-nice kid like P.J. And the saddest thing of all is P.J. is like some little stray puppy just begging for attention from my dad. More than anything in the world P.J. wants a dad. No, my dad isn't a psychopath with a gun, but he sure is a jerk.

I reach the gym doorway that leads back to the hallway and realize for the first time how thirsty I am. I bend over the drinking fountain and take a long drink. The water is luke-warm and tastes a little rusty, but it feels good in my throat.

I step into the hallway and tiptoe toward the staircase. If I go upward I will be in P.J.'s hallway. If I take a right and then a left I will be in the primary wing of the building, where the kindergarteners, first and second graders have their class-rooms. I think of Faith Garrity and how scared she was and I imagine that all the other little kids are, too. Faith, though, would be with her mom and dad now, while the rest of the kids are stuck in their classrooms not knowing what is going on out here.

I can't be sure that the man is still up in P.J.'s classroom. If it was Beth's dad, he may have grabbed Natalie and was off in search of Beth. He could be roaming the hallways right now. I duck into the space beneath the steps, sit down and try to decide what to do next.

My stomach makes a sloshing sound; it's empty except for the gallon of water I just drank. I've lost about fifteen pounds since we've moved here and when I look at myself in the mir-ror I barely recognize myself. My eyes look too big for my face and the spot at my throat looks like it's been hollowed out with an ice cream scooper. I can't say I look very good, though some of the girls at my old school who talked only about how fat their faces or thighs or butts looked would be impressed with my transformation. It's not exactly a diet I would recommend to others: the Watch Your Mother Get Her Skin Burned Off Diet.

Ever since the fire, the smell of any kind of meat cooking makes me sick. All I can think about when my grandpa is fry-ing bacon or making sloppy joes is the sizzle of my mother's skin. I threw up for twenty-four hours after the fire trying to get the ashy taste out of my throat and the horrible, sweet smell of her hair and skin burning out of my nose.

When Grandpa was driving P.J. and me to the airport to catch our flight to Iowa he wanted to stop at a fast-food place.

He said that he and Grandma Thwaite rarely ate out—maybe
once every few weeks at the only restaurant in Broken Branch.
Plus, Grandma didn't approve of the nutritional value of such
establishments. *While the cat's away...*he said. As he pulled up
to the drive-through of a Buster Burger the thought of the car
filling up with the smell of grease and burgers made my stomach lurch. Out of the blue I told him that I was a vegetarian
and that I didn't eat meat products of any kind. P.J. looked at
me as if I'd sprouted antennas or something. Grandpa laughed
at me and I think that's when I decided to hate him. I already
didn't like him because of all the things my mother had told
me about growing up with him as a father, like how strict and
sarcastic he was, but right then and there I decided I would
loathe him. His laugh was my mother's. Sweet and slow like
taffy being pulled. But it didn't sound right coming from his
mouth and didn't earn him any popularity points with me.
"Well, a vegetarian on a beef cattle farm." He laughed. "This
is going to be entertaining."

I sat in the car while he and P.J. went into the restaurant
to eat. I fell asleep wondering what in the world I would be
eating for the next how many weeks until my mom got better and we could go home.

Right now I think about curling up in a little ball like
Grandpa's dog, Roxie, does. It would be so wonderful to
close my eyes and then wake up a few hours from now with
this whole thing over. But P.J.'s upstairs and all those kindergarteners are down the hallway. I stand and decide to go up
to P.J.'s room and see what's happening. If the man is in the
classroom, I'll sneak back downstairs and tell all the little kids
and their teachers that it's safe for them to get out. Unless, of
course, there is more than one man in the school, but that
thought is just too awful to imagine.

Meg

I spare about ten more seconds watching Faith and her parents before making my way into Lonnie's to talk to Eric Braun, the officer stationed there. Faith's father holds on to her like he will never let go again. Her mother strokes Faith's hair and smiles while tears roll down her cheeks.

Two statements that Faith had made were nagging at me. The first being that the gunman had at least five cell phones. Why in the world would anyone have five phones with them? The second thing that struck me was that Faith said she had seen the gunman before but didn't know him. Broken Branch is a small town. Two churches, one school, one grocery store. Everyone pretty much knows everyone else by name in town. The gunman has to be someone on the periphery. Someone who has a connection to Broken Branch but most likely doesn't live here.

I need to get back to the school and check in with the chief. I still haven't had the opportunity to talk more with Gail Lowell and haven't even spoken with the school principal. I feel at loose ends; the little information I have is fragmented and disjointed, doesn't make sense. An unknown gunman with five cell phones and an unknown motive, and one teenage girl who had the opportunity to escape but runs back into the school.

I step inside Lonnie's and the warm air feels good against my face. Instantly I am surrounded by parents and family members of the children still inside the school, begging for any information. I've got none to offer, so I simply keep my face emotionless and keep repeating, "I've got nothing new to tell you" and "No injuries have been reported." My friends and neighbors are not impressed and turn away from me, their mouths pinched tight with frustration. They slump down in their booths and resume watching the TV affixed to the wall, hoping to gather information from news reporters and speculators who know less than we do.

I see Braun in a corner booth talking with Dennis and Alise Strickland. They have three children at the school. A sixteen-year-old boy—a sophomore—and two daughters, twins who are seventh graders. Eric looks relieved when I approach while Dennis and Alise get up from their seats wearing the same dejected look as everyone else in the room.

"Can't you tell us anything?" Alise asks me. "Please?"

"Everyone is working very hard to get every single person out of the school safely." I can tell by the looks on their faces that these aren't the words they want to hear.

"I don't understand why no one is going into the school. Why is everyone just standing outside waiting?" Dennis Strickland asks. Dennis manages the local feed store. He normally has an easy smile and laid-back personality that serves him well in working with the local farmers, but now he is understandably tense and has no pleasantries to offer me.

"I know it's hard to be patient," I say, reaching for Alise's hand. "But there are protocols and procedures for these situations." Dennis shakes his head and stalks away and Alise gives me an apologetic look.

"Will you *please* let us know if you learn anything?" she asks.

"Of course," I assure her, and she walks away. I settle into the booth with Eric and from the way he is rubbing his forehead I can tell that as the parent liaison he probably has gotten the most difficult of duties.

I need to get back to the school so I dive right into my questions. We'll have time after this is all resolved to commiscrate. "Do you have any information on two students by the names of Augie Baker and Beth Cragg?"

"I can answer the Beth Cragg question right now. Her grandmother is right over there." He nods toward a booth where a woman of around sixty-five is sitting with three other men. "When Beth didn't step off the school bus with the other kids from her class, Beth's mom, Darlene, lost it. Started crying and yelling. Fortunately, Darlene's dad was with her and took her home. She's got two girls in the school right now. Beth is an eighth grader and Natalie is in third."

"What about Beth's father? Where's he at in all this?" I know from calls I've made to the Cragg farm that there is a history of domestic violence.

"No one is quite sure where Ray Cragg is right now. No one has seen much of him since Darlene left him and moved into town." Realization spreads across Eric's face. "Are you thinking that Ray might have something to do with this?"

I shrug. "Could be. Beth never came out of the school with her classmates. There's a history of domestic abuse, the dad isn't present." I look around the café. "I mean, everyone who has a child unaccounted for is right in this room, right? So where is Ray Cragg?"

"Are you going to follow up on it?" Eric asks.

I lean back in the booth and shake my head. "I don't know. How can we not check on it? But who are we going to send over to the Cragg farm? Everyone has their hands full as it is."

"I don't know, Meg," Eric says in a low whisper. "He could be the guy. Have you ever seen Darlene after one of his rages? I got called one night and he had beaten the shit out of her. Maybe the fact that she finally said enough and left and took her daughters away from him made him go nuts."

"You're right," I say. "This is the best lead we have so far. I'll head over there next."

"By yourself? No way, Meg," Eric says, shaking his head from side to side.

I brush aside his worry with a wave of my hand. "If it's Cragg he'll be in the school, right? I'm just going over to his farm and do some looking around. If he's there, great. If not, then maybe we know what we're looking at here and that's a hell of a lot more than we have right now."

"Okay, be careful and make sure you tell the chief where you're going."

"Yeah, yeah. Real quick, what about this Augie Baker? What do you have on her? She had two opportunities to get out of the school and she didn't take advantage of them."

Eric checks his list, flipping pages attached to his clipboard. "Yeah, got it here. Augustine Baker. Will Thwaite's granddaughter. Thirteen. Recently moved here from Arizona along with her brother—" he riffles through some more papers "—P. J. Thwaite."

"Parents?" I ask.

"Mother and father are in Arizona. The mother was badly burned in a fire and the kids came here to stay with the Thwaites while she recovers."

"Okay. I'll see if I can contact Will Thwaite."

"You don't have far to look, he's sitting in the back with Verna."

I clap Eric on the shoulder. "Thanks, I'll just go on over and have a quick chat with the two of them and then head over to the Cragg farm. Hang in there. Hopefully this will all be over soon."

"Yeah." Eric rubs his eyes. "Give me a trespassing or a cow tipping any day over this."

As I make my way over to the table where Verna and Will are sitting, Lonnie, the café's namesake and owner, a squat, heavy man with stringy gray hair pulled back in a ponytail, approaches with a steaming Styrofoam cup of coffee and presses it into my hand. "Here you go, Meg. You look like you could use something to warm you up."

"Thanks, Lonnie," I say, taking a sip of the blessed liquid. "And thanks for letting us use your café as a place for the families to gather. We couldn't do it without you."

"Bah, of course. We're glad to help."

"At least business is good," I joke lamely, reaching into my pocket for some money in order to pay Lonnie for the coffee.

"No charge," he says, shaking his head. "I can't charge these folks for coffee and pie when this could very well be the worst day of their lives."

"Thanks, Lonnie," I say. "That's very kind." He shrugs the compliment off, limps away, his heaviness causing a hitch in his step, and returns to filling coffee cups and making people smile. Once again I am reminded why I love Broken Branch and why I chose to remain here to work and raise Maria. I only hope we can get each and every one of those students and staff sitting at the school out safely. Otherwise, potentially, ninety percent of Broken Branch's youth could be erased in one fell swoop. Despite the warmth of the café and the hot coffee in my hand, I shiver at the thought. If that happened, Broken

Branch will become a ghost town, would die and wither away. We can't let that happen. *I* can't let that happen. Maria needs to come home, to her town, her school, her friends. To me.

Holly

"Maybe I'll be able to go outside for a little while when Augie and P.J. get here," I tell my mother hopefully when she returns to the room. I haven't been outside for nearly eight weeks, can only see the Arizona sky through my hospital window.

"Maybe," my mother says doubtfully. I know she's worried about the heat and the fierce Arizona sunshine. For the rest of my life I'm going to have to carefully cover my damaged skin to avoid sunburn. "Oh," my mother says, reaching into her purse and pulling out her cell phone. "I wonder who this is?" She presses the phone to her ear. "Hello," she says in the overloud way I've learned she uses while on her cell phone. Before the accident, the last time I saw my mother, I didn't even own a cell phone and my mother certainly didn't. She covers the mouthpiece. "It's Gloria Warren," she whispers, and gets up to leave the room. "I'll be right back."

Meg

As I approach the table where Verna Fraise sits, the men rise from their seats and remove their hats in greeting. "Gentlemen, Mrs. Fraise," I say.

"You have news on my grandchildren?" Verna asks hopefully.

"No, no," I say apologetically. "But I do have a few questions for you."

"We'll let you be, then," Will Thwaite says, stepping away from the table, and the other men start to follow him.

"Actually, Mr. Thwaite, if you could stay..." I say.

He hesitates for a moment, but settles himself back into his chair.

Will Thwaite must be at least seventy years old, but looks younger. He looks healthy in that vibrant, ruddy way of those who work in the outdoors. He is barrel chested and bow-legged, stands at about five foot ten inches, though he seems much larger. His face is deeply lined with a scattering of red patches that look, even to my untrained eye, like the beginnings of skin cancer. He is wearing his work clothes, coveralls, a barn jacket and brown leather boots caked with mud. He absentmindedly begins stirring cream into his cup of coffee and waits for me to speak.

Verna, on the other hand, doesn't give me a chance to ask any questions as she has many of her own. "You don't have any idea where Bethie is?" she asks. "Why she didn't come out with the rest of her class?"

"I don't," I admit. "One of her classmates commented that Beth was exceptionally upset during the lockdown—"

"What would you expect?" Verna interrupts. "A man with a gun comes barging into the school. Of course she would be very upset. I would be worried if she wasn't."

"That's the thing," I say, lacing my fingers together and laying them on the table in front of me. "Not one of the students who came out of Beth and Augie's classroom even knew that there was actually an intruder in the school. They knew they were in lockdown, but no one saw a gunman." Verna blinks at me through her thick-lensed glasses but doesn't respond. I decide to get right to the point. "Your daughter and son-in-law are separated, correct? And a divorce is pending?"

"Yes," Verna says warily, and fear springs to her eyes.

"I'm wondering," I begin carefully, trying to find the right words. "I know that sometimes in divorces there can be heated discussions about child custody."

"You're wondering if Ray Cragg could be the one in the school with a gun because Darlene won't let him see the girls," Will Thwaite says bluntly. Beside him, Verna seems to deflate.

"I am wondering exactly that," I say, looking back and forth between the two of them. "We've got a school full of children trapped in that building and no one seems to know who would have any kind of motive to storm in there with a

gun. Right now, Ray Cragg seems to be the only parent unaccounted for."

Verna's eyes well with tears and she dabs at her face with
a crumpled-up napkin. "I've been trying to get ahold of him
since this happened. Ray has treated my daughter terribly
and I'm glad she's divorcing him." Verna presses her lips together and struggles to continue. "Ray loves those little girls
and I can't imagine that he would hurt them, but now I don't
know." She shakes her head resolutely as if to convince herself. "No, he wouldn't hurt his girls, ever."

"But he would hurt his wife, right? Has hurt her and can't
do that anymore. Darlene has a restraining order against Ray,
so for all purposes he can't get to her, at least not physically."

"You think that Ray might threaten to hurt his girls in
order to get back at Darlene?" Will asks.

I shrug. "I don't know. That's why I'm asking you, Mrs.
Fraise."

Verna cups her age-spot-speckled hand beneath her chin,
her fingers covering her mouth, which is trembling with emotion. She nods. "It's possible. It's possible Ray could do that."

"Okay, I'll check it out and get back to you as quickly as
I can. In the meantime, Darlene is doing okay? Someone is
with her?"

"Yes, my husband, Gene, is with her. She was so upset when
Beth didn't come out with the other children. She's sure something bad has happened to her."

I turn my attention to Will Thwaite. "Your granddaughter
and Beth are friends?" I ask. "Could that explain why Augie
didn't come out the window with the other children?"

"I know that Augie and Beth are friendly," Will says. "But I
wouldn't say that they were best friends. Augie and her brother
came to stay with us about eight weeks ago and she wasn't
very happy about leaving Arizona. Her mother was...was in-

volved in an accident and Augie and P.J. are staying with us until she gets better."

"So you don't think that Augie would have stayed in the school to be with Beth?" I ask.

Will shakes his head. "More than likely Augie was trying to go and find P.J. Those two are as thick as thieves, though Augie would never admit it. She looks after that boy like she's the mother. And that girl is as stubborn as cement. She gets an idea and doesn't let it go. Runs in the family, I think. You find P.J. and, more likely than not, Augie will be right there with him."

"That may be why she ran back into the school after she brought Faith out. What grade is P.J. in?"

"Third grade, Mrs. Oliver's room," Will says. "There's Cal Oliver over there, Evelyn's husband." He points to a thin, long-legged man with a white beard and a bald head sitting by himself at a corner table. I've never formally met Mr. Oliver, but he's a familiar face. A cell phone sits on the table in front of him and he just stares at it as if willing it to ring.

"I need to get going now," I tell Will and Verna. "Thank you for your help. I promise I will let you know as soon as I learn anything about your grandchildren." I'm halfway across the room when a thought strikes me.

"Mr. Thwaite, one more thing," I say apologetically. "P.J. and Augie have different last names. What can you tell me about their fathers?"

"Well, it couldn't be Augie's dad. He was the one who called us to come get them. As for P.J.'s father, never met him. As far as I know, he's never been involved in P.J.'s life. I don't think that P.J. even knows his name."

Out of the corner of my eye, throughout my conversation with Will and Verna, I could see Ed Wingo puffing up like a blowfish trying his damnedest not to interrupt. He can't hold it in any longer and shakes a finger at me. "What the hell is going on out there? I don't think you could find your own ass if you tried."

As much as I'd like to give Ed a piece of my mind, I know it's useless. "We're doing the best we can," I tell him mildly, and this makes him even angrier.

"Oh, shut up, Ed," Verna says before he can say another word.

"I'll be in touch," I say, and rush out of the café into the snow. At least an inch has fallen since I've been in Lonnie's. Now we have two possibilities. Ray Cragg seems to be the most obvious suspect, and it's a long shot but maybe P. J. Thwaite's biological father wanted to come reclaim his son. At least I won't go back to the chief empty-handed. I sweep the snow from my windshield with my arm and climb into the car. A blast of cold air from my heater greets me when I turn the ignition. I try to put a call into dispatch, but there is no answer. Obviously communication is still a mess. I consider using my cell phone to check in with Chief McKinney, but decide against it. First I want to check out the Cragg lead and the chief has more than enough on his plate right now.

Will

Will said a quick goodbye to Verna and the others. "Where are you going?" Verna asked with concern.

"I need to go check on the calves. Daniel's trying to deal with all that on his own." His throat felt thick and raw and he wondered if it was from biting back the tears he felt forming when Augie didn't come through the café door or if he might be coming down with something.

"I'll call you if I hear anything," Verna promised, unashamedly allowing her own tears to fall freely.

Will pushed open the café door and was met with a blast of bitter air and snow that scraped against his skin. He welcomed the harshness of it, a meager punishment for the way he had acted toward Augie recently. He was supposed to be the adult, the mature one. Instead, he teased the poor girl. Thousands of miles away from her home without her mother, and he had the gall to tease her about her hair, her eating habits, the way she dressed.

He sat in his truck, trying to decide what to do next. He had no intention of going back to his farm yet, knew that Daniel would handle things there just fine. He needed to call Marlys and he wanted to go see for himself what Ray Cragg was up to. He was fishing inside his pocket for his cell phone when it rang, another decidedly inappropriate ringtone programmed in by Augie.

Marlys.

"Will," came Marlys's tearful voice over the line. "Gloria Warren just called me. What's going on there? Are P.J. and Augie in the school? What about Jenny?" she asked about Todd's wife.

Will silently cursed himself for not calling Marlys earlier and then spoke. "Marlys, I am so sorry I didn't call you, there is no excuse. I should have realized that some busybody in this town would be just itching to call you and break the news. I went to the school and it was a madhouse there and then everyone went over to Lonnie's and I thought about calling you a hundred times—"

"Will," Marlys said sharply. "If you find yourself in a hole, the first thing to do is stop digging." Will stopped. "Just tell me what you know about what's going on," she finished more gently.

"I don't have any news, Marlys," Will said helplessly, and rubbed his eyes. "I know they haven't come out of the school yet. Some of the kids have, but not P.J. and Augie."

"It's on the news here," Marlys said incredulously. "Gloria called me and I found a television in one of the family rooms at the hospital and Broken Branch School is right up there on the screen with police tape. They even had a shot of Jay Sauter's RV in the parking lot. But they aren't *saying* anything.

They aren't telling us who's in the school and what they want. I don't even know if they are theys. What's going on?"

"You know about as much as I do, Marlys. I've heard everything from it's an expelled student, a fired teacher, a terrorist. Verna even thinks it could be Ray."

Marlys was silent for a moment and Will thought that perhaps she had hung up on him in order to get on the next flight back to Broken Branch. "I can see that," Marlys said softly. "What should I tell Holly?" She paused. "I don't even know *if* I should tell Holly," Marlys said more to herself than to Will. "They have to get out of there okay," Marlys finally said with vehemence. Will knew what she meant. They at last got to see their daughter, meet their grandchildren. Yes, it took a catastrophe for that to happen, but it did and this was their chance, Will's chance, to make things right again with Holly. There was no way that he could walk back into her hospital room without the children she entrusted to him.

"Don't say anything to Holly just yet, Marlys," Will said. "I'm going to do whatever I can to find out exactly what's going on. It won't do Holly any good to worry. She needs to concentrate on getting better. I'll call you with an update every hour, okay?"

"Okay," Marlys answered, though she didn't sound convinced. "On the TV it looks like it's snowing pretty hard there," she finished. Will allowed himself a small smile. If Marlys was talking weather he knew she had forgiven him.

"It's snowing like a son of a bitch," Will said with relief, then tucked the phone into the front pocket of his coveralls, pulled out onto the highway and began the twenty-minute drive over to the Cragg farm.

Meg

I try Randall one more time with no luck and Stuart keeps on sending me these inane text messages. I knew that Stuart was passionate about getting his story, going to extreme measures. A few years ago, the *Des Moines Observer* arranged for Stuart to travel to Afghanistan and join an Iowa Army National Guard Unit. He reported the undercurrent of terror as well as the mind-numbing mundaneness of day-to-day life in a war zone through the eyes of twenty-one-year-old Specialist Rory Denison. Stuart's article focused on the unlikely love story between a young Afghani girl and Denison. It was a touching story and even brought tears to my jaded eyes when Stuart shared it with me early in our relationship. Sadly, Denison was killed by a roadside bomb, leaving the young girl pregnant and alone back in Afghanistan. After the article was published, Denison's family tried relentlessly to find the young girl and their grandchild, but to no end.

Stuart won the Pritchard–Say Prize, cementing himself as Iowa's highest honored investigative reporter.

After recovering from the initial shock of reading Stuart's latest investigative piece detailing the attack and rape of Jamie Crosby and his unapologetic explanation, I called her. I knew I had to handle the discussion carefully. From the tone of the article, it appeared as if Jamie was a willing participant in the interview, enthusiastic even. That wasn't the Jamie I knew. Jamie was reserved, hesitant to share the painful details, but in the article little was left to the imagination. The crux of the story was accurate, but certain aspects just didn't fit.

"I saw the article," I said when Jamie answered her phone, careful to keep any judgment from my tone, though I was disappointed that she would talk to Stuart, any reporter. The article could come back to haunt her, compromising the case when it went to trial, if it even got that far.

"I know," Jamie said, and I could hear the worry in her voice. "I didn't say things the way he made them sound. It's terrible. People will think I'm terrible." She began crying.

"No one knows it's you, Jamie." I tried to soothe her. "The paper can't release your name. It's going to be okay," I murmured, even though I had no right to tell her that.

I listened to Jamie weep for a few moments and then asked the question that I really didn't want to know the answer to: "Jamie, why did you talk to the reporter?"

Jamie sniffled and cleared her throat. "He seemed so nice and he said you and he were really good friends. I thought it was okay."

It was worse than I thought. Stuart not only located Jamie through me, followed me to her house the night she called me in a panic, but he had the gall to use my name to wheedle his way into her good graces. Making her trust him.

"Oh, Jamie," I said softly. "I know him but he most definitely isn't my friend. I swear to you I never, ever talked to him about your case, never mentioned your name, never suggested he talk to you."

"I know." Jamie swallowed hard, her voice thick with tears. "The thing is, he was so nice, but the story wasn't even right. I didn't say half of those things, not in the way he made them sound, anyway."

"Jamie, I will get to the bottom of this, I promise," I told her. "Don't talk to anyone else. Everything will turn out okay."

That conversation was two weeks ago and I had been digging around, making some calls, talking to some people, learning more about Stuart than I wanted to. When it came to his news stories, he was ruthless. This wasn't the first time he wooed a victim into giving him the exclusive scoop into their ordeal. Their willingness to open up to him only really benefited one person. Stuart Moore.

Now not only did Jamie have to deal with the rape, but her brothers were locked in the school with a gunman with unknown intentions. How much more could one family take? We need to get the students out of the school before night falls. There are only a few hours of daylight left. I imagine all those kids in a pitch-black school, huddled in corners, not able to see what is going on. I hesitate for only a moment as I approach County Road B. I can turn right and go back to the school or turn left and head to the Cragg farm. "Left, it is," I mutter to myself, and take a deep breath.

Will

The Cragg farm, like the Thwaites', was a century farm. Will remembered Theodore Cragg, Ray's father, as a serious, frugal man who lived for farming and had hoped that his four boys would also. Three of the Cragg boys left Broken Branch to pursue other ways of life and only Ray stayed behind to continue his father's legacy. But while Ray was an excellent cattleman, loved his animals, loved the earth, he was no businessman. Rumors had been floating around town that Ray was on the verge of losing the farm that had been in his family for well over one hundred years. Two seasons of drought followed by a summer of record rains had put the Craggs heavily in debt. Theodore Cragg, who still lived with his son, was quite vocal regarding his son's perceived mismanagement of the farm. There were several times while at Lonnie's or while chitchatting with a group of farmers at the feed store, Will would witness Theodore berating his son in front of the others. Will now wished he would have stepped in, told the old man to shut up, that many farmers faced difficult years but somehow pulled themselves, their farms, out of the depths of ruin. Back in '88 Will and Marlys sat on their front porch one afternoon and watched helplessly as the rich, golden yellow cornstalks bleached to bone-white from the unrelenting August sun. All farmers, it seemed, could be one step away from foreclosure, but he and Marlys persevered, as did the land; the following harvest was a humdinger.

Will parked his truck in front of the house. Will was struck by how lonely the property looked. The Craggs had two young daughters. There should have been traces of their presence, Easter decorations on the windows, sleds, toys, something that indicated children had been here. Verna had mentioned that Darlene and the girls had moved out, but Will had figured it was just for a few days, until tempers cooled. Will knew that the elder Cragg was an old son of a bitch with a nasty disposition, but Ray seemed more easygoing, had more of a sense of humor. Not according to Verna. She described Ray Cragg as a violent, jealous man. Goes to show you, Will thought, how you never really knew what went on behind closed doors.

Will had been a guest in the Cragg house several times and he walked to the side entrance and knocked on the door that he knew led to the kitchen. No one answered but he could hear the sharp yips of the Craggs' dog. He was just about to give up and head back to the café when he caught sight of the golden Lab through the door's pane-glass window. The dog sniffed manically at something on the floor, alternately barking and whining. Will pressed his face against the glass to get a better look. Bright red droplets speckled the white linoleum of the kitchen floor. Blood, Will thought with a growing sense of alarm. He rushed back to his truck, flung open the door and got inside. He fumbled inside his coveralls for his phone and dialed a nine and a one before hesitating. A phone call to the police right now would mean that someone would have to leave the school in order to respond, leaving the already short-staffed department with one less police officer to assist the children trapped inside the school.

He didn't even know where the blood had come from. The dog could have an injured paw, old Mr. Cragg could have cut himself making a sandwich. Will snapped the phone shut and, without considering the consequences, grabbed his shotgun from the seat beside him and returned to the Craggs' side door. He tested the doorknob, which swung open easily. The dog wagged his tail at Will as his paws skittered through the bright red droplets leaving scarlet streaks, like a toddler's messy finger painting, across the floor.

"Go on outside, girl," he urged the dog, pushing her gently out the door. There were a few dirty dishes in the sink, a half-filled cup of coffee on the kitchen table. "Ray!" Will called out. "Theodore! It's Will Thwaite down here." Will cocked an ear and listened for any response but was only met with silence. He made his way slowly through the kitchen to the living room where a large console television was turned to a soap opera, the volume muted. Will felt the hairs on the back of his neck stand up. Surely someone must be home. He peeked inside the dining room and then the small bedroom that Ray used as an office. A computer filmed with dust sat on an equally dusty desk. Piles of mail, bills by the looks of them, sat unopened. Will backed out of the office and stood in front of the set of stairs that led to the second floor, knowing that if he ascended those steps he wouldn't be able to exit the house easily. He took a deep breath and forced himself upward. Just as he reached the top step he heard a cry coming from below.

"Anyone there?" he called out, his breath quickening within his chest. "You okay?" Another moaning sound. Will went back down the steps and followed the noise to a closed door just through the office. A bathroom, Will thought, trying to remember the layout of the house.

"Who's there?" Will called through the door. "Are you okay in there?" He felt his grip slip on the shotgun, transferred it to his other hand and wiped his palm against his pants. He pushed open the door with a quick movement and shuffled backward, afraid of what he was going to see.

Theodore Cragg was sitting on the floor of the bathroom, a wadded-up towel soaked with blood pressed against his head. "Theodore," Will gasped, rushing toward the elderly man and kneeling down next to him. "What happened?"

Theodore pulled the towel away from his scalp, revealing a deep gash that would surely need stitches. "Ray," was all he managed to weakly croak before his eyes fluttered closed.

Mrs. Oliver

Mrs. Oliver opened one eye, lifted her chin and found the gunman and P. J. Thwaite staring down at her. The man still looked concerned. P.J. did not. Mrs. Oliver rolled over onto her back and reached out her hand for the man to help her up. He shook his head and walked toward her desk and opened her purse. P.J. reached down and grasped Mrs. Oliver's hand and braced his feet in order to pull her up.

When she was finally upright, she patted her hair and noticed sadly that more Bedazzler beads had fallen from her chest. "I'm okay, everyone." She smiled encouragingly, but inside she was cursing. The man was at her desk, pawing through her purse. She wondered what he would do when he found her cell phone. Would he say, "Don't believe in cell phones, huh?" and then toss it into the air like one of those clay pigeons and blast it to smithereens like they do in trap shooting? Or maybe he would just shoot her. She was seriously considering collapsing to the floor again when P. J. Thwaite sidled up next to her and she felt something drop into the large pocket of her jumper. P.J. allowed a small grin to creep onto his face and then returned to his seat. The man, finished with her purse, tossed it aside and looked at Mrs. Oliver.

"You going to make it?" he asked her in a manner that made Mrs. Oliver know that he really couldn't have cared less whether or not she expired in front of her students.

"I'll be fine," she responded, comforted by the familiar weight of the phone in her pocket. "I'll just sit over here and rest."

"Good idea," he said. "I've got a call to make."

So do I, thought Mrs. Oliver to herself.

Augie

The hallways are so quiet that it's hard to believe that there are any students or teachers even in the building. For a second I wonder if maybe I'm the last one left in here, if everyone else is already at home saying to one another, *Whew, that was a close one.* If maybe Grandpa came and picked P.J. up, stopping off at Lonnie's for a cheeseburger and fries before driving home. P.J. might wonder about me, stop in the middle of slurping on his chocolate shake and say, *I wonder what happened to Augie?* And Grandpa would shrug and say, *Well, she did make life interesting around here for a while.* Of course I know this wouldn't really happen, but if there ever was a third wheel in a group, I'm it. I guess I can kind of understand how P.J. felt whenever my dad came over to our house to pick me up and we shared all these inside jokes that P.J. knew nothing about. Grandpa and P.J., from the moment they met, were best buds. And it completely irritated me. Here I had given up living in my hometown, being with my friends, being near my mother, all for P.J., and he was ditching me for an old man and his farm. Whenever Mom talked about her father there was an edge to her voice. *Be thankful for having me as a parent,* she would say. *All I did was work, work, work on that farm growing up.* She told us all about how she could never take part in after-school activities or spend time at her friends' houses because of all the work Grandpa had her doing. *And the smell,* she would say, pinching her nose.

Even before we met our grandparents, P.J. and I had already had a long discussion about what we thought our Grandma and Grandpa Thwaite were going to be like. And together we decided we weren't going to like them. But within an hour P.J. had two new best friends. This shouldn't have surprised me, P.J. likes everyone. He's like a puppy dog that way, almost begging people to love him. But at least I was being loyal to our mother. Saying goodbye to her was the worst. You'd think that a person would feel comfortable leaving someone with their own mother, but I didn't. Grandma Thwaite is a stranger to me. To my mom, really. They haven't seen each other in over fifteen years and only talk a few times a year. So I was very surprised to see my mom's eyes tear up when Grandma walked into the hospital room. *Mom,* she said, like it was candy on her tongue. I blame the drugs. I wanted to say, *Are you kidding me? This is the lady who you said never stood up to your father, she let him make all the decisions, made her a shadow of a woman.* Funny thing is, Grandma Thwaite looks nothing like a shadow woman. She is big and round with pink cheeks and has a loud, happy laugh.

So even though my brother and my mother decided to act like everything was all sunshine and roses, I decided to take up where my mom left off. There was no way I was going to let that man walk all over me. Still, though, every day before we left for school in the morning, he tells me to look after my brother, and as much as I'd like to tell the old man to shove it, I do look out for P.J. Not because Grandpa tells me to, but because I always have.

Mrs. Oliver

Mrs. Oliver covertly fingered the cell phone in her pocket. She knew how to text others but her fingers seemed so large and clumsy against the tiny keys she rarely attempted it. She thought about just pressing some numbers and hitting the send button, but who knew who would receive the call. Then there was the problem of actually speaking. She didn't know how she would be able to hide a conversation from the gunman. She wondered if she could create another diversion. She looked over at P. J. Thwaite, who was looking back at her and raising his eyebrows at her as if to say, *Make the call already*. Mrs. Oliver raised her eyebrows in response. P.J. scratched his head and began stretching out his neck, dipping it to one side and then the other in a strange snake charmer sort of way. He continued on in this way until the man glared at him in irritation.

"What the hell are you doing?" he asked P.J.

"I was just trying to see what color of eyes you have," P.J. answered innocently.

"Preparing to pick me out of a lineup?" the man asked with a snort.

"No, I..." P.J. looked at his teacher in confusion.

"You won't have to worry about lineups," the man said, and Mrs. Oliver felt the pills that she swallowed creep back up into her throat. "Blue," the man snapped at P.J. "My eyes are blue," he said shortly, and then reached into his backpack for a bottle of water.

"P.J., don't," Mrs. Oliver said.

"Are you sure you've never been to Revelation, Arizona?" P.J. asked, ignoring his teacher. "It's just outside of Phoenix."

"Nope, never been there."

"You'd remember my mom. She's so pretty. She's got brown hair. I know that doesn't sound pretty the way I'm saying it, but it is pretty. It's all shiny and soft. She's got blue eyes and she's skinny, but not too skinny." P.J. leaned forward in his desk. "You would have known her about nine years ago, I guess." The man decided to ignore P.J. and took another swig from his water bottle. "Were you in the marines? You look like you could have been a marine. My mom said my dad was a marine and had to go to the war. Were you ever in the war?"

Mrs. Oliver was so enraptured in P.J.'s account that she didn't immediately think to make the call.

"Listen...Parker," the man said almost kindly, glancing down at the nametag on P.J.'s desk.

"My name is P.J.," P.J. told him stiffly, risking a glance at Mrs. Oliver, who was busily fiddling around in her pocket. P.J. had asked her many times to please make him a new name tag that said P.J., rather than Parker.

"Okay, *P.J.,*" the man amended. "I've never been to Revelation, Arizona. I've never met your mother." A flash of understanding lit his eyes. "And I am most definitely not your father here to kidnap you away so we can live happily ever after. Have you ever taken a look in the mirror? We look nothing alike. I have blue eyes. You say your mother has blue eyes. Two blue eyes don't make a brown eyes. Your eyes are brown. Get over it, Parker. If your dad hasn't come looking for you by now, he isn't ever going to. Now shut up and leave me alone."

A storm of emotions skittered across P.J.'s face and finally settled on anger. "Well, I'm glad you're not my dad," P.J. said in such a low voice the man had to strain to hear him. "My dad was a marine and he would never come into a school with a gun and scare people. You're a jerk."

The man, to P.J.'s embarrassment, laughed. "I've been called much worse things, Parker, but I suppose you're right. I am a jerk. Now shut up."

"My name is P.J.," P.J. said dejectedly, and plopped back into his seat and buried his face in his arms on top of his desk.

Mrs. Oliver, meanwhile, wanted to weep for P.J. The man could have been a bit gentler with the boy. She also realized what a sacrifice P.J. had made for her and his classmates. P.J. had never once in the weeks he had been enrolled at the school ever uttered anything about a father. He spoke of his mother, sister and grandparents. But never his father, though the other students asked P.J. about him. P.J. would only shrug his shoulders and quickly change the subject.

Because P.J. had distracted the man for even just a few seconds, Mrs. Oliver was able to press the first name on her contact list and press Send. With any luck, Cal was listening to their conversation right now.

Will

"Theodore." Will lightly shook the older man's shoulders and his eyes opened, unfocused and still heavy. "Theodore, Ray did this to you?" Will asked. Theodore nodded, his double chins quivered in agreement. "I'm calling for help." He gingerly relieved Theodore of the blood-soaked towel and replaced it with a clean one that he pulled from the towel rack and pressed gently against Theodore's head.

Once again, Will pulled his phone from his coveralls and, without hesitation this time, dialed emergency. Busy. "Jesus," Will muttered, disconnecting and trying again. Once again he was greeted by the monotone beep of a busy signal.

Will looked around helplessly. Theodore Cragg had to weigh at least two hundred and fifty pounds. There was no way that Theodore was in any shape to walk to Will's truck on his own accord, and it didn't look like Will would be able to get the man there without help.

Will debated on which of his sons to call in order to help

get Theodore to the hospital over in Mason City. Todd lived in Broken Branch, but it wouldn't be right to pull him away from the situation at the school and news of his wife's safety. His next option was to call his eldest son, Joe. The drawback was that Joe lived thirty minutes away on a farm outside of Walton and Will wasn't sure that Theodore could wait that long for medical care. Will finally settled on calling his friend Herb Lawson, who promised to work on getting help to the Cragg farm.

The next call Will had to make was more difficult. He dialed Verna's number. His wife's best friend answered on the first ring. "Any news on anything?" she asked breathlessly.

"Now listen, Verna," Will said, trying to keep his voice from shaking. "You need to make sure that Darlene is in a safe place."

"Why?" Verna asked in confusion. "What's going on?"

"I'm here at Ray's and Theodore's got a nasty lump on his head. Said that Ray was the one who gave it to him. Ray's nowhere to be found."

"Oh, Lord," Verna said fearfully. "I've got to call Gene and Darlene. I told you that man is crazy."

"You do that and I'll make sure that Theodore gets to the hospital. And, Verna, you take care of yourself, too. Marlys needs you, you hear?" Will swallowed back a flood of emotion. What more could this awful day bring?

Meg

The road conditions have deteriorated rapidly and I can barely see the pavement in front of me. It's approaching four o'clock and I have no idea of what's going on back at the school. I suddenly am nervous about heading out to the Cragg farm without officially letting anyone know. I could end up stranded in a ditch and freeze to death. Cragg could be on a violent bender and shoot me when I show up at his house unexpectedly without backup. What if something big is happening at the school and I should be there assisting?

I try Randall, the dispatcher, again and finally I hear his familiar voice, a little hoarse from all the talking he's been doing the past few hours. "Hi, Randall, it's Meg. Just checking in."

"Meg, where are you? You've been off the radar for a while," Randall says a bit snippily. "Chief McKinney has been looking for you."

"I've been trying to call in," I say defensively. "I haven't been able to get through to you."

"I know," Randall says, his tone softening. "It's still crazy. Parents and kids in the building have been calling nonstop. The parents are asking me what is going on and wondering why the hell we can't get their kids out of the school. I try to explain that we need to keep the phone lines clear and information will be shared as soon as it's available, but it doesn't matter."

"Is there any progress?" I ask. I'm about five miles away from the Cragg farm and my palms begin to sweat.

"Chief McKinney tried to make contact with the intruder by phone and with the bullhorn, but the guy never responded. But from the 9-1-1 calls from within the school I've been able to get a sense of which classrooms appear to have had absolutely no contact with the intruder."

"Which classrooms are those?" I ask, my heart thumping loudly as I think of Maria's schoolmates.

"Surprisingly, no one in the high school wing has seen or heard a thing. So as of now it looks like nine grade levels have had no contact with the intruder of any sort. Plus, the 9-1-1 calls from the primary wing of the building, that's kindergarten through second grades, indicate that there has been no sighting of a gunman."

"Okay, what about third through eighth grade?" I ask as I turn onto the gravel road that leads to the Cragg farm.

"That's the strange thing," Randall says in a puzzled voice. "Initially, that's where we were receiving the most 9-1-1 calls from. Then all of a sudden nothing. No calls were coming in from those classrooms and the students' parents and the teachers' spouses started calling in saying that they couldn't reach—"

"The gunman collected all the phones," I interrupt. "Faith Garrity said that when she saw the man in the hall he dropped several phones. I bet you anything he avoided the high school wing so as not to be overpowered by the older students, collected all the phones from the middle school kids and either didn't bother to go to the younger grades because they most likely don't have cell phones or because he was interrupted before he could get to them."

"That makes sense," Randall says. "Listen, you better call the chief, he really wants to talk to you."

"Will do. And, Randall, I'm doing a welfare check at the Cragg farm right now, okay? So if you don't hear from me in half an hour, send someone out here."

"What the hell, Meg? Why are you going way out there?"

"I got some information that leads me to believe that I need to do a check on the Cragg farm. That's all I know right now, okay?"

"Okay, but you better call me in thirty minutes. Call my cell—at least I know you'll be able to get through to me. And call the chief!" he shouts as I disconnect.

Mrs. Oliver

Mrs. Oliver stood and went to P.J.'s side, the trill of the cell phone as it dialed Cal smothered by her hand and the denim of her jumper. P.J.'s tirade stopped as suddenly as it began. The man regarded her incredulously. "Sit back down. Now!"

"I'm just checking to make sure P.J. is okay. You've upset him terribly."

"He's fine," the man scoffed, looking down at P.J., who still had his head down on his desk.

"This is ridiculous," Mrs. Oliver said loudly, chin down, trying to direct her voice toward the phone. "How dare you march into my classroom, with a gun no less, and terrify my students for no apparent reason. Thankfully no one is hurt. And then poor Lucy. Shameful the way you locked her in the closet." Mrs. Oliver knew she was taking it a bit too far, but she couldn't seem to stop herself. Now that she had an outside audience she wanted to make sure she provided as much information as she possibly could. "You said this was all going to be over soon. Why isn't it?" Mrs. Oliver took a cautious step toward the man. She fiddled with the fabric of her dress, trying to casually pull the pocket open, hoping that the conversation was audible to Cal.

"Go sit down," the man repeated in a low, menacing tone.

"I will once you tell me what is going on here, when you are going to let us go."

Suddenly the man reached out and grabbed the front of Mrs. Oliver's jumper, sending the remaining rainbow-colored beads skittering across the tile. Mrs. Oliver squawked loudly, more in dismay at the thought of all of Charlotte's hard work on her jumper ending up on the floor than in fear. "Sit down and shut the fuck up or I will shoot you and every one of these kids in the head!" the man sputtered, his nose nearly touching her own. And to prove his point, he pressed the barrel of the gun against her temple.

From her pocket came Cal's voice shouting, "Evelyn, Evelyn, are you all right?" For the first time, Mrs. Oliver realized that this might just be the very last time she would ever hear her husband's voice.

The man looked curiously downward toward the source of the voice, reached roughly into her pocket and pulled out the cell phone with Cal still shouting helplessly for his wife. "I love you, Cal," she managed to say before the man pressed the end button. Mrs. Oliver squeezed her eyes shut as the man ground the barrel of the gun into her cheek and waited for the deafening blast.

Augie

I decide not to take a chance by telling the primary teachers that the man with the gun is upstairs. Who knows if he is still in there or if there's another crazy person running around the school. I would die if someone got hurt because I said it was safe for them to leave the school.

I take a deep breath and begin my climb up the steps, and because I left my soggy shoes in the gym, the cold floor tiles prickle at my feet. I have no idea what I'm going to do when I get up there. It's not like I can knock on the door and politely ask to be let in. I don't particularly want to get shot.

I've only taken a few steps upward when I hear a door open and a soft voice rasping out to me, "Hey, what are you doing?" I trip forward and bang my knee on the step in front of me. I twist my body so that I'm sitting and rub at my kneecap. It's one of the second-grade teachers, peeping her head around the classroom door. I put a finger to my lips and glance over my shoulder to see if anyone above has heard us. "Is it safe?" she asks. She is young and hugely pregnant. She looks exhausted and is leaning on to the door frame like it's the only thing holding her up. I shake my head no and she bites at her lip like she's trying not to burst into tears. "Does he have a gun?" she asks. I nod. Her eyes grow wide with terror and she looks up and down the hallway. "Do you know where he is?" I point upward, still not saying a word. "Get down here, come in here with us," the teacher says through clenched teeth. "Hurry, he might come this way."

I shake my head and push myself up from where I'm sitting. I don't rush because I'm not afraid that she is going to come after me. I can easily outrun her and her basketball-size belly. "Come back," she says more loudly than she means to because she claps a hand over her mouth and then whispers, "Please." I shake my head no one more time, and turn my back on her. Slowly, quietly, I make my way back up the steps toward P.J.'s classroom, not quite knowing what I'm going to do once I get there.

The last time I had to save P.J. was the night of the fire. I was in my room, texting my friend Taylor, making plans to go to a movie later that night, when the smell of garlic crept underneath my bedroom door making my stomach growl. Mom was making dinner and sautéing vegetables in olive oil on the stove and P.J. was at the kitchen table, working on his science project, painting Styrofoam balls to look like the different planets.

"Hungry, Aug?" my mother asked as she dumped a bowl of chopped zucchini into the pan.

"As usual," P.J. said in a snotty voice.

"What's your problem?" I shot back. He ignored me, but I didn't let it go. "Look who's talking. At least my belly isn't hanging over my pants."

"Shut up," P.J. mumbled.

"Hey," our mother said. "Both of you, knock it off. Augie, will you get me a hot pad out of the drawer?"

"Why don't you ask lardo over there?" I asked. "He's the one who could use the exercise."

"Ha, ha." P.J. glared at me as he got up and opened the refrigerator, pulled out a gallon of milk and smacked it down on the counter next to where our mother was stirring the zucchini. "At least I don't have a zit-covered face that causes people to vomit."

I think about what I did next every single day. It was only a Styrofoam ball; I knew it wouldn't hurt him, even if it hit him in the face. "Shut up, loser," I hollered as I threw the ball in his direction. I didn't even throw it hard, just tossed it.

"Aha!" P.J. raised his hands in victory as the ball missed him. Instead, it hit the open bottle of olive oil that my mother instinctively tried to catch before it fell to the ground. I could see the thick, yellow oil spill from the bottle and onto my mother's hands, shirt, even onto her hair. P.J. was still laughing at me when my mother slipped on the oil that had dripped to the floor and tried to balance herself by grabbing onto the kitchen counter, knocking the pan of zucchini onto the ground and covering herself with more oil. It happened so quickly. Her sleeve barely touched the burner, but when it did, instant flames crawled up her arms like a scurrying bug. I can still see my mother's face the second before the fire jumped to her hair; her mouth was frozen in surprise, a perfect round Cheerio, but it was her eyes I will never forget. The shock, the *this can't be happening to me* look.

The fire ignited everything that had been touched by the spilled olive oil, like a strange game of dominos, a stack of newspapers and magazines left on the counter, the corner of the curtains, the kitchen cabinets. By instinct, my mom went to the sink and began trying to put out the fire by running water over her hands, splashing it onto her face, but my one year of Girl Scouts came back to me. Oil and water don't mix. Flour. I grabbed the rooster-shaped canister that my mom found last year at the Phoenix swap meet, pried off the lid and threw the flour all over her. The white powder covered her face, putting out the flames that had eaten up the hair on the left side of her head and leaving her left ear a charred mess. I gagged at the smell of burned hair and skin, but tried to scatter the remaining flour from the rooster over her arm, which was still on fire.

"Stop, drop and roll!" I heard P.J. yelling, and my mother must have, too, because she fell to her knees and writhed around on the floor until the fire was out. The curtains and the kitchen cupboards were still burning and a thick smoke filled the room and my lungs. My mother staggered to her feet and yelled for P.J., who had suddenly disappeared. I promised to find him and pushed her toward the front door.

So here I am again, trying to find P.J. and pull him to safety. At least this time it's not my fault.

Mrs. Oliver

Mrs. Oliver was glad, at least, that she had the opportunity to tell Cal she loved him but was ashamed that her actions could be the reason that her students would never be able to utter those same words to their own families. She expected the blast to be louder and she expected pain. Instead, all she heard was a sharp rap and felt nothing. So getting shot was blissfully pain free, she thought to herself. Mrs. Oliver dared to open her eyes, and in the space beneath the gunman's arm, she saw the classroom door being opened. The pressure against her cheek fell away and a voice pierced the silence.

Meg

I pull up adjacent to the lane that leads to the Cragg home and put the cruiser into Park and kill the lights. I want to make sure I can easily drive away if I need to. I notice that the snow that covers the lane looks recently disturbed, making me believe that someone has driven through here in the past hour. A truck lightly frosted with snow is parked in the driveway, but this doesn't mean much; most farmers have several vehicles for their use and Cragg could have left earlier in the day. The truck could also belong to Ray's father, who, against everybody's better judgment, still drives.

There are no lights on in the Cragg house that I can see, but a shaggy golden retriever sits on the front steps of the house trembling. Great, a dog. He looks friendly enough, but I open my glove box and retrieve a few dog treats that I keep in there just for this purpose. The dog's tail thumps the ground at my approach and I snap the dog biscuit and toss half to her. She swallows it in one bite and looks expectantly up at me for seconds.

"Hold on, girl," I tell her as I join her on the steps. The Cragg house is a lovely two-story, painted white with black shutters. Below are window boxes that I imagine are filled with pansies and geraniums in the summer months, but now are filled to the brim with snow. I allow the dog a moment to sniff me and when I'm certain she's not going to attack I press the doorbell. I listen for any sounds but hear nothing but the whine of the wind and the dog's snuffling breaths. I open the screen door and pound on the thick oak front door with my fist. Nothing. "Where is he?" I ask the dog, as if she might be able to answer me. When I get none, I walk back down the steps and over to the front window. I stand on my tiptoes in order to peek through the window. The living room is dark; there are a few soda cans and beer bottles strewn around on a dusty coffee table. It's not a disaster area, but is neglected enough for me to be able to tell a woman isn't living here.

I walk to the side entrance of the house and see that while the screen door is shut, the inside door is ajar. "You stay," I order the dog as I step into the kitchen. A reddish smear of some unknown substance is smattered along the floor. Drying blood is my first thought and I pull my Glock from my holster. I move to what appears to be a home office. There are the usual papers and clutter that fill a home office, but my eyes are drawn to a large gun safe in the corner of the room. I pull at the metal handle and it swings open easily. The safe is designed to hold several shotguns, all nestled in their correct green-velvet homes. One empty space glares conspicuously up at me. It isn't large, just the right size for a handgun. "Jesus," I mutter. "It *is* Ray Cragg."

"I think you're right," comes a voice from behind me, and I whirl around, raising my firearm as I do so, my finger instinctually pressing against the trigger as I take aim.

Will

"Don't shoot!" Will called out as he saw Officer Barrett level her gun at him.

"Goddammit," she barked, clutching at her chest with her empty hand. "That's a damn good way to get killed."

Will steadied himself against the desk, heart hammering in his chest, his fingers leaving imprints in the dust. "I'm sorry," he gasped, hoping that he wouldn't die of a heart attack after avoiding death by gunshot.

"What the hell are you doing here?" Officer Barrett asked venomously as she shakily returned her firearm to its holster.

"Verna Fraise was worried about her son-in-law. I knew you all were busy with the school so I came over to check things out," Will explained, realizing as he heard the words said out loud what a stupid thing it was to come here. He took a shuddering breath and continued. "I found Theodore Cragg in there—" he gestured toward the bathroom "—bleeding. He said his son did it."

Officer Barrett pushed Will aside and entered the bathroom. Theodore Cragg was slumped against the wall, barely conscious, a bloody towel pressed against his forehead. "Your son did this?" Barrett asked Cragg, who nodded woozily. She turned back to Will. "Did you call an ambulance?"

Will shook his head. "I tried, several times. I couldn't get through to 9-1-1. I figured the lines were tied up with families trying to get information. That or maybe the storm knocked out some telephone lines. I did get through to Herb Lawson just fine. He was going to try and get an ambulance over here."

"Did you see any sign of Ray?"

"No, none. But I've only checked down here. I didn't make it upstairs or to the outbuildings."

"I'll make a quick sweep of the upper level. Keep trying for an ambulance," she ordered, and then disappeared.

Meg

After I clear the upper level of the Cragg house and once the ambulance has arrived to take Theodore Cragg to the hospital, I head back outside. The golden retriever nudges her nose into my leg; I give her the other half of the dog biscuit and check her dog tag for her name. Twinkie. "What do you think, Twinkie?" I ask. "Where do we look next? The big scary barn on the right or the big scary barn on the left?" I run my gloved hand through the dog's shaggy coat and make my way toward the smaller of the outbuildings. I check my watch; I only have five minutes before I need to call Randall back. I pick up the pace, grateful that I'm wearing my knee-high winter boots. Still, a sharp, cold wind pushes me toward the red, peeling structure and I begin to jog toward the barn door, Twinkie running ahead of me, stopping every few yards to make sure I am still following her. She reaches the barn well before I do and begins to whine and scratch at the red door. I try to run faster but the snow is deep, my legs are aching and my chest feels as if it's going to burst.

Twinkie looks up at me with mournful eyes and a sense of foreboding comes over me. I slowly pull at the handle of the door and it opens a fraction of an inch and then is blocked by a pile of snow that has drifted around the base of the door. I kick the snow away with my boot and pull the door open wide enough for Twinkie to squirm through. Immediately she begins barking, a rapid desperate baying. I look at my watch again. Two minutes until Randall calls in the cavalry. "Police," I call out. Nothing but the dog's yapping. "Police," I say again, this time more loudly but my words are still drowned out by the dog's barking. "Quiet!" I shout, and Twinkie immediately quiets and squeezes back through the door to my side. "You sit," I order, and she does. I clear away more snow so I'm able to open the barn door as wide as it will go. Gun at the ready, I peer around the corner into the barn. The musty smell of hay fills my nose and minuscule bits of dust hang in the air around my head.

I step inside, look around the dim interior and pause at what lies in front of me. I lower my Glock, pull out my cell phone and speed dial Randall.

Augie

I just make it to the top of the steps when I see Beth standing in front of P.J.'s classroom door. Her long brown hair has come loose from her ponytail and it looks like she's been crying. I try to get her attention by waving my arms at her, but she doesn't notice me. She knocks twice on the glass window in the door as she twists the knob and steps into the room.

"Dad?" I hear her say. "Please don't."

Meg

"Jesus, Meg," Randall says, relief in his voice. "I was just about to call the chief. He would have castrated me if someone had to leave the school to come looking for you."

"Randall," I try to interrupt.

"I can't believe you put me through this. I've had enough stress for one—"

"Randall," I say more forcefully. "Ray Cragg gave himself a 9 mm skylight. I need Fred." Fred is our medical examiner investigator.

There is silence on the line.

"Randall?" Still no response.

"Randall," I snap. "Stay with me here. I need the MEI at the Cragg farm."

"I'll call Fred, but you have to call the chief."

"Fine." I press the end button and look over to where a man sits—Ray Cragg, legs splayed, head lolled forward. I bend down to get a better look at what remains of his face, the lower half obliterated. His eyes, though lifeless, are opened wide as if surprised that he did this awful thing to himself. To his family. Splatters of blood and tissue cling to the bales of hay that he is resting against and I'm thankful that I'm the one who found him this way. At least that horror was spared from his family. I cringe at the thought of one of his daughters finding him in this state. I hear footsteps behind me and I whirl around, "Stay out!" I order.

The footfalls abruptly stop and I see Will Thwaite standing in the doorway, his hand on Twinkie's collar. "Jesus," he rasps, his gaze falling on the grotesque figure behind me.

"Go on outside, Mr. Thwaite," I say gently. "I'll be right there."

Mrs. Oliver

"Beth?" A small voice came from the back of the room. Mrs. Oliver spun around, the man's hand still gripping her upper arm firmly. Natalie Cragg looked up at her older sister in surprise, the tail of her braid damp from where she had been sucking on her hair nervously.

"Jesus H. Christ," the man said in defeat. "What kind of town is this? Doesn't *anyone* know who their father is?" Beth stood in stunned silence looking from her little sister and back to the gunman. The man dropped Mrs. Oliver's arm and shoved her aside, sending her crashing into the iron radiator beneath the window. A sharp pain spread from her hip down the length of her leg. The man grabbed Beth by her ponytail and forced her to her knees, waving the gun around carelessly. "Who else is out there?" the man asked.

"No one, j-just me," Beth stammered. "I thought...I thought you were..."

"I'm not your fucking father," the man spat, yanking the

ponytail violently, causing Beth to cry with fright. "You better not be lying to me." He was breathing heavily and had a
dangerous expression on his face.

"I'm not, I'm not lying," Beth assured him desperately.

Mrs. Oliver felt that things were spiraling quickly out of
control and hobbled back toward the man. "Can't you see
she's terrified?" Mrs. Oliver said. "Look at her." The man's
eyes seemed to clear a bit and he released Beth's hair and she
collapsed into a sobbing heap on the floor. Mrs. Oliver bent
down and whispered soothingly in her ear. "Go to Natalie
now, Beth. It's going to be okay. See—" Mrs. Oliver tenderly
brushed Beth's hair away from her sweaty forehead "—it's not
your father. Go on and sit with your sister now." Beth nodded
and, still crying, joined her sister in the back of the classroom.

A burning rage grew in Mrs. Oliver; she straightened her
spine, drawing herself up to her fullest height, trying to ignore the stabbing pain in her hip. She turned to the gunman.
"Lay one more hand on one of these children—" Before she
could finish her sentence the man reared back his hand. Mrs.
Oliver's last thought before he cuffed her soundly on the side
of the head with the gun was that once again Cal was right—
the easiest way to save face is to keep the lower half shut.

Meg

The medical examiner investigator, Fred Ramsey, lives only about twenty minutes from Broken Branch and should be here shortly. I quickly decide that no one is going to disturb the body so I hike through the snow back to my car, with Twinkie on my heels, in order to meet Fred and the ambulance and warm up. I settle Twinkie into the backseat, well aware of the crap I'm going to get for being a softie, but I can't leave her out in the cold; the temperature is dropping quickly and the winds have picked up. It must be below zero with the windchill factor and I can only imagine how logistically difficult it is over at the school. I dig into my glove compartment and pull out the plastic bag filled with dog biscuits and give them all to Twinkie, who makes short order of them and then curls up into a golden ball and closes her eyes. Exactly what I'd like to do right about now.

I'm taking notes regarding my discovery of Ray Cragg's body, the interior of the cruiser is finally warm enough for me to remove my gloves and I can actually feel my toes again when my cell phone buzzes. I'm hoping it's Maria but the display reads *Stuart*. My curiosity gets the best of me and I answer. "Yes, Stuart? Very, very busy here."

"Hi, Meg," Stuart whispers. "Two quick questions for you—"

"No comment, no comment," I answer in a bored voice.

"Ha. Good one. No, seriously. This one is off the record if you'd like," he says softly.

"Oh, I like," I respond, angry at myself for getting pulled into Stuart's orbit again. "Why are you whispering, Stuart?"

"I don't want Bricker to hear my conversation. He's always trying to home in on my stories. Question one. Do you ever miss me?"

"How's your wife doing, Stuart?" I snap.

"Okay, sorry. She's fine."

"I'm happy to hear it. You used up one of your questions."

"I kind of have the feeling you haven't heard this news yet." Stuart hesitates as if maybe continuing this conversation isn't such a good idea.

"Spit it out, Stuart."

"Have you heard about your ex-husband?"

I straighten in my seat. I can see a vehicle moving slowly through the snow toward the Cragg farm, its headlights barely a glint against the brightness of the snow. "What about Tim? Is he okay?"

"That's the thing. No one seems to know where he is. My sources tell me that a call came into the Waterloo P.D. and that he just up and disappeared."

My mind is whirling. Where could Tim be? It's not like him to take off, especially when he has a visit with Maria.

"Meg," he says gently, tenderly, as if he still cares about

me. "My source speculated that maybe, just maybe, he's the guy in the school."

"That doesn't make sense," I say out loud before I remember I'm talking to a reporter, a reporter I once thought I could love, but certainly don't trust. "No comment," I say, and disconnect. If I find out who the hell Stuart's source is, I'm going to arrest him myself.

As the car comes closer I recognize Fred Ramsey's white SUV. Trailing behind him is another car that looks to be a Stark County sheriff's vehicle.

My feet feel like lead. I'm still in shock from Stuart's words. Tim, the intruder at Maria's school? No way. Stuart is messing with me. I force myself from the car to greet the men.

"Fred," I say, "thanks for coming so quickly. The body is this way, in the barn." I move to lead Fred to the barn when the sheriff's deputy steps from his car. Unusual for a deputy from another county to work a scene. I try to tell myself that it's because this is an unusual day, unusual circumstances, but a ripple of fear moves through my limbs.

"Officer Barrett?" he says formally. I nod. "I'm Deputy Sheriff Robert Hine from the Stark County Sheriff's Department. We're assisting your department because of all that's going on over at the school. Your chief wants me to take over here so that you'll be able to head back into Broken Branch."

"Did he say why?" I ask.

"No, ma'am, just that you are to report to the command center at the school."

I climb back into my car and, with shaking hands, I slide the gear into Drive. I hear Twinkie yawn in the backseat. I've forgotten about the poor dog. I don't have time to take her to animal control or to take her to Darlene Cragg's house without having to explain why I have her in the first place.

Mercifully, the snow has stopped for the time being but the

winds continue to blow, making visibility difficult. I try to call Tim's cell phone but it goes directly to voice mail. "Tim," I say, "please call me right away when you get this message."

I call Judith, Tim's mother, hoping to get more information, but she isn't answering, either. I consider calling Maria, but I don't know what she knows. I don't want to worry or upset her.

I know Tim's not the man in the school. There's no reason for it. He doesn't own a gun, doesn't have a mean bone in his body. That isn't the man I was married to.

As much as I don't want to, I put a call in to Chief Mc-Kinney.

Will

Will thought that he would be tied up at the Cragg farm for hours giving his statement to the sheriff's deputy about how he came to be in the Cragg home, found an injured Theodore, how that led to the discovery of Ray's suicide. Surprisingly, the officer simply took Will's statement, wrote down his contact information and sent him on his way.

He decided to drive back to the farm, check in with Daniel on how the calving was going. At times there were complications with calving in the best of weather, but in bitter conditions like this it could be deadly. He knew he should head back to Lonnie's, but the thought of sitting and just waiting made his skin itch. The Cragg farm was just minutes from Will's place but drifts of snow were scudding across the roads in erratic sheets, making visibility difficult. Just as Will was nearing his farm, faint headlights winked weakly from an approaching vehicle. Daniel. And he had the cattle trailer hitched to his truck. The two vehicles stopped, and Will powered down his window. The cold was relentless and instantly he was chilled through.

"I'm heading over to Dr. Nevara's. Number 421 is in distress and I'm thinking she's going to need a C-section," Daniel explained. "Herb Clemens is watching over the others, so no worries there."

Will felt a rush of gratitude toward his friends and neighbors; they could always be counted on. Whether you needed help planting your corn or birthing calves, they were there. "I'll follow you to Dr. Nevara's and then head back to Lonnie's." Will paused, trying to decide whether or not to tell Daniel about Ray Cragg's suicide. It could wait, he figured. Best if Verna and Darlene learned about it before the town at large.

Will turned his truck around, careful not to slide into the snow-driven ditches, and followed Daniel along County Road J that led to Dr. Nevara's vet clinic, which was on the western outskirts of Broken Branch.

If it hadn't been for Daniel, Will would have missed the black tires and chrome wheels of the car, flipped upside down in the ditch, nearly completely drifted over with snow.

The two men clambered from their vehicles, the ground knee-deep with snow in some areas and bare in others. Together, using their hands, they pushed the snow away from the driver's side window of the upended car, in hopes of seeing inside. When they finally cleared an area big enough to see, Daniel pressed his face against the window, trying to shield the glare of the snow. "There's a man inside," Daniel confirmed, reaching for his cell phone. "He's not moving."

As Daniel tried to raise help, Will peered inside the car. The man was upside down, held in place by his seat belt. Blood dripped from his nose and one of his legs was dangling at an odd angle. Will tried to still his own labored breathing so he could focus on the man's chest, hoping to determine if he was breathing. After a moment, he could discern the faint rise and fall of the man's chest. He was alive.

"They want to know if he's breathing," Daniel shouted above the groan of the wind.

"He's breathing," Will confirmed. "He's unconscious and looks like he has a broken leg."

"They'll be here as quickly as they can," Daniel said once he disconnected. "They're sending a wrecker from town and an ambulance from Conway. Do you recognize him?"

"No," Will answered. "But it's hard to tell. He's in pretty bad shape. I hope they get here in time."

Augie

I see Beth disappear into the classroom and I try to imagine what it would feel like believing that your father could love you so much he would resort to kidnapping a classroom full of kids. Then I have another thought, one that leaves my stomach feeling sickish. Maybe it's because Beth's dad hates her mother so much. Maybe this was his way of getting back at her. Would he shoot his own daughters out of hate for his wife? You hear about that on television sometimes, the woman who smothers her six-year-old for being sassy or drowns her eight-month-old in the bathtub, or the dad who shoots his entire family and sets the house on fire.

My knees feel weak at the thought and for the first time all day I'm really scared. The kind of scared that begins as a knot in your chest and gets bigger and bigger until that's all there is and there is no room left for air. The same kind of scared I felt the day of the fire. It's the scared that comes from knowing how badly and how easily we can hurt another person.

I know that there is no way I can go into that classroom. I was stupid to think I could actually get P.J. out of there all by myself. The man with the gun probably wouldn't let us leave, anyway. What would I say? "Excuse me, but it's getting close to supper time and I need to get my little brother home." He would probably laugh and tell me to sit down and shut up. Maybe even shoot me.

I figure the best way to help P.J. and everyone else in the classroom is to just sit down outside the door and wait and listen. Maybe I'll hear something that could help the police. I tiptoe along the hall and crouch down in the little area beneath the drinking fountain, which is right next to P.J.'s classroom. I lean against the cold wall and pull my knees up to my chin and try to make myself as small as possible. Hopefully the man doesn't get thirsty and come out and find me sitting here.

Mrs. Oliver

I t's not the pounding, throbbing pain in her jaw that awakened Mrs. Oliver, though that certainly had a rousing quality. It was the children and their welfare, as it always was, that brought Mrs. Oliver out of the miasma of semiconsciousness and forced her to pull herself up from the ground and into an empty desk. The man was most definitely losing control—the way he grabbed Natalie Cragg's sister, the way he had struck her with the gun—Mrs. Oliver couldn't leave the students alone with him. She was vaguely aware of a wet warmth trickling along her check and down the length of her neck. She tentatively touched the side of her face and wasn't surprised to find that when she pulled her fingers away they were coated with blood. "I'm okay," she tried to tell the children, but her jaw seemed unhinged somehow and all that tumbled from her mouth was an optimistic sounding but garbled jumble. She looked around for something with which to wipe her fingers, sticky with blood, and settled dejectedly upon her denim jumper. Through the one eye that wasn't swollen shut, Mrs. Oliver found that her students, along with Beth Cragg, were all staring at her in alarm and she gave them a lopsided smile and a thumbs-up. The man looked at her with a mix of irritation and admiration. He must have thought she was no longer any threat to him, because he left her where she sat and pressed his phone to his ear. Mrs. Oliver concentrated on staying upright and her abruptly ended phone conversation with Cal. He would most assuredly contact the police with what he heard. Any moment now they would burst through the classroom door, or a bullet sent by a trained sniper expressly for the man would shatter the window and pierce his forehead.

She would be transported to the hospital, but not until all the students were safely reunited with their families. Cal would be there to meet her. He would lean low over the hospital bed and smile down upon her and tell her that she was the most beautiful woman he had ever seen. Just as he had done so many years earlier after she had given birth. With one hand Cal held her swollen fingers and in the nook of his other arm was George's baby.

To her surprise, Mrs. Ford encouraged the brief courtship between Evelyn and Cal. "Evelyn," she said shortly after the disastrous dinner when Evelyn had retreated to her room, "you know there's nothing wrong with being happy."

"What do you mean?" Evelyn asked.

"George would want you to be happy." Mrs. Ford's chin trembled with emotion. "He would want someone who is a good and kind man to help raise his child."

Evelyn rotated her head from side to side trying to shake the thought away. It seemed too cruel, too soon. "Now, Evelyn," Mrs. Ford gently chided her. "It's obvious to see that

Cal Oliver is crazy about you. You are young and you have a lifetime in front of you."

"But I still love George," Evelyn said in a small wounded voice.

"Of course you do," Mrs. Ford said, wrapping an arm around her daughter-in-law. "And you always will. That's the wonderful thing about the human heart, there's room enough for all kinds of love."

Evelyn couldn't answer, couldn't explain how she still felt devoted to George but how an electrical spark of joy would course through her veins at the sight of Cal.

"Promise me one thing, Evelyn," Mrs. Ford asked gently. Evelyn nodded and sniffed. "Please tell the baby all about George. Tell him...or her," Mrs. Ford amended, "that his father was a sweet boy who loved numbers and Coca-Cola. That he was smart and a little bit silly. That he died in a faraway place because it was the right thing to do." Evelyn could feel the top of her head become damp with Mrs. Ford's tears and she clutched more tightly to the older woman's hands.

"I will tell him," Evelyn said, because she was sure that the child she was carrying was a boy. "I will tell him and you will, too."

Evelyn and Cal were married just a few weeks after she gave birth to Georgiana Elizabeth Ford. She was surprised when the doctor had told her she had given birth to a healthy baby girl, but that was quickly replaced with a deep-seated gratitude. Amazing, really, how this tiny pink-faced being came into this world less than a year after her father left it. *What a gift,* Evelyn kept saying to herself. And as if reading her mind, Cal looked down at both of them and then upward. "I'll take good care of them," he whispered. "I promise."

Meg

"Dammit, Meg," the chief spits into the phone. "What the hell have you been up to?"

I know I need to speak fast, keep it short and to the point. "I had reason to believe that Ray Cragg could have been the intruder in the school. I went to investigate and found him on the floor with a gunshot to the face." I stroke Twinkie's flank while I wait for Chief McKinney's reaction.

"So Ray Cragg is really dead?" the chief asks softly.

"Yes, an apparent suicide. Ray's father, Theodore, was injured by his son. An ambulance just took him away." Twinkie looks up at me with mournful brown eyes. Ray Cragg lost everything—his wife, his children, his life—but his dog still loved him.

Chief McKinney sighs heavily. "This day just keeps getting better and better. Did the sheriff's deputy arrive to relieve you yet?"

"Yes, he's there. He said you wanted me back at the school ASAP."

"Yes, head on back over here as quickly as you can, but drive safely."

I hesitate before continuing. "Chief, have you heard anything on the scanner about my ex–husband?"

I am met with silence. Not a good sign. "We'll talk when you get back here," he finally says.

"Chief, you can't think—"

"Just come on back to the school, Meg," he says wearily.

Will

Will tried to stay outside next to the flipped car in case the man trapped inside awoke, but the cold drove him back to his own vehicle. He sent Daniel on his way, so he could get the distressed cow to the vet before she gave birth. In the scheme of the world, in this day, the life of one cow and her calves didn't matter much, not in comparison to the lives of his grandchildren and daughter-in-law.

Will decided to take a moment to call Marlys. He had promised to call her every hour with updates, but with the fiasco at the Cragg farm he was late.

"Any news?" Marlys asked by way of greeting.

"Nothing new at the school," Will answered, and turned the heater in the truck down so he could better hear his wife.

"But..." Marlys began.

"Ray Cragg committed suicide."

"No!" Marlys exclaimed. "Those poor children."

"Yeah, now I'm sitting on County Road B waiting for a wrecker to help someone who flipped his car." Will pressed his fingers to his temple. He felt the beginnings of a monstrous headache.

"I'm sorry," Marlys said soothingly.

"Well, I'm in a much better state than Ray and this guy in the Ford." Will tried to lighten his voice. Marlys already had so much to fret about, he didn't need to add to her worries. "How's Holly doing? Does she know anything about what's going on?"

"No, but I don't like keeping this from her," Marlys said ferociously. "Holly's made a lot of mistakes, but she's a good mother to Augie and P.J. and loves them more than anything."

"Maybe we should tell her, then," Will said pensively. "You want me to talk to her?"

Marlys was quiet for a moment. "Let's wait a bit longer. She is so looking forward to seeing the kids tomorrow. I don't want to ruin that for her. For goodness' sake, Will, how much can one person go through? It's just got to be okay," Marlys finished with determination.

"Okay, we'll wait," Will assured her. "Just keep her away from the TV, I'd hate for her to hear about it that way. Listen, I gotta go. I see the wrecker and the ambulance. I'll call you back in a little while."

"I love you, Will." Marlys's voice trembled with emotion and Will wanted nothing more than to pull his wife into his arms and tell her it was going to be okay.

"Love you, too," was all he could manage. Bracing himself against the cold, Will stepped outside and waved his arms, flagging down the wrecker and the ambulance.

Holly

Most days I absolutely hate my physical therapist, Gina. She lets me whine and moan all I want, but she doesn't let me get by with any excuses. If I tell her I'm tired, she tells me too bad. If I say I'm in too much pain, she tells me to suck it up. Today, when I tell her I have an infection, she says, "What's that have to do with the price of eggs?"

I can't help laughing. "That's *exactly* what my dad always said when I was growing up."

"Smart man," Gina says, tapping her head.

My dad was, *is,* one of the smartest men I ever met, not that I'd ever tell him that. He was so practical, though, that it drove me crazy. He could never just do something for the fun of it. There was always a bull to buy, a calf to be born, a crop to be harvested, a piece of machinery to be fixed. I remember once, when I was fifteen, my boyfriend at the time and I snuck out into one of the sheds. After fooling around for a while, we decided that it would be fun to take my father's brand-new John Deere tractor for a little ride. The thing didn't go any faster than five miles per hour, but he completely had a conniption.

"It's not like we even hurt the thing," I remember protesting after he caught us and grounded me for two weeks.

"What's that have to do with the price of eggs?" he had shot back, just like he always did.

"Get some rest," Gina finally says when she realizes that she isn't going to get anything more out of me during this physical therapy session. "We'll hit it hard again tomorrow. You want to be good and strong when those kids of yours get here."

I smile at the thought. "I can't wait," I tell her. "It seems like forever since I've seen them." I wonder if my father had ever been so anxious to see me, wonder if he is looking forward to seeing me tomorrow. I know I didn't make things easy for him, I know I was oversensitive and overcritical when it came to my father. But how does a kid compete with a cow? If once, just once, my father would have said, "Holly, won't you please come home? I miss you." I would have been on the next plane back to Broken Branch. But he never did. That's the difference between the two of us. When it comes to my kids, I know what's important.

Mrs. Oliver

Mrs. Oliver's tongue felt dry, thick and swollen, like a sock had been shoved into her mouth. The man was pacing methodically in the front of the classroom, frequently checking his cell phone and growing increasingly agitated with each passing minute.

Mrs. Oliver knew that this whole episode would need to come to an end soon. If it didn't, someone, maybe many, would be dead, and she couldn't fathom the thought that it could be a child. She rapped soundly on the top of the desk with her knuckles and the gunman looked irritably toward her. "What?" he asked impatiently.

Mrs. Oliver tried to form the words she knew she needed to say. Her mouth still didn't work correctly. Her jaw was obviously broken, maybe shattered. She made a writing motion with her hand and the man nodded. Carefully she lifted the lid of the desk and quickly scanned the contents of the messy desk: textbooks, a pair of scissors, broken crayons, pencils, notebooks. As she retrieved a pencil and a notebook she pulled the scissors more closely to the desk's opening. The man watched her warily as she closed the desk and opened the notebook to a clean page. She concentrated on keeping her hand steady and in her normally tidy script Mrs. Oliver wrote shakily, "I will stay. It's time to let the children go now."

The man stared at the words for a long time but finally gave one short nod. Mrs. Oliver breathed deeply and sighed in relief, wincing at the stab of pain as the stream of cool air crossed over her broken teeth.

Meg

It's nearing six o'clock, already it's getting dark and sunset will arrive in just over an hour. Beyond the police tape, despite the weather, two news vans are parked, puffs of exhaust cloud the air. "Keep your head down," I tell Twinkie, who snuffles softly in response. A few reporters of indiscriminate genders are bundled up in large parkas with fur-trimmed hoods, and are facing shivering cameramen and speaking into microphones. Their attention turns briefly to me as I drive by, but seeing that I'm just a lowly Broken Branch public servant they quickly forget about me.

The sentries, a pair of police officers from a neighboring department, wave me into the school parking lot and I pull up as close as I can to the RV that has become the makeshift command center. I remove my coat and tuck it around Twinkie, hoping that her fur and my jacket will keep her warm and content.

The frozen air and brisk wind instantly sweep away any

body heat I've conserved and by the time I burst into the RV without knocking, I'm shaking with cold. Chief McKinney, Aaron and a man I don't recognize look up at me when I enter. The chief's face is grim and I ready myself to get a tongue lashing for the way I went off to the Cragg farm without following protocol.

"Sit down, Meg," he says gently.

I look first to the chief, then Aaron and finally to the unknown man. None of them can look me in the eye.

Augie

Even though my hiding place beneath the drinking fountain is uncomfortable and my neck is twisted at an awkward angle, I somehow keep zoning out. Not sleeping, but I feel strange, numb. Every once in a while I hear a loud noise from P.J.'s classroom and I am startled awake and bang my head on the drinking fountain. I'm not quite close enough to understand any of the conversations in the classroom. I've heard some crying and shouting. I'm not sure why the police haven't come into the school yet, but I figure they probably know what they are doing.

Meg

I lower myself into the nearest seat. The RV has been effectively transformed from a recreational vehicle to command center. There's a laptop and a police radio on the kitchen counter and blueprints of the school are spread out over the breakfast nook table. Chief McKinney hasn't told me what's going on yet, but I refuse to believe that it might have something to do with Tim.

"Meg, this is Terry Swain, a hostage negotiator from the state police, and we've got Anthony Samora, who leads the state tactical team, on the phone. The weather prevented him from making the trip."

Samora's tinny voice comes over the speakerphone. "I tried, though. Roads are terrible. Now let's get down to business." I swallow hard, afraid of what's coming next. "Just about forty minutes ago, we got word that your ex-husband, Tim Barrett, was reported missing by his mother. He told her that he was called into work unexpectedly this morning, and when she didn't hear from him after several hours, she called his place of work."

Chief McKinney leans forward and rests his forearms on his knees. "Meg, Tim was never called into work today."

I try to keep my tone even and neutral. "I'm not sure what my ex-husband's fibbing to his mother has to do with me."

"Now, Meg," the chief says uncomfortably. "I know that your divorce with Tim was difficult, that you had some custody issues to iron out."

"Most divorces are difficult, Chief," I say, irritated that my personal history is being pulled into this discussion. I cross my arms in front of me. "Most divorces involving children involve custody issues. We worked that out a long time ago."

"Officer Barrett," Terry Swain, the hostage negotiator, says, "let's get right to it. You had a contentious divorce with child custody issues, your ex-husband lied about his whereabouts and has been off the radar for several hours, and we have a hostage situation in the school where your daughter attends. And she just happens to be absent today."

"She's absent because she is spending spring break with her *father*. It doesn't make any sense that Tim would be in that building!" My voice rises and I forcefully try to lower it. "There has to be a logical explanation."

Swain stares intently at me for a moment as if trying to read my face for any hidden information. Anthony Samora pipes in over the phone line. "You're right. That in itself doesn't lead us to that scenario."

I lift my hands in exasperation. "Then what? What could possibly lead you to believe that my ex-husband, that Tim, would be involved in this?"

"Fifteen minutes ago, Terry tried to make another contact with the intruder," the chief explains. "He got on the bullhorn and reached out to the man, asked him what he wanted, what his demands were."

My mouth has gone dry. Looking through the RV's windows, my eyes lock onto the school building.

"We got a call a few minutes later, from a cell phone belonging to—" Swain checks his notes "—a Sadie Webster."

"Sadie Webster?" I say in confusion. "Doug and Caroline Webster's daughter?"

Swain nods. "Yes, the call came from Sadie's phone, but the caller definitely wasn't a twelve-year-old girl."

"Who was it, then?" I ask.

"We don't know," Swain admits, and I immediately relax.

"So this is all conjecture? You have no proof that Tim is the gunman in that school?" I laugh in relief. "Jesus, Chief, you scared the hell out of me."

"Meg," Chief McKinney says seriously. "We don't know who the caller was, but we do know that it's all over the news that your ex-husband is unaccounted for." Damn, I think to myself. Stuart was right. "We also know," McKinney continues, "that the man in the school has only one demand at this time."

"And what is that?"

"He asked specifically for you."

"For me?" I ask in disbelief. "Why would he ask for me?"

"Have you had any differences of opinion with Tim lately?" the chief asks, leaning in close to me. He is trying to be kind about this, fatherly.

"No, Norman," I answer fiercely, using the chief's first name. "I already told you that things are fine between Tim and me." I cross my arms and shake my head. "In fact, he invited me to spend spring break with him."

"And you said no," Swain states. It isn't a question.

"I said no," I say simply.

"Was he angry about that?" the unseen Samora asks.

"No, he was fine with it." I'm exasperated and pissed off. "Why are you wasting time on this? Tim would never do something like this. He doesn't even own a gun!"

"Right now there's a man with a gun in that school." Swain points toward the school and then to me. "And all we really know is that you have some kind of connection with him."

"Okay," I say, trying to sound more reasonable. "If you really think this person is connected to me, then look at someone besides Tim. Someone I arrested at one time, or my brother, Travis, for instance. He'd be a hell of a lot more likely to do something like this than Tim." In the past, I had confided to the chief the complicated history I had with my brother. How Travis's juvenile delinquent behaviors and shady friends kept our family held hostage, so to speak. At least until Officer Demelo came along and for the first time let me know I could fight back using the justice system. Good thing she did, because at that point in my childhood I truly felt like I was capable of smothering Travis in his sleep with a pillow.

"I haven't seen Travis in over ten years and haven't talked to him in seven. The last interaction with my brother was most certainly not warm and fuzzy. His final words to me were, 'Why are you such a bitch? You think you are so much better than me, don't you? I hope you're enjoying your happy little family while you can because I will never forget this, Meg.'"

"What happened between you two?" Swain asks.

I hate rehashing the bad blood between Travis and me. Frankly it is all so embarrassing to me as a law enforcement officer, but lives are at stake so I let out a big breath and explain. "Seven years ago I got a call from the Waterloo Police Department. An officer there said he had Travis in custody for drunk driving. Travis gave him my name, told him I was a police officer, said I would vouch for him, come bail him out." I rub my eyes at the memory. I felt nothing at the time. Not one iota of pity or sadness for the state of my brother's life. Just a dull resignation. He would never change. "I told the officer that I could not and would not bail my brother out."

"That's it?" Swain asks unsatisfied. "He threatened your family over a DUI?"

"No, there's more. After I hung up the phone with the officer and he told Travis he was out of luck, Travis freaked out. Punched the officer in the nose, broke his nose, went for his sidearm, ended up tearing some tendons in the officer's hand. Travis ended up being charged with a slew of crimes and has spent the past seven years in prison. Got out last November."

Swain shrugs. "So he said something in anger seven years ago. He called you from jail pissed off. Not unusual."

"I got that call last week."

"We'll check on it," Chief McKinney says, nodding toward Aaron, who writes something down in his notebook.

"I still think you're making a big mistake, but let's say it is Tim or my brother or whoever, what do you want me to do?"

The men look at one another. But no one speaks.

"Well?" I lift up my arms in defeat. "Do you want me to call him? Already tried it, no answer. Do you want me to get on the bullhorn and try to reason with him from out here? I will be happy to do it. I need a little direction here, guys."

"He wants to see you," the chief says in a tired voice.

"Fine, I'll go in there. No problem," I say, standing, but the men remain seated, still looking unsettled. I glare especially hard at Aaron, who hasn't said a word yet.

"It isn't protocol," Samora says, "to send an officer who hasn't been trained in tactical operations into a building."

"Right, I get that," I agree, "but I am an officer, I've started my tac training and if it gets those kids out of the school safely, I don't understand what the issue is."

"The issue is we've got six available officers here that will make up our makeshift little rapid response team and their lives are on the line once they enter that building," Swain says harshly. "We need to make sure every single officer that goes in there knows what they are doing."

"But if I go in there on my own, find out what he wants, then no other officers get hurt. Whoever it is," I say, glancing at Chief McKinney, "won't feel threatened by me. I'm just one person."

"I don't like it," the chief says, getting up to pour himself another cup of coffee from a thermos sitting atop the counter. "No shots have been fired. There are no reports of injuries. The lockdown plan says we fall back and wait. I don't want to go in there and force the situation."

"So we have to wait for someone to get shot or hurt before we can move?" I ask. "I can see that for a typical situation, but obviously whoever is in there has a beef with me, not with anyone in the school."

"We don't know that for sure," Chief McKinney says, handing me a cup of steaming coffee. "We just know that he wants to talk to you."

"I think she's right," Samora says. "Maybe she'll be able to talk him down."

"Or get herself killed," Swain counters. "I don't like this at all."

"How did he contact you?" I ask.

"A different cell phone," Swain says. "Belongs to a kid named Colton Finn, a seventh grader. We think he went into all the classrooms and collected as many cell phones as he could."

"I figured as much." I nod. "That makes sense. First he knocks out all the landlines and then takes all the cells he can.... Limits communication with the outside world."

There's a knock on the RV door and Officer Jarrow pokes his head in. "Hey, Chief, I've got a Cal Oliver here who says his wife called him from the school. He's pretty upset. You want to talk to him?"

"Absolutely," the chief says. "Let him in."

Mrs. Oliver

Mrs. Oliver cradled her jaw in her hand. The light pressure seemed to keep everything held in place and kept the discomfort to a dull ache rather than sharp bursts of pain. She looked at the man who, remarkably, by a nod of his head, had agreed to let all of the children go. She didn't know what this meant for herself, but didn't really care, just as long as her students got out the door safely. She wondered if, before this was all over, she would get the chance to learn why the man had invaded her second home, her classroom, where she spent most of her waking moments. She had the feeling that the whole episode was bigger than she was, bigger than the students in her classroom, but in all the time she had spent with the man on this day, she hadn't been able to piece together his reasoning for his actions. He was certainly interested in that phone of his. He had been furiously texting and making calls, so someone outside of this room was most definitely involved, but whether it was an accomplice or a victim, Mrs. Oliver couldn't tell.

"It's time," the man said. Mrs. Oliver saw the weariness in his eyes, but not just from the exhaustion that came from the events of the day. His eyes had no life to them, no hope, and this more than anything prodded her into action.

Mrs. Oliver stood swiftly, causing a dizzying rush of pain to stream through her jaw and hip, and hobbled to the door. She clapped her hands sharply together and all heads snapped up. "Up," Mrs. Oliver managed, forcing her mouth open wide enough to let the brief word escape. The students stood without hesitation. She pointed to her own eyes and every pair of eyes in the room met her own. Mrs. Oliver scanned each of her students' faces, tried to memorize every freckle, every gap-toothed mouth, each tousled head. It was just too bad, she thought to herself, that the last image they would have of their teacher would be one of her in a wrinkled, stained, formerly Bedazzled denim jumper. She imagined that her hair was a fright and her face...well, she could tell without seeing herself that she must look monstrous. She snapped her fingers once and pointed to the classroom door and the students immediately walked swiftly but in an orderly manner past the man with the gun, their eyes never leaving their teacher's, to the door.

"Beth," Mrs. Oliver mumbled through her broken teeth, and Beth, still weeping softly, came to Mrs. Oliver's side, clutching her little sister's hand. "Take the children," Mrs. Oliver said, holding on gently to Beth's arm. Beth nodded in comprehension. "Go and don't look back." Mrs. Oliver looked at the gunman and then her eyes flicked toward the closet door where Lucy was locked away with the chair wedged beneath the doorknob.

The man shook his head. "No." Mrs. Oliver wanted to

argue with him, but could tell by the finality in his voice that negotiations weren't an option.

"Go, now." Mrs. Oliver pushed lightly on Beth's shoulder and in a straight, single-file line, just as she had taught them, her students were leaving.

Meg

Everything about Cal Oliver is long. He is tall with long limbs, long fingers, long nose, long narrow face made longer by his downturned lips. He stoops as he enters and looks uncertainly around the RV.

"Cal," Chief McKinney says, standing and holding out his hand for Cal to shake. Before he can introduce each of us, Cal is going on and on about a phone call.

"Wait a second, Cal," the chief interrupts, "please take a seat and start at the beginning."

Cal perches himself on the edge of a metal folding chair and takes a deep breath. "I was over at Lonnie's," he begins, "when my cell phone rang. Right away I see it's from Evie." At Swain's questioning look he adds, "My wife, she's the third-grade teacher at the school." When the man nods in understanding he continues. "Right away I can hear a boy yelling. It was hard to hear exactly what he said, everything sounded muffled." Mr. Oliver runs a hand across his bushy white eyebrows that frame his watery blue eyes. I wonder if they are wet from age, the biting cold or worry. "Then I hear Evie talking real loud saying something about how thankfully no one was hurt and about someone named Lucy in a closet."

"Your wife told you no one was hurt?" I ask.

"It wasn't like she was talking to me, but more like she was talking for my benefit. Anyway, she also said something about how he had no business in her classroom."

"She didn't know who he was?" Chief McKinney asks. Mr. Oliver shakes his head helplessly.

"She didn't say a name, but I just don't know." Mr. Oliver pulls a carefully folded handkerchief from his coat pocket and swipes at his nose. "Then I heard a scuffling noise and then Evie screamed." Mr. Oliver bows his head so low that his nose is nearly touching his knees, his shoulders shaking with quiet sobs. "She told me she loved me and then she was gone."

Augie

Something is happening inside the classroom. There is the scraping sound of chairs being pushed and feet running across the floor. I hold my breath and try to make myself as small as possible, but if the man comes out in the hallway I will be pretty hard to miss.

Suddenly the classroom door is open and Beth steps out. She is holding her little sister's hand and, without even glancing my way, she is moving down the hallway. I watch as the kids walk quickly and then they are moving faster and faster until they are running. I am trying to find P.J.'s feet through the blur of tennis shoes that are echoing like thunder down the hallway. My heart skips a beat when I realize that I don't see him. Still the children are streaming past me and there is no P.J. "Hey," I call out from my spot under the drinking fountain. No one even slows down. "Hey, where's my brother? Where's P.J.?"

Something happened once that classroom door opened and

the kids in P.J.'s room came out. Suddenly all the doors in the hallway open and heads are peeking out. Teachers look up and down the hallway, but once they see Mrs. Oliver's classroom rushing down the stairs it's like an invitation. Soon the hallways are crowded with students and I am trapped in my spot beneath the drinking fountain. I must have missed him, I think to myself. He must have run right past me. He is in that crowd of students heading out to the parking lot right now. I wait until there is a break in the traffic so I can pull myself up and not get trampled by a bunch of third and fourth graders. And once again I find myself all alone. The hallway is completely deserted. I spin around in disbelief. How could I have not seen him? His bright red Converse high-tops are impossible to miss. Without thinking I move toward Mrs. Oliver's classroom. The door is shut, but I press my nose against the window in the door to see inside. My stomach drops and then the door is opening and I am being pulled inside.

Meg

Chief McKinney gently hands Cal Oliver off to a victim's advocate, in this case Father Adam, who volunteered to assist. "Everyone is doing their best, Cal," Father Adam kindly explains when Cal balks at the thought of leaving. "Let's go on back to Lonnie's and wait. Chief McKinney will call you as soon as he has any information. Right, Chief?" Father Adam looks pointedly at Chief McKinney and he nods.

"As soon as we get any news about Evelyn, you'll be the first to know," he promises. "We are all working hard to end this whole thing with the best possible resolution."

Cal steps out of the RV and into the swirling snow with a lost and bewildered expression, leaning on to Father Adam for support.

"This has got to end," the chief says miserably. He looks hard at Swain. "Doesn't the implied threat that Cal heard over the phone give us cause enough to send the tac team into the building?"

"He's talking," Swain explains. "As long as we're participating in a dialog with the man and no one has gotten hurt, we keep negotiating with him."

"But it's me he wants. Let me go in there and talk with him," I say with more conviction than I feel.

Swain shakes his head. "Listen, we'll get you in phone contact with him, but there is no way you're going into that school building, especially if you're the target. We're not going to endanger innocent children, teachers and officers because you want to play hero."

"Then let me go in there alone. If you think this is Tim holed up in there, what are you worried about? I'm not. Tim has never hurt me, would never hurt me in a million years and certainly would not hurt Maria in this way." My face is burning from anger and from Swain's condescending attitude toward me.

"Let's make phone contact with him first," Chief McKinney says, trying once again to get us back on track. "You'll recognize Tim's voice, then we'll know for sure."

Something clicks into place within my brain. The phone. If it was truly Tim in that school and it was me he wanted, he would have simply called me. Why would he care whether or not I recognized his voice? It didn't make sense. No, this wasn't Tim. "You said the intruder called you asking for me, right?"

"Yes," Swain agrees. "He called using one of the students' cell phones."

I pull out my phone. "Why didn't he just call me, then?" I pause as I look at my phone. "It looks like I got several texts earlier from an unknown number. What was the student's cell number?"

Aaron flips through his notes and rattles off the number.

"Why didn't you look at the texts?" Swain asks, annoyed.

"I didn't know I even got them," I explain. I try to keep the defensiveness out of my voice but fail. "Besides, I've been a little busy, Swain," I say, not caring that I sound insubordinate. "The chief frowns on taking personal calls during a standoff."

"What's it say?" the chief asks. The three men gather tightly around me and peer down at my phone.

I read the first text out loud. "Barrett. Alone. 6:30 p.m."

"It's six-twenty," Swain says, glancing at his watch.

"I've just thought of someone else," I say suddenly. McKinney, Gritz and Swain look at me expectantly. "Matthew Merritt."

"Greta Merritt's husband?" Samora's incredulous, disembodied voice fills the air and I glance down at the speakerphone. I'd forgotten Samora was listening in.

"Yes," I say, shaken by the possibility. "I was the one who took the initial report. I was the one to convince the victim to press charges, I was the one who read Merritt his rights while Gritz cuffed him." What I didn't bring up was the news articles and interview that Stuart had done with the victim. No one knew that it was through me that Stuart found Jamie. If anyone had reservations that Merritt was a monster, all doubt was erased after reading the article Stuart had written. "Maybe Merritt is getting back at me this way. He definitely is a desperate man. He's lost his wife, his family, his freedom and a chance at the governor's mansion." The men look at one another dubiously, but are considering the possibility.

Before I even finished reading the news article I had Stuart on the phone. "How did you do it?" I asked. He knew exactly what I was talking about, didn't even try to play dumb.

"I heard you talking to her on the phone."

My mind whirred, trying to pinpoint the date and location of the phone call. When realization dawned on me all I could say was, "Oh." Stuart had spent the entire night at my house only once since we met. Maria was at a slumber party at a friend's house and wouldn't return home until the following day. It was late when Jamie called me. Stuart and I had been sleeping, curled up together as if we had slept that way for years. His arms wrapped tightly around me, his chin on my shoulder, his hands resting on my stomach. We fit together perfectly. Or so I thought. When my cell phone rang, I eased myself carefully out of bed so as not to wake Stuart. Since I had taken her to the rape crisis center, walked her through the steps to pressing charges against Matthew Merritt and promised her that everything would be okay, she had trusted me. During that phone call she tearfully told me that she kept having nightmares, that she knew Mr. Merritt was going to get back at her. He had told her he would hurt her, hurt her family, if she ever told anyone.

"Matthew Merritt will not hurt you again," I reassured her. "I won't allow it. You can do this, Jamie, and you have a lot of people who are here to help you get through this. I know it isn't easy.

"Do you want me to come over?" I asked after several minutes of listening to her quiet cries.

"Could you?" she said hopefully. "Please?"

I left a note for Stuart, just saying that I had to go out on police business and I would be back soon.

That was the night Stuart learned that Jamie Crosby was raped by Matthew Merritt. He had his story. The biggest one of his career.

"We'll check on the Merritt angle," Swain promises, "but I can't imagine him going to this extreme."

My cell phone chimes, startling all of us, and two more high-pitched pings follow. "There are three more texts," I say, and a wellspring of fear spreads through my veins. BANG, reads the second text. I press the button again with shaking hands. BANG. BANG.

Augie

When I peek through the window I find a man staring back at me. His blue eyes send a shiver down my back. My heart leaps and I try to turn to run away but my stocking feet cause me to slip and, before I know it, the door opens and I'm being yanked into the classroom.

"Who are you?" the man asks, still holding me by the arm and looking me up and down.

I see P.J. with his back pressed against the blackboard. His teacher, Mrs. Oliver, who looks like she was hit in the head with a baseball bat, is standing with her arms around two other kids, a girl with black, messy hair and a short boy with a bowl haircut and braces.

Everyone is looking at me with their mouths hanging open and I realize I must look like a crazy person. I don't have any shoes on, I'm wearing a sweatshirt that is ten times too big for me and I'm peeking into a classroom where there is a man with a gun. "Who are you?" the man asks again.

"Au–Augie," I stutter. "That's my brother." I point to P.J.

"Do you think I'm your dad, too?" the man asks, and my mind tries to make sense of his words. I look at P.J., who is staring down at his red Converse tennis shoes.

P.J. He probably did think this nut job was his real dad. He is always looking at men on the street, staring at their faces. For a long time he would ask our mom question after question. *What color was my dad's hair? What color were his eyes? Was he tall or short?* The only information he could get out of her was that when they met he was a marine and was heading to Afghanistan.

P.J. finally gave up asking when our mother lost her temper, started crying and told P.J. she would tell him his father's name when he turned eighteen and in the meantime he should realize just how good he had it even if it was only the three of us. "You could be stuck on a farm in Iowa having to do chores for three hours a day, shoveling cow shit!" she hollered before locking herself in the bathroom. I wonder what she'll do on P.J.'s eighteenth birthday when he holds out his hand for the little slip of paper with his dad's full name, address and phone number written on it. P.J. has a mind like an elephant. He never forgets anything. Though my mom has never said these words, I don't think she has any idea who P.J.'s father is.

The man looks at me suspiciously but realizes very quickly that I'm too young and puny to be an undercover police officer or something. "Can we go now?" I ask, and P.J. starts moving toward me.

"No, not yet." The man shakes his head.

"But you said," P.J.'s teacher begins. Her face is black and blue and swollen and her words come out sounding like *Buh you seh.*

The man holds up his hand like he wants her to be quiet.

"Patience," he says. "I need you for just a little bit longer, and if they do as I say, you'll be free to go."

I wanted to ask who has to do what he says and what happens if they don't do it. The little girl starts to cry, her shoulders shaking while the boy with braces is biting his lip, trying not to cry, and looking up at his teacher, waiting for her to tell him what to do next.

"Take a seat," the man says, and I watch P.J. carefully. He just looks mad. I've seen this look before. It's the same look he gets whenever I push him too far or tease him too much. P.J. doesn't get mad often, but when he does, watch out. I shake my head hard at him and give him my *don't you dare* look. We all move to the front row of desks and sit down. "She should be arriving any time now," the man says, and sits down on the teacher's stool and closes his eyes.

I might be able to take him, I think to myself. I'm fast when I want to be and all I have to do is leap out of my desk and land on top of him, knocking the gun out of his hand. I sneak a look at Mrs. Oliver and she is giving me the same *don't you dare* look I gave P.J.

"Who should be arriving?" Mrs. Oliver asks. The bruised side of her face is swelling up even more and looks deformed like something out of *Phantom of the Opera*. It sounds like she is talking through a big wad of bubble gum.

"The person all this is for," the man says, and spreads his arms out wide.

"What if she doesn't come?" Mrs. Oliver asks. "The police won't let anyone in, we're in lockdown."

"She *is* the police," the man says with a mean smile.

Meg

I look at the text messages and each *bang* on the screen drops with a thud into my stomach. "I'm going to call him," I declare. "I'll be able to recognize Tim's or Travis's voice, then we'll know for sure."

The three men look at one another. "Do it," Samora says, and I press the send button. The phone rings four times before there is silence. *Call ended* blinks back at me. A few seconds later my phone beeps signaling a new text message.

I'm waiting, it reads.

Let the kids go and i come in, I type.

You have 5 min.

Who r u?

4 min.

"He's still got kids in there," I say, looking at Aaron, Swain and the chief. "I've got to go."

"No way," Chief McKinney says. His normally well-groomed mustache has drooped over his mouth, covering his lips.

"I'm going in," I say sharply, standing. "I need a vest," I say, pointing to a bulletproof vest sitting in a corner of the RV.

"Now wait a minute," Swain says, standing also. He is as wide as he is tall and his bulk looms over me. He has a very calm, soothing voice that must come in handy as a hostage negotiator. "The minute he shoots someone in there, it's all over for him. We'll be inside in seconds. He must realize that."

"I don't think we can take that chance," I say, lifting the vest and threading my arms through, the solid heft a comfort. "If it's Tim—and that's a big if—I can talk him down. I'll be able to get everyone out safely."

"There is absolutely no way I can authorize this," Swain says.

"What choice do we have?" I ask, looking him in the eye. "What if I don't go in there and someone gets killed? That isn't an option."

"Meg," the chief says warningly. "Don't even think about it."

We all look out the window at the same time, as a low rumbling sound slowly gathers volume like a stampede of spooked cattle. We move to the windows of the RV, framed by the mustard-yellow curtains, and watch with a mix of relief and apprehension. A sea of children spill into the parking lot.

"Jesus," Chief McKinney says as we all rush toward the RV's door.

This is my chance. While everyone is scrambling toward the mass of kids fleeing the building, I move toward it. I hear Aaron holler after me, but I ignore him. This is going to end, and end now.

Mrs. Oliver

Mrs. Oliver struggled to keep her eyes open. It wasn't that she was tired, though that was true. She felt like she could lie down and sleep for a week straight and decided that was exactly what she was going to do once she got home. Her head ached so badly that the only relief she felt was when her eyes were shut, but she didn't dare let the man out of her sight. He was nearly trembling with anticipation now, though Mrs. Oliver couldn't determine if it was an eagerness filled with fear or excitement. Maybe both. According to the man, a police officer was on her way up to the classroom right this minute, but the confusing thing was that the man had *requested* her presence. It made absolutely no sense. The only female police officer she knew was Meg Barrett, Maria's mother.

Mrs. Oliver tried to focus the eye that wasn't nearly swollen shut on each of the children. They all appeared to be on the edge of losing it and her heart welled with affection. For

Charlotte, who was now crying piteously into her hands, her one mistake was bending down to retrieve a scattering of jeweled beads that had been yanked from Mrs. Oliver's jumper as she exited the classroom. And poor Ethan, because he was so small for his age, his short strides and the fact that his desk was located in the corner of the classroom farthest from the doorway, he, too, was still there. P.J., on the other hand, could have been one of the very first children out of the classroom, but for some reason he hung back and waited for Mrs. Oliver. Now both P.J. and his sister, Augie, were trapped in the classroom with the madman. She wondered what Will Thwaite was thinking right now. Most likely all of the other children who had raced out of the classroom were reunited with their families. She pictured Will standing outside in the sharp wind waiting for his grandchildren to emerge. She thought of Holly Thwaite, remembered her as a vivacious child, full of mischief, her body always vibrating in anticipation of the possibilities the world had to offer. Mrs. Oliver always knew that Holly would leave Broken Branch and she wondered if Holly, recovering in Arizona, had any knowledge of what was happening today to her own children in the town where she was born, in the classroom where she dreamed of a different life.

Holly's daughter is eyeing the door, and Mrs. Oliver knew what she was thinking. She tried to tell Augie to hold still, but her mouth hurt too much and all that came out was a weak gurgling sound. Augie, a look of determination on her face, rushed the man and tried to swat the gun from his hand, but he raised his gun above his head and deftly stepped aside. As she stumbled, he grabbed Augie by the scruff of her neck and began to drag her across the room.

"Hey!" Augie protested as P.J. tried to pull his sister from the man's grip. Impatiently the man pushed P.J. to the ground and pulled Augie toward the closet.

Mrs. Oliver limped toward the man, figuring that this was it, he would surely kill her now, but she couldn't stand by and watch him manhandle these children. "Stay there," he ordered, and something new in his voice caused Mrs. Oliver to freeze and watch helplessly, while for the second time that day he shoved a child into the closet and then locked the door.

Meg

Ignoring Aaron and not daring to glance back, I dash across the snowy parking lot. The sky is bruised-looking and is getting darker. It has stopped snowing and the wind has died down as if it is holding its breath to see what will happen next. My heart is pounding as I make my way toward the school, stepping in the well-trod paths that the fleeing students created as they ran from the building and toward the gym entrance where I encountered Augie Baker earlier. Using my flashlight I smash the glass in the door in order to let myself in.

I think of Maria and what I would have done differently if she would have been in school today. Chief McKinney probably would have sent me home with the explanation that I was a victim, that I couldn't be professional, objective, knowing that my daughter was being held by a gunman. I wonder if I would have followed his orders or would have refused. I say a silent prayer of thanks that Maria is miles away from here, safe and sound with Tim's parents. I feel a wave of doubt wash over me and consider for a moment the possibility that Tim is upstairs in Maria's classroom with a gun, holding children and a teacher hostage, demanding my presence for some unknown sin I've committed. Was it because I refused his invitation to spend spring break with Maria and him? I can't believe that's true. While Tim and I have had our moments, haven't always liked each other, we've always loved each other in our way. I brush away the thought and mentally prepare for one of four scenarios. One, the man upstairs is someone I arrested in the past, someone with a grudge. Maybe I sent him to jail for drugs or domestic abuse, or driving while under the influence. Two, it's my ex-con brother. Three, it's Matthew Merritt, the rapist. The fourth and most unlikely scenario is it's my ex-husband, the man I married, the man who is a wonderful father to my daughter, and in some deep spot in my heart someone with whom I believe I still might actually end up growing old.

I know that my four minutes to get up to the classroom have already come and gone so I try to move more quickly, my eyes and flashlight darting from left to right, each shadowy corner concealing something sinister. I approach the set of stairs that lead up to the classroom, a walk I've made several times with Maria, open-house night, parent-teacher conferences, the winter program. I can't help thinking that I may step into that room and end up coming out on a stretcher.

An anxiety-filled whisper greets me as I begin my ascent. "Is it safe?"

I spin around, gun in hand, and instinctively raise it, then aim the beam of my flashlight at the source of the sound. It's a young woman, her head poking out from a classroom door. "Police," I order. "Don't move." She freezes, but relief floods her face. "Go back into the classroom," I say, "and lock the door. Keep the lights off. This will all be over soon."

"My name is Jessica Bliss, a first-grade teacher," she says in a rush. "Please tell my husband I love him."

"You'll be able to tell him yourself," I say gently, wondering if I will ever be able to say those words to anyone ever again.

Augie

It is pitch-black in the closet so I use the backlight from one of the cell phones I grabbed off the floor after they fell out of the man's pocket to see. My hands are shaking as I try to remember my mother's number. All I want to do is hear her voice. I want to tell her how sorry I am about the fire, how everything was my fault.

I manage to dial my mother's cell phone number and the ring vibrates in my ear as I wait for her to answer her phone. "Hello?" Finally, I hear her voice, tired and small.

"Mom," I say, gasping for air as if my lungs are still filled with the smoke.

Holly

I'm in that lovely space between consciousness and sleep. I feel no pain thanks to the morphine pump and I can almost believe that the muscles, tendons and skin of my left arm have knitted themselves back together, leaving my skin smooth and pale. My curly brown hair once again falls softly down my back, my favorite earrings dangle from my ears and I can lift both sides of my mouth in a wide smile without much pain at the thought of my children. Yes, drugs are a wonderful thing. But the problem is that while the carefully prescribed and doled-out narcotics by the nurses wonderfully dull the edges of this nightmare, I know that soon enough this woozy, pleasant feeling will fall away and all that I will be left with is pain and the knowledge that Augie and P.J. are thousands of miles away from me. Sent away to the place where I grew up, the town I swore I would never return to, the house I swore I would never again step into, to the man I never wanted them to meet.

The tinny melody of the ringtone that Augie, my thirteen-year-old daughter, programmed into my cell phone is pulling me from my sleep. I open one eye, the one that isn't covered with a thick ointment and crusted shut, and call out for my mother, who must have stepped out of the room. I reach for the phone that is sitting on the tray table at the side of my bed and the nerve endings in my bandaged left arm scream in protest at the movement. I carefully shift my body to pick up the phone with my good hand and press the phone to my remaining ear.

"Hello." The word comes out half-formed, breathless and scratchy, as if my lungs were still filled with smoke.

"Mom?" Augie's voice is quavery, unsure. Not sounding like my daughter at all. Augie is confident, smart, a *take-charge, no one is ever going to walk all over me* kind of girl.

"Augie? What's the matter?" I try to blink the fuzziness of the morphine away; my tongue is dry and sticks to the roof of my mouth. I want to take a sip of water from the glass sitting on my tray, but my one working hand holds the phone. The other lies useless at my side. "Are you okay? Where are you?"

There are a few seconds of quiet and then Augie continues. "I love you, Mom," she says in a whisper that ends in quiet sobs.

I sit up straight in my bed, wide awake now. Pain shoots through my bandaged arm and up the side of my neck and face. "Augie, what's the matter?"

"I'm at the school." She is crying in that way she has when she is doing her damnedest not to. I can picture her, head down, her long brown hair falling around her face, her eyes squeezed shut in determination to keep the tears from falling, her breath filling my ear with short, shallow puffs. "He has a gun. He has P.J. and he has a gun."

"Who has P.J.?" Terror clutches at my chest. "Tell me, Augie, where are you? Who has a gun?"

"I'm in a closet. He put me in a closet."

My mind is spinning. Who could be doing this? Who would do this to my children? "Hang up," I tell her. "Hang up and call 9-1-1 right now, Augie. Then call me back. Can you do that?" I hear her sniffles. "Augie," I say again, more sharply. "Can you do that?"

"Yeah," she finally says. "I love you, Mom," she says softly.

"I love you, too." My eyes fill with tears and I can feel the moisture pool beneath the bandages that cover my injured eye.

I wait for Augie to disconnect when I hear three quick shots, followed by two more and Augie's piercing screams.

I feel the bandages that cover the left side of my face peel away, my own screams loosening the adhesive holding them in place; I feel the fragile, newly grafted skin begin to unravel. I am scarcely aware of the nurses and my mother rushing to my side, prying the phone from my grasp.

Will

After the highway patrol, the wrecker and the EMTs left, Will was free to go. He couldn't stand the thought of returning to his own home, not until his grandchildren were safely by his side, so he drove his pickup back to Lonnie's. The snow had stopped and the roads were much better, but when he arrived Verna was nowhere to be found and the officer stationed at the café told him that he didn't know if she had been notified about her son-in-law's suicide. Though it will probably be little consolation to her, Will imagined that Verna and her family would prefer this outcome to Ray being the perpetrator in the school. Now he found himself once again sitting at a scarred, sticky table, drinking coffee, trying to pass the time. Shaken from the day's events, he stared at the newspaper opened in front of him but he wasn't able to concentrate.

There was the rumble of tires and all eyes snapped to the window. Another school bus was pulling up in front of the café. "There are more kids!" someone shouted, and there was the familiar rush to the door to greet the children. He was pushing back his chair to join the group when his phone vibrated. It was Marlys. He knew he should answer it, but he wanted to see if Augie and P.J. were on this bus. He wanted more than anything to give Marlys the joyous news of her grandchildren's safe return. His phone stilled and he joined the crowd at the window. His heart leaped when he saw Beth and Natalie Cragg step out of the bus and he searched each face for P.J. and Augie, but they were not among the children. In frustration, he elbowed his way toward Beth and Natalie in hopes of getting some information. He also didn't want them to hear about the death of their father from anyone but Darlene or Verna.

"Beth, Natalie," he called out to them, and their eyes brightened upon seeing a familiar face.

"Mr. Thwaite," Beth cried, running toward him clutching her little sister's hand. "Have you seen my mom or dad?"

Will shook his head, not wanting to lie, but not wanting to reveal too much. "Your grandma was here earlier. You stay here with me and we'll wait until she comes back. She knows this is where the kids are being dropped off." Will guided them back to his table. "Have you seen P.J. and Augie?" Will asked, not able to hold the question in any longer.

Beth and Natalie both nodded. "He still has them. In the classroom." Beth can't look at Will and began to cry. Natalie wrapped her arms around her sister and buried her face into her stomach.

The room tilted precariously and Will grabbed a chair to steady himself. "Are they okay?" he asked, feeling the blood rush from his face.

"I don't know." Beth shook her head and wiped her eyes with her sleeve. "He let everyone go but a few kids. He said something about waiting for someone to come to him, then he would let them go."

"He hit Mrs. Oliver," Natalie said tremulously. "He made Lucy go into a closet."

Will looked around in hopes of catching Officer Braun's attention. Another child was animatedly talking to him and Will realized it could take a while before he got to interviewing the Cragg children. "Sit down and we'll get you something to eat." Will raised a finger and a waitress came over. "Order whatever you want, and I'll try and call your grandma." Will stepped away from the table and found a somewhat quiet corner of the café where he could make his call while still keep an eye on the kids. Verna's cell phone went right to voice mail and Will left a brief message. "Verna, it's Will Thwaite. Beth and Natalie are at Lonnie's. They are safe. They don't know anything about what has happened at their father's home. Call me back."

Will weaved unsteadily in and out between those families who had been reunited and those who still anxiously awaited news of their children, and sat down next to the Cragg girls. The waitress had brought the girls cups of hot chocolate and Natalie was blowing away the curling steam that rose above the mug. Beth slouched in her chair, staring sightlessly out the window. "You doing okay?" Will asked as he sat down. The girls nodded silently. "Did you know the man who came into the classroom? Have you seen him before? Can you describe him?" he said, leaning in so close to Natalie that he could count the freckles on her nose. Natalie cringed and Beth narrowed her eyes, placing a protective arm around her sister. Will pulled back, seeing how his barrage of questions had overwhelmed them. "I'm sorry," he said apologetically. "I'm just so worried about Augie and P.J."

They sat in silence for a while. Natalie took tiny sips of

her hot chocolate; Beth nibbled at the French fries Lonnie brought over to the table. "He was tall," Beth finally said. "With brownish hair. I've never seen him before." She swallowed hard and glanced at her sister. "I was just so happy it wasn't my dad that I didn't take a good look at him." Will busied himself with stirring a packet of sugar into his already cold coffee. He couldn't bear to look at them. In a matter of hours, maybe minutes, they would learn that their father didn't have the strength or the foresight or whatever one might call it to stay in this world for them.

"He had on brown pants," Natalie remembered, "and nice shoes."

"Well, when Officer Braun has a minute, you can tell him all of this. I know it will be very helpful." Will wanted to leave. He wanted to drive over to the school, crash through the barriers that had been set up to keep traffic away and pound on the RV where Chief McKinney was sitting and waiting. Waiting for what? he wondered. For someone to get shot? He couldn't leave the Cragg girls, though, not until Verna or Darlene got here. He looked around for Lonnie in hopes that he could replace his tepid coffee for a fresh cup, when he saw Natalie staring down at the newspaper that had been tossed carelessly aside when the bus arrived.

"What is it?" Will asked. "What's the matter?"

"That's him," Natalie said in excitement. "That's the man." Will followed the path of her small, slender finger tipped with bright blue nail polish to the newspaper and the black-and-white photo of a smartly dressed man with intense eyes and a hint of a smile.

"Are you sure?" he whispered.

"Uh-huh." She nodded solemnly. "I'm sure.

Mrs. Oliver

Mrs. Oliver, as much as she has tried to, couldn't see this unfortunate situation ending well. The man with the gun had a manic gleam in his eye and had been muttering to himself, every once in a while saying, "It's almost over now."

Her jaw was throbbing and two children were locked in the supply closet, and the three remaining children were terrified, so much so that Charlotte had vomited in the trash can. Mrs. Oliver had always been a woman of action. She had given birth to her first child while in teacher's college, had three more children within a matter of six years, could change a flat tire, had once chased down a group of teenagers on skateboards that had knocked over old Mr. Figg outside the grocery store. She most certainly should have been able to handle this deranged interloper, but somehow couldn't. *Don't do it,* she could hear Cal whispering in her ear. *He has a gun, Evelyn. For once go with the flow.*

Mrs. Oliver, most definitely, was not a flow-goer. By her calculations, she had one last chance to make things okay. She inched slowly toward her desk, the man being preoccupied with his cell phone once again, nervously tapping his foot and rubbing at his forehead. *Evelyn,* she heard Cal's exasperated voice as her fingers reached for the stapler. It wasn't the cheap plastic kind that cost $8.95 in the school supply catalog the teachers ordered from each year. This stapler was a heavy-duty MegaSnap industrial all-metal stapler circa 1972 that Mrs. Oliver had specially ordered. Her hand wrapped around the cool metal throat of the stapler, dithered for just a second before she heaved it at the man. She watched with self-satisfaction at the surprising strength of her sixty-five-year-old arm as it sailed through the air. If he had looked up a fraction of a second later, the man would have most certainly been felled by the stapler. Mrs. Oliver could almost hear her students twenty years later: *Yes, a stapler. She overtook the man with a stapler, can you imagine?* Well, they wouldn't have to. The man did look up, his eyes narrowing at the sight of the stapler winging toward him and with no hesitation raised his gun and pulled the trigger three times, striking the wall closest to the closet door. Mrs. Oliver moaned at the sight of the damaged wall, terrified at the thought of how close the bullets came to hitting Lucy and Augie. The man glowered at Mrs. Oliver and with one swift punch struck her in the chest, knocking her to the ground.

"Don't make me kill you," the man growled, pointing the gun at her head.

Meg

I hear the unmistakable sound of gunfire from above me. "Shit," I mutter, and scramble up the steps. I thumb the mic at my collar. "We've got shots fired. Repeat, shots fired."

There is a crackle of static and Chief McKinney's voice is in my ear. "We'll be right there as soon as we can. Stay put, backup is on the way. And, Meg," the chief says in a rush, "it's not Tim in there."

I hesitate, my head is reeling. While I knew deep down that Tim couldn't be the man, I can't wrap my head around who could be summoning me to the classroom and needing a room full of hostages to get me there. I want to ask how he knows this, where Tim has been all this time, but there's no time. "Ten-four," I respond, knowing that I should stop and wait for reinforcements, but I continue upward. It must be my brother. Son of a bitch. All I can think of are those poor children and their teacher in that classroom. Despite the bitter cold outside, sweat trickles down my back and I wipe a bead of perspiration from my forehead. My breath comes in uneven hitches, and I focus on inhaling and exhaling in smooth, even streams. I move in long strides, peering in classroom windows as I pass.

This wing of the school seems deserted and I know Mrs. Oliver's class is the last room on the left. I hear a child's inconsolable crying as I move closer. It's the sound of great fear, terror, but not of pain. This particular child, at least, isn't hurt physically. I pause twenty yards from the classroom, press my back against the wall and look back in the direction I came from, sorely missing the comfort of backup. I should wait for the tac team, but press forward.

"I'm here!" I call out. My voice sounds too high, too unsure. "Is everything all right? I thought I heard gunfire." There's no response. "Is anyone hurt?"

"No," bellows a male voice. I don't recognize the speaker. I want to try and keep him talking, see if I can figure out who he is before I step into that room.

"I'm here, just like you asked. How many are in there with you?" No answer.

"Listen," I say, trying to keep the impatience out of my voice. "I want to talk to you, but I need to know you aren't going to shoot me the second I come in."

Again silence. Then a child's voice. "There are three kids and a teacher in the room. And the man. No one is shot. It was an accident."

I radio Chief McKinney. "False alarm, stand by." And then to the man in the classroom, I say, "Okay, I'm going to walk in the room now. I'm alone and unarmed," I lie as I slide my firearm into the shoulder holster hidden beneath my jacket and glance over my shoulder at the dark, empty hallway. Thinking of Maria and wishing I had the opportunity to talk to her one more time today, I take a deep breath, square my shoulders and step confidently into the doorway.

Will

Will was still examining the picture of the man in the newspaper, the man Natalie insisted was the gunman, when once again his phone buzzed.

"Yeah," he said absentmindedly, trying to recall where he had seen the man before. The name beneath the photo didn't ring a bell.

"Will." Marlys's frantic voice assaulted his ears.

"Marlys? What is it? Is Holly okay?" Will asked.

"What's going on there? Holly talked to Augie, said there were gunshots." Will had to concentrate to understand his wife. He couldn't make sense of her words. Holly, Augie, gunshots? "She's hysterical," Marlys said, not too far from hysteria herself. "The doctors had to sedate her. Will, what's happening?"

Will didn't know what to say. He looked up and saw Officer Braun also talking on the phone. Their eyes met; Braun looked at Will with a mixture of pity and resignation and began walking toward him. In that instance Will knew that what Marlys was telling him was the truth. "I'll find out what's happening and call you back," Will told his wife weakly, and then disconnected.

"Stay here, girls," he told Beth and Natalie. "Your grandma will be here soon." He moved across the sticky floor and met Officer Braun in the center of the restaurant, unclenched his fingers from the newspaper and tried to smooth away the creases as he showed it to the officer.

"This is the man," Will said hoarsely, pointing to the crumpled photograph.

"Who is he?" Braun asked, furrowing his brow.

"I have no idea," Will answered. "But I'm going to find out."

Holly

I try to pull myself from the fog of morphine that a nurse has injected into my IV. "Shhh, now," I hear her say. "Calm down, Holly, if you're not careful you'll tear your skin grafts. You don't want to go through all that again, do you? You've come so far."

I slap weakly at her hands, trying to push her away from me, trying to get out of the bed, to get to my children. I should never have let them go so far away from me. I want to grab Augie and shake her and tell her that accidents happen, that I didn't blame her for the fire, for my injuries, that I'm only grateful that she and P.J. were not hurt. My head feels light and my mother's face comes into my field of vision. "Mama," I say, something I haven't called her since I was five.

"I know," she says, chin trembling. "I know."

Augie

After we hear the shots, the little girl in the closet with me pounds on the door with her fists and then slams herself up against it, trying to get it open. "Shhh," I tell her. "It's going to be okay." But I know it won't be. She is crying so hard she's having trouble breathing.

"Shhh, I'm supposed to call 9-1-1," I tell her. "My mom said to call 9-1-1." I'm shaking so hard that my teeth knock together. I dial the three numbers and a man answers but I can barely hear him because of the little girls' cries. Finally I just blurt out, "I'm in the school, in Mrs. Oliver's room, and he's shooting. I'm in the closet with another girl. Please send help, please." Then I hang up hoping that he at least got a little information that is useful.

Finally, the little girl's cries become quieter and she curls up in the corner. I shine the light from the phone next to my face so she can see me. "I'm Augie." I sit down next to her and shine the phone light so I can see her better. Her face is blotched white and red and she is making soft hiccuping noises and sucking her thumb.

She pulls her thumb out and says, "I'm Lucy," before she stuffs it back in her mouth.

I can hear someone crying on the other side of the door but it's not P.J.'s crying. "P.J.," I yell through the door. "P.J., are you okay?"

"I'm okay, just a misfire," I hear him holler back, and I slump to the floor in relief. *Just a misfire,* I think to myself, *only P.J.*

"The police are coming," I tell Lucy, hoping that it is true.

Lucy starts sniffling. "What if he starts shooting again?" she wonders out loud.

"Just hang on, we'll be out of here in a few minutes," I promise her. I look down at the cell phone and see that the battery is running low. I quickly enter my mother's number but after four rings it goes to voice mail. "Mom," I say. "It's Augie. P.J. is okay. I'll call you back in a little bit." I stop, wanting to tell her more but not sure what to tell her. "I'm sorry," I finally whisper. "I'm so sorry."

From the classroom comes another voice. A woman. "It's you?" she says loudly, like she doesn't quite believe it. "Why?"

Will

The snow has started falling again, but more softly, as if all the bluster has gone out of the storm, like a child in its last throes of a fit, Will thought. When Holly was little she had the worst temper tantrums. Will often found himself laughing, despite his frustration, at the way Holly would open her mouth as wide as she could and wail, just like a newly born calf bellowing for its mother. His laughter would only fuel Holly's rage and she would hold her breath until her back arched and her face turned a frightful shade of blue. Marlys would swoop her into her arms, begging her to breathe. "Ignore her," Will would chastise. "The more attention you give her, the more she'll do this." Will wondered now if that is truth. Maybe if he had carefully lifted Holly onto his lap and held her close to his chest, softly singing a half-learned lullaby from his own childhood while gently rocking her to and fro, things would have turned out differently between the two of them.

"Jesus," Will lamented to the sterling-silver-and-garnet Seven Sorrows rosary draped over the rearview mirror, its beads lightly clicking against one another. The same rosary that his mother had pressed into his hand just before he left for basic training. He remembered singing to the newborn calves in distress, their mothers suffering from uterine torsion or prolapse. Couldn't he have afforded his own daughter the same courtesy? He drove recklessly through the snow-driven streets, dark and deserted, back to the school. He didn't care if he had to drive through the blockades or break into the school; he was going to bring his grandchildren home. Bring them home to his daughter.

Mrs. Oliver

Mrs. Oliver feigned death, sprawled out on the floor after the man had shoved her and pointed the gun at her head. She tried to still her breathing, tried to let her muscles go slack. *Evelyn,* she heard Cal chide her. *What were you thinking?*

I don't know, she mentally answered her husband. *For once, I really don't know.* She remembered sitting in front of the television with Cal, watching news coverage of a natural disaster somewhere far away, but still she sat there with tears rolling down her cheeks. *Evie, don't cry,* Cal had told her. *We're always one breath away from something, living or dying, sometimes it just can't be helped.* She wondered what her children would say at her funeral. Would they be bitter of all the hours she spent with other people's children, resentful of the restless nights she spent worrying over some other eight-year-old's neglectful father, abusive mother, reading disability, social ineptness? Would they linger over the class photographs hung with care on the walls of their childhood home, counting and comparing the number of pictures where their mother was posing with strange children versus the ones with her own flesh and blood?

A woman's voice punctured Charlotte's crying and the poor girl is instantly quiet. "It's you?" the woman asked incredulously. Mrs. Oliver dared to unscrew one eye to see what was happening. The man had turned away from her, the gun still held tightly in his hand, but now he was pointing it at P. J. Thwaite's temple, his elbow crooked around the boy's neck. Mrs. Oliver painfully raised her head, trying to get a better look at the new arrival. Officer Barrett, Mrs. Oliver realized, Maria's mother. Was this the person that the man had been waiting for? It didn't make sense, though, nothing about this terrible day had.

Charlotte and Ethan looked expectantly at their teacher, waiting for her to do something. Mrs. Oliver wanted to shrug her shoulders as if to say *I've got nothing,* but her body hurt too much. But their eyes did not veer from hers, their gazes did not waver. They were waiting for her, waiting for their teacher to do something, anything.

Meg

"Stuart?" I say in disbelief, staring at the man. "What are you doing? Put that gun down. Are you crazy?"

"Crazy?" The man gives a mirthless laugh. "I guess you could say that? Partially in thanks to you, Meg."

"What do you mean? I don't understand." The sight of Stuart standing in this classroom, holding a gun to a little boy's head, takes my breath away.

"You haven't heard? Haven't got a chance to read the newspaper today yet, huh?" Stuart asks lightly as if we were having this conversation over appetizers and beers.

"No, I haven't heard. Why don't you fill me in? I'm more than a little confused." Without taking my eyes off of Stuart, I try to assess the situation. Mrs. Oliver, injured on the floor. One male, one female child standing off to my left, apparently uninjured, one male child being held hostage.

"In a matter of a few months I've lost my wife, my children and my job and I owe it all to you, Meg." Stuart grasps the boy's neck a little tighter, the barrel of the gun grinding into his temple.

"Stuart," I say as calmly as I can, "let the kids go and you can tell me all about it. Please, they don't have anything to do with this."

"I had you going there for a bit, didn't I?" Stuart flashed an angry smile. "Made you think that your ex-husband was the man in here, didn't I?"

"No," I answer. "Never for a minute did I think Tim would do this. Why did you tell me that he was a suspect?"

"He was. For about five minutes. My source—" He sees the doubt on my face. "Yes, I do have a source from the sheriff's office and he told me your mother-in-law called and said he disappeared suddenly. My source was the one who suggested Tim could be the gunman. I thought it was kind of funny."

"Tim would never do this," I say again, and then add, "And I never thought you could do something like this, either."

"My wife threw me out. Because she found out about our affair," Stuart continues as if I hadn't spoken. I want to amend his statement. I want to say, *You had an affair, Stuart. Not me. I didn't know you were married and had three kids, remember?* But I don't say anything. My job is to keep him calm and keep him talking until the tac team can get into position or until I can get to my gun and fire a shot.

"I didn't tell your wife about us, I promise you that, Stuart. I didn't say a word."

Stuart makes a snorting sound and gives a half chuckle. "No one else knew, Meg. It had to be you. Twenty-two years of marriage and she threw me out."

Duh, I want to say, but instead I hold up my hands in surrender. "I'm so sorry, Stuart, but I never initiated any contact with your wife. She came to me."

"My kids won't talk to me, I'm living in a shitty hotel. My

wife had a lawyer who was more than willing to cut off my balls in order to get her the settlement she wanted."

Something about the way Stuart was talking about his wife in the past tense sends a shiver of dread through me. "Stuart," I ask, afraid of the answer. "What did you do? What do you mean your wife had a lawyer? Did she drop the divorce?" Stuart just smiles condescendingly at me and raises his hands in a *could be* gesture.

"Then, when I went into the newspaper yesterday, the editor in chief was waiting for me. Apparently someone has been doing some investigations of their own."

"Stuart, I have no—"

"Shut the fuck up, Meg," he shouts, causing the boy in his grasp to whimper. "Someone has been making calls and asking questions about my work. They've decided that I embellished the truth in my article on the girl who was raped and now they think I made up the whole story about the time in Afghanistan."

All the while Stuart and I have been talking, the hostage, a boy I recognize from Maria's school winter concert, has kept his eyes on my face. His glasses have been knocked askew and his shaggy hair is standing on end but his gaze has been unwavering. "Stuart, why don't you let P.J. go," I say, taking a stab that this little boy is Will Thwaite's grandson. "You know his mom is real sick, don't you? Was burned badly in a fire. Come on, he's been through enough. Let the kids go. I'm here, isn't that what you wanted? You think I'm the one who made those calls and got you fired." As I'm trying to reason with Stuart, I see P.J.'s eyes slide to the floor where his teacher is crumpled. She is slowly, inch by inch, trying to pull herself toward Stuart. Jesus, I think to myself, I hope she doesn't do anything stupid.

Mrs. Oliver

Mrs. Oliver's entire body felt battered. Her breath sent a spasm through her jaw and her injured hip pulsed with pain. But what hurt more was the realization that she failed to protect her students.

This horrid man, now holding a gun to P.J.'s head, obviously had no intention of leaving this room alive and didn't appear to care who he ended up taking with him. She wished she had one more opportunity to talk with her children and with Cal. She wanted them to know how happy her life had been, how loved she felt. She wanted her children to know that even though she had a room at home filled with artifacts from her life as a teacher—photos, homemade ornaments, carefully worded letters and meticulously drawn pictures by her students over her forty-year teaching career—what she prized most was her children's love.

Deliberately, painfully, she slid her hand across the floor until one fingertip grazed the cool metal of the Mega-Snap stapler.

Augie

I feel around the closet for a light switch but all my hands find are stacks of construction paper and baskets that are filled with markers and crayons. A shiver travels down my back and I reach behind my neck to knock away what I'm sure is a spider when my fingers graze a string hanging from the ceiling. I pull the string and a lightbulb pops on. Lucy covers her eyes with her hands at the brightness. I look around the closet trying to find something that will help us get out of here but there is nothing.

The voices in the classroom are getting louder and louder. "This is all your fucking fault!" the man shouts. "My job, my wife, my kids, all gone!"

I can't understand what the woman is saying, but it must have made the man furious because he yells, "One by one, Meg, and it will be all your fault!"

"What does he mean?" the girl asks me. "What's he going to do?"

"I don't know," I admit. But what I do know and don't say out loud is if the man opens this closet door, there is nowhere for us to run. I look above me and see a large vent. I look back at Lucy. "I think I have an idea," I say.

Will

When Will pulled into the school parking lot, everything was so still and quiet he thought for a moment that everyone had gone home, that the standoff was over. As he drew closer, he could see that the police were still very much present, as were the ambulances, their vehicles glazed over with snow. Will pulled up next to the RV and, still holding the newspaper, got out of his truck and pounded on the RV's door. No answer. Will looked back at the school. The parking lot was eerily quiet and void of movement. Only the telltale wisps of exhaust from the ambulance tailpipes gave any indication that someone was inside.

Something had to be happening inside the school. Will reached back into his truck, retrieved his shotgun and jogged to the front entrance of the school. Locked. He made his way around the perimeter of the school, trying doors, all locked, until he came to a first-floor window whose screen had been kicked out. He carefully set the gun on the windowsill and with shaky arms tried to hoist himself up onto the low sill and pull himself inside. His boot slipped on the slick brick and he couldn't find his footing. He was just about to try again when he heard the chilling click of a gun being cocked.

Meg

"Stuart," I say in a low voice, trying to placate him. "I can see you're upset. But please, please, don't take it out on these kids and their teacher. Let them go."

"You know they are going to take the Pritchard–Say away from me? I'll have to pay back the hundred thousand dollars." He shakes his head. "I don't have the money anymore. I spent it on a goddamn house for my wife."

"Stuart, please…"

"I had hoped Maria would have been here today," Stuart says bitterly. "I knew that if Maria was here, you would come right away."

My heart clenches at the mention of Maria's name. "I still came, though," I say in a small voice. "See, I'm here." I'm hoping that our meager tac team is in place, already moving this way.

"Yes, but if Maria was here and I had a gun to her head, what would you do, Meg?" Stuart asks.

I look at Stuart in disbelief, but choose my words carefully. "I would do just what I'm doing right now, Stuart, try to talk with you, try and help you," I say when what I want to say is, *If you had a gun to my daughter's head I would blow your fucking head off, you crazy son of a bitch.*

Stuart snorts and shakes his head. "No, you wouldn't, Meg." He taps the barrel of the gun on the top of P.J.'s head.

"If you shoot him, you will go to prison for the rest of your life," I say. "Kid killers aren't real popular in prison, Stuart."

"You and I both know I'm not coming out of here alive, Meg. The only good thing that will come out of it is that you get to live with the knowledge that the death of these kids and their teacher is all because of you." The magnitude of what Stuart is saying crashes down on me. He lured me here. He lured me into this classroom, would kill as many of the hostages as he could before I could get to my weapon.

"Why?" I say again helplessly, all the while trying to think of a way to take him out before he got his first shot off.

"Because I can," he answers coldly.

Augie

I climb up to the vent near the ceiling using the shelves screwed into the closet walls as stair steps. "Hand me a pair of scissors," I tell Lucy, and she digs through a box on one of the shelves until she finds one and passes it up to me. I'm trying to unscrew one of the four bolts that hold the cover on the vent when I hear the man say something about killing the kids and I drop the scissors to the ground. Lucy quickly picks them up and hands them back to me.

"What are you doing?" she asks.

"We're going to hide you in there," I tell her. She looks at me doubtfully. "Listen, if he opens up that door and is pointing a gun, you're going to want to be up here." She nods and I start unscrewing the bolt again with the scissor tip. The bolts loosen more easily than I thought they would and in just a few minutes I have all four unscrewed. "I'm going to pull the cover off the vent and hand it to you. You think you can grab it from me?" I ask.

She nods and I hand her the vent cover. "Climb up here with me, Lucy." She looks at me doubtfully but carefully uses each shelf as a stepping-stone until she is standing next to me. "I'll give you a boost in and, whatever you do, don't come out until I tell you to."

"You're not coming in, too?" she asks. "Please come with me," she begs.

"We both won't fit," I tell her. "You'll be safe, I promise. He won't waste time looking up here for you." Lucy gives me a long, sad look, but does as I ask and pulls herself into the dark, dusty vent until I can only see the bottom of her tennis shoes. "I won't put the cover on, Lucy. I'll just move this stack of papers in front so he won't see you, okay?"

"Okay," comes her scared voice.

"Remember, stay put until you know it's safe." I push a pile of colorful construction paper in front of the open vent. I climb down, trying to listen to what is going on in the classroom. It's quiet. Too quiet. Somehow I have to get to P.J. I twist the knob and throw my body against the door and the chair moves just a bit.

From above me in the vent, Lucy is calling, "What's happening?"

"It's okay, don't worry," I tell her, lying flat on the floor to peek beneath the narrow opening at the bottom. I can't really see anything, just the chair legs. I look around the closet. There has to be something I can use to get out of here. In the corner I see a long, thin, wooden meter stick and grab it. Sliding the stick beneath the door, I try to shove it against one of the chair legs. The chair slides forward, just a little bit, away from the door. I do the same to the other leg and it moves, just a centimeter. Using the stick and going back and forth I shove at the legs until I see the chair nearly tip over but then land upright, just a few inches away from the door. Carefully

I try the knob; it turns and the door bumps into the chair, but it isn't blocked anymore. All I have to do is push it all the way open and I'll be out of the closet and back in the classroom with P.J.

Will

"Don't move," came the voice from behind Will. "Drop the gun, put your hands over your head and turn around slowly."

"I'm just trying to find my grandkids," Will explained, but he did as he was told.

"Jesus," the officer said once he could clearly see Will's face. "Mr. Thwaite, what the hell are you doing?" It was Kevin Jarrow, one of the part-time officers on the Broken Branch police force. Will went to lower his hands but Jarrow kept his gun aimed at him. "Keep your hands up," he ordered.

"I'm just trying to find P.J. and Augie," Will tried to explain. "Augie called my daughter from inside of the school. She heard a gun go off." Will looked at Jarrow imploringly. "I couldn't stand it—I had to find out what was going on."

"That's exactly what we're trying to do and we don't need any interference. Jesus, I could have shot you." Jarrow bent over and picked up Will's shotgun from the ground, emptied the barrel of bullets and dropped them into his pocket.

"Really, Kevin, I meant no harm. But I have to get my grandchildren out of that school," Will said, allowing Officer Jarrow to pat him down. Satisfied that he didn't have any other weapons, Jarrow led him back to a squad car, settled him into the backseat and told him to stay put. "I don't want to cuff you, Mr. Thwaite, but I will. I need to focus my attention on the school and can't waste my time babysitting you, got it?" he said severely.

Will nodded miserably. "I'm sorry."

Jarrow softened his voice. "Just stay out of trouble. We're doing all we can to get everyone out of the school safely." He soundly shut the car door and left Will sitting alone, helplessly trying to look out windows that were thickly covered with snow, blocking his view of the school.

Will's phone vibrated. Seeing that it was Marlys, he was tempted to ignore the call, but knew that he couldn't do that to his wife. She was just as scared and starved for news as he was. He just didn't know how he was going to tell her that he had nearly been arrested for trying to break into the school with a shotgun and had no information on her grandchildren. "Hello," he said, trying to infuse confidence into his voice.

"Dad?" came a tearful voice, and Will's stomach plummeted. "Please tell me Augie and P.J. are okay."

Mrs. Oliver

Mrs. Oliver pulled the heavy stapler slowly toward her, its heft a comfort beneath her hand. This was her last chance, she figured. If she could distract him just for a second, she knew that Officer Barrett would be able to reach her gun and put an end to this terrible day, maybe even put an end to this terrible man.

With difficulty Mrs. Oliver raised herself first on her elbows, then her knees. Her first thought was to swing the stapler as hard as she could to knock the gun from his hand, but she wasn't sure she had the strength to disarm him.

"Stuart," Officer Barrett pleaded, "let P.J. go. You don't have to kill innocent people to get what you want. You want to commit suicide? Just point the gun at your own head. You don't need me to shoot you."

It happened so quickly, Mrs. Oliver didn't even have time to flinch. The man turned and without hesitation pulled the trigger. The stapler dropped from her fingers and she was thrown backward from the impact. Sprawled out on her back, Mrs. Oliver looked down curiously at her hand, which had suddenly become useless, and at the stream of blood pumping from her arm. Just as quickly, the man turned away from her and aimed the gun at P.J.'s head. "No," she tried to shout, but her mouth had finally stopped working, her unhinged jaw frozen in place. She closed her eyes against the impending gunshot. She was so sorry and her only comfort was that she would be there, in death, to guide the children into the light or wherever it was they were going to go.

The sound wasn't as loud as she thought it would be, but muffled and far-off sounding. She hoped, rather absurdly, that maybe this meant that the gunshot wouldn't have hurt so much for P.J. as it did for her.

Augie

I trip as I push open the door and as I'm falling I see the man holding a gun to P.J.'s head. I try to call out to him, but my voice catches in my throat as I fall to the floor. I hear Lucy's screams echoing from out of the vent. The man turns and points the gun toward me and I see the surprise on his face. I cover my head with my hands and the sound of another gunshot explodes in my ears. Suddenly I can't seem to hear anything but the ringing in my ears and when I dare to look around for P.J. all I can see is blood everywhere.

Holly

I've calmed down enough for the nurses to leave me alone and I finally convinced my mother to give me her phone. "Dad?" I say again, and at his silence I know things are anything but okay. "Please," I beg.

My father clears his voice before speaking. "I don't know anything else, Holly. I've tried to find out exactly what's going on, but no one's telling me anything. I'm so sorry." I crumple as his voice cracks.

There are no words spoken as we both cry for a minute. I don't think I've ever heard my father cry before, never heard him sound so helpless. "Tell me about them," I finally whisper. "Tell me what I've missed."

My father sniffles a few times and when he speaks his voice is thick and filled with emotion. "Oh, Hol, you've got the best kids," he begins, and I lean back into my pillow and nod into the phone as he talks. Yes, I do, I think. I really do.

Meg

The second that Stuart turns away from me, I reach into my holster to pull out my Glock. I see Maria's teacher fly backward as a bullet rips through her shoulder. By the time Stuart turns back toward P.J., I'm shouting for the kids to get down and P.J. instantly drops to the floor and scurries behind the teacher's desk. A noise comes from behind Stuart and for a brief instant Stuart pauses; his head turns toward the sound and Augie Baker stumbles from the closet. Stuart has the girl in his crosshairs and without hesitation we both take aim and pull our triggers.

Will

"You should have seen P.J.'s eyes when he saw the calf drop," Will told Holly while he sat in the back of the locked squad car, chuckling at the memory. "That kid could easily be a large-animal vet."

"Or a farmer," Holly said softly.

"Could be," Will agreed, unable to conceal the pleasure in his voice at the idea of P.J. raising cattle one day. "And that Augie," Will went on. "Hasn't eaten one bite of meat since she came here. But smart as a whip. Her teacher told me last week he's never seen a more talented writer than Augie."

"Really?" Holly asked. "He said that?"

"He sure…" Will paused. "Wait a sec, Hol. Something's happening."

"Don't hang up, please don't hang up," Holly begged. "Tell me what's going on?"

"I'm not sure, I can't tell. Hold on." Will pounded on the window, hoping to knock snow from the glass so he could see.

"What's going on?" He heard Holly crying through the phone. "Please, Dad, tell me what's happening," she whimpered.

The snow that clung to the window fell away at his pounding and he could see a flurry of activity at the front of the school. Police officers racing into the school with guns drawn. "Dear God," Will whispered.

"Dad!" Holly shouted. "Dad, please!"

Will raised the phone back to his face. "It's nothing, Holly. False alarm." There was silence except for Holly's soft sobs. "Yeah, and Mr. Ellery said Augie should be in advanced placement classes when she gets to high school," Will went on calmly as a stretcher carrying Evelyn Oliver emerged from the building. "Plus, I was thinking, maybe if you'd like to spend some time here this summer, P.J. might like to show a calf at the county fair. He's got a doozy picked out. A beaut of a Hereford."

Holly sniffed. "Maybe. I think P.J. would really like that."

"Yeah, I think so, too," Will said as two children stepped out of the school into the gray dusk. Not P.J. He held his breath. "I think that Augie would have fun at the fair, too. Maybe she'd like to raise some rabbits." The door opened again and three police officers appeared. A struggling figure squirmed in their grasps.

"P.J.," Will breathed with relief. "It's P.J."

"Thank God." Holly wept. Then, after a moment, "Where's Augie?"

Augie

I touch my face and when I look at my fingers they are covered with blood. A lot of blood, but I don't feel any pain. I've heard of that happening, it's the shock. I wonder if I'm going to die. I squeeze my eyes shut and think of my mom. She's going to be so sad. She won't have anyone left except my grandparents and suddenly I hope more than anything that she forgives my grandpa. Then someone is at my side and I decide I'm not going to die quietly. I start kicking and screaming. "It's okay, it's okay!" a man shouts. "I'm the police!" I stop moving and yelling and dare to open my eyes. A policeman with the biggest mustache I've ever seen is standing over the top of us. "It's all over now. You're safe. Stay down. We want to check you over, okay?"

I ignore him and jump to my feet. "P.J.?" I can hardly say his name, I'm so dizzy. I don't see him anywhere. The officer holds on to my arm, trying to keep me from falling over.

"P.J.'s safe, he's already out of the building. We'll take you right to him once we check you over. Now lie back down."

I look around the classroom. There is blood everywhere. "No need to look at that, now," the policeman says, trying to block my view. I can't help it; I sit right down again on my butt and start to cry. Hard.

Will

W ill watched helplessly through the squad car window as P.J. continued to fight the officers as they led him out of the school. "Holly, let me call you back," he told his daughter.

"Don't you dare hang up, Dad," Holly cried. "If you ever loved me, you will not hang up that phone."

Will blinked in surprise. He never once believed that his daughter doubted his love for her. It was always the other way around. Will never could quite figure out what he needed to do to garner his daughter's respect, her love. "I won't hang up, Hol," he promised. "Hang on, I'm going to set the phone down on the seat, see if I can get someone's attention." Will laid down the phone carefully and once again began to pound on the squad car window. "Hey," he yelled at a sheriff's deputy who was passing by. "That's my grandson!" The deputy looked at him quizzically. "My grandson," Will repeated, pointing at P.J., who was still trying to get back into the school.

The deputy consulted with Officer Jarrow, who came over and released Will from the locked car. "P.J." Will rushed over to his grandson, who buried his face in his grandfather's stomach. "P.J.'s okay," Will told Holly. "He's right here."

"Thank God," Holly cried. "Can I talk to him?" Will passed the phone to P.J. and grabbed the arm of an officer who was hurrying by.

"I'm looking for my granddaughter, can you help me?"

"Sorry, sir." The officer shook his head. "We've got hundreds of kids to reunite with their folks. Just be patient."

Over the officer's shoulder Will saw the front door of the school open once again and Augie's crimson head and tearstained face appeared. A small, equally frightened-looking girl was at her side. Will's heart clenched when he saw the bloody cloth pressed to her head, the smears of blood on her face, hands and clothes. Augie's frantic eyes settled on her grandfather and then on P.J.

Will reached for the phone in P.J.'s hand and in a trembling voice spoke to his daughter. "Augie's okay, Hol. She's right here with us."

Will reached out for his granddaughter. "It's okay, Augie," he said gently, pulling her into his arms. "It's time to get you home."

Meg

Thank God Stuart was never much of a hunter. He missed Augie, but the shot hit the floor, sending sharp fragments into her face. She needed a few stitches but was just fine. Though I wouldn't recommend it, the fact that Augie finagled her way out of the closet distracted Stuart just enough that I could take him down. My shots were better, though not by much. My first shot took his left ear off and my second hit him in the ribs. Not enough to kill him, but the way he was crying and writhing around I knew it hurt like hell. Served him right.

In my mind there were many heroes that day and I wasn't one of them. The students in Mrs. Oliver's classroom showed more bravery than any child should ever have to. Augie Baker was determined to get to her brother despite placing herself in great danger. She also had the presence of mind to get the little girl who was locked in the closet with her up and into the vent in order to keep her safe. Except for the fact that she was terrible at following orders, Augie would make a great police officer one day. But who am I to give lectures about following orders.

It took three officers to get P. J. Thwaite out of the classroom, down the steps and out of the school. He kept hollering for his sister, but we had to assess her injuries before we moved her. No matter that the officers promised him that someone would bring her out soon, he still carried on. It was a great relief to see both Augie and P.J. reunited with their grandfather. I even passed Twinkie, the Craggs' dog, who had been camping out in the backseat of my cruiser, off to Mr. Thwaite. He would get her to the Cragg girls. A small consolation after the suicide of their father, but a comfort.

Mrs. Oliver's injuries were much more severe and by the time the EMTs got to her, she had lost a lot of blood and her breathing was shallow. I could tell just by looking at her pale face that it would be a miracle if she survived.

The eighth-grade teacher, Jason Ellery, was found in a janitor's closet with a large gash in his head, and the maintenance man, Harlan Jones, was found tied up in the boiler room. There were a lot of traumatized kids, but except for Evelyn Oliver, no one else was seriously injured.

Tim, hearing about the lockdown on the news, told his mother and Maria that he was called into work so as not to worry them. Instead, ignoring the abysmal road conditions, made his way to Broken Branch to see what was going on at the school and to see if he could be of help to the other emergency workers when his car slid on the ice and flipped into a ditch. Thankfully, Will Thwaite and Daniel Tucker came upon the accident, finding Tim. He spent a few days at the hospital over in Conway, has a few broken bones and a concussion, but he's going to be okay. He's going to stay with me and Maria until he's back on his feet again.

Even though we were confident that Stuart was working alone, it took hours to sweep the building to make sure
no other gunmen were present and that all the kids and staff
were accounted for. By the time Stuart's gunshot wounds
were treated and he was transferred to the county jail, we had
learned a lot more about his very rapid downward spiral. Stuart, in the end, turned out to be a cheater, a liar and a murderer. Boy, can I pick 'em. I'll never know if Stuart purposely
targeted me in order to get inside information on the Merritt
rape case and to get access to Jamie Crosby, but it wouldn't
surprise me. After reading the article he wrote chronicling
the rape and talking to Jamie, it was clear that the story was
wrought with inaccuracies and downright lies. I made a few
phone calls and it came to light that many of Stuart's stories,
after very close scrutiny, were nothing more than the products
of his imagination and ambition. Case in point was the article
he wrote as a result of the time he was supposedly embedded
with the Iowa Army National Guard Unit. When asked, no
one could actually verify that he was where he said he was
and no one could recall the supposed forbidden love affair between Specialist Rory Denison and the young Afghani girl.
In fact, there was no evidence, anywhere, that proved there
was a young woman.

The morning of the standoff there was a full article, along
with a file photo of Stuart receiving his Pritchard-Say Prize,
in the *Des Moines Observer* describing Stuart's fake stories and
subsequent firing, and that must have completely sent him
over the edge. His wife's body was discovered soon after Stuart was apprehended. She wasn't the perfect little wife who
would stand by her man, so he killed her, before moving on
to the school. I disrupted his almost perfectly executed scheme
of making up news stories to further his career, pad his wallet
and stroke his ego. Once that all collapsed, he went after me

in the way that he knew would hurt me the most. He went to Maria's school and lured me there in hopes of holding her life over my head. He would kill Maria, then himself and leave me shattered and alone. If all worked the way he had planned, he would be the biggest news story that Iowa has seen in a long time, even in death. Instead, he is sitting in jail, sans one ear, awaiting trial. Somewhere along the way Stuart had lost his soul. I'm hoping that I'll get a chance to talk to him, try and find out exactly why he did what he did. How he changed from this likable, even lovable man, to a liar and cheater, to a murderer.

As for me, I'm hopeful that I'll still have my job after disobeying Chief McKinney by going into the school on my own. Once the kids were safely out of the building and the ambulances had left, one carrying Mrs. Oliver, the other Stuart, the chief told me that was the most stupid-assed thing one of his officers had ever done. Then he gave me a big hug. There were hours of questions to be answered and mountains of paperwork to be completed. A small price to pay. But I think I'll be okay. After all, I did take the bad guy down.

Mrs. Oliver

Mrs. Oliver was confused, which she thought was entirely unfair since her church-going mother and father had promised that when she reached the gates of heaven everything would be illuminated, all of life's mysteries solved. First of all, she thought it would be warmer, that her surroundings would be bathed in a golden light. However, she was shivering, and when she opened her eyes, instead of seeing her deceased mother or father, George or even P.J., who she thought was most certainly dead, Mrs. Oliver found Cal standing over her. "Oh, he killed you, too," she tried to say but found that she had no voice.

"Your jaw is wired shut," Cal told her as he gently touched her cheek. "You're in the hospital. You've been asleep for nearly two days. He shot you in the shoulder, too, but you're going to be okay." At the troubled look in her eyes, Cal squeezed her uninjured arm. "The kids are okay. The officer shot him before he could hurt anyone else. Georgiana is here and the boys are on their way."

Georgiana leaned into her line of vision. "Hey, Mrs. Oliver," she said, smiling down at her mother with George's eyes. "You couldn't retire like everyone else, could you? You had to literally go out with a bang." Mrs. Oliver gave her daughter a hint of a smile and shrugged painfully.

"You took good care of those kids, Evie," Cal said as he pulled a chair up beside her bed. "All the parents are sending flowers and balloons, look." Cal gestured to a corner of the room where bouquets of sunny daffodils, spiky blue hyacinths and pink roses filled a small table, while silver Mylar balloons, emblazoned with get-well wishes, lazily bobbed overhead.

"Looks like Dad is going to have to give up his den so there's room to frame all the pictures and letters your students are sending you," Georgiana said, holding up a pile of papers. Mrs. Oliver shook her head sharply and a small grunt of pain escaped through the wires. She had so much she wanted to tell Georgiana, but couldn't. "I know, Mom," Georgiana said with a little laugh. "I know."

She was so very tired that all she could do was blink up at her daughter.

"You rest now, Evie," Cal whispered into her ear, and brushed his lips lightly against hers. "Go to sleep. We'll be waiting right here for you to wake up."

Mrs. Oliver felt her eyelids grow heavier and heavier and she wanted nothing more than to sink into a deep, dreamless sleep, but before she did, using her good hand, she lifted the sheet, peeked beneath and frowned at the hospital gown she was wearing.

"Don't worry, I didn't let them throw it away," Cal reassured her. "The nurses had to cut it off you. Georgiana washed it up the best she could, but you won't ever be able to wear it again." Mrs. Oliver nodded once to show her approval.

"Go to sleep now, Mom," Georgiana whispered, resting her lips briefly on her mother's forehead.

From outside the hospital window, Mrs. Oliver thought she could hear the soft plop of water from the dagger-sharp icicles that had clung to every eave in Broken Branch for the past four months. She could see that the snow had finally stopped and watery streams of sunshine struggled to breach the iron-fisted snow clouds that had softened to a dove gray. Mrs. Oliver smiled as the sweet scent of hyacinth filled her nose and she could almost feel the mild caress of a Chinook dance across her skin before she closed her eyes and slept.

★ ★ ★ ★ ★

ACKNOWLEDGEMENTS

As always, enormous gratitude goes to my agent, Marianne Merola, for her wisdom, guidance, attention to detail and her friendship. Thanks also to Henry Thayer for his behind-the-scenes support.

A thousand thanks to my editor, Miranda Indrigo, whose insights and suggestions are always spot on. Thanks also to all the folks at MIRA Books—especially Margaret O'Neil Marbury and Valerie Gray. I'm so proud to call MIRA my home.

Thank you to John and Kathy Conway and Howard and Shirley Bohr for opening up their homes and farms to me as I researched the novel. I always enjoy our time together.

Much appreciation goes to Mark Dalsing, whose advice in regard to police procedure and his early readings of the manuscript were invaluable.

A heartfelt thank-you goes out to my parents, Milton and Patricia Schmida, my brothers and sisters and their families, for their generous support and enthusiasm.

Much love and thanks to Scott, Alex, Anna and Grace—I couldn't do it without you.

If you loved *One Breath Away* don't miss

THESE THINGS HIDDEN

by bestselling author
Heather Gudenkauf

Read on for a preview!

Allison

I stand when I see Devin Kineally walking toward me, dressed as usual in her lawyer-gray suit, her high heels clicking against the tiled floor. I take a big breath and pick up my small bag filled with my few possessions.

Devin's here to take me to the court-ordered halfway house back in Linden Falls, where I'll be living for at least the next six months. I have to prove that I can take care of myself, hold down a job, stay out of trouble. After five years, I'm free to leave Cravenville. I look hopefully over Devin's shoulder, searching for my parents even though I know they won't be there. "Hello, Allison," Devin says warmly. "You all set to get out of here?"

"Yes, I'm ready," I answer with more confidence than

I feel. I'm going to live in a place I've never been before with people I've never met. I have no money, no job, no friends and my family has disowned me, but I'm ready. I have to be.

Devin reaches for my hand, squeezes it gently and looks me directly in the eyes. "It's going to be okay, you know?" I swallow hard and nod. For the first time, since I was sentenced to ten years in Cravenville, I feel tears burning behind my eyes.

"I'm not saying it will be easy," Devin says, reaching up and wrapping an arm around my shoulders. I tower over her. She is petite, soft-spoken, but tough as nails, one of the many things I love about Devin. She has always said she was going to do her best for me and she has. She made it clear all along that even though my mom and dad pay the bills, I'm her client. She's the only person who seems to be able to put my parents in their place. During our second meeting with Devin (the first being when I was in the hospital), the four of us sat around a table in a small conference room at the county jail. My mother tried to take over. She couldn't accept my arrest, thought it was all some huge mistake, wanted me to go to trial, plead not guilty, fight the charges. Clear the Glenn family name.

"Listen," Devin told my mother in a quiet, cold voice. "The evidence against Allison is overwhelming. If we go to trial, chances are she will be sent to jail for a very long time, maybe even forever."

"It couldn't have happened the way they said it did." My mother's coldness matched Devin's. "We need to make this right. Allison is going to come home, graduate and go to college." Her perfectly made-up face trembled with anger and her hands shook.

My father, who had taken a rare afternoon away from his job as a financial adviser, stood suddenly, knocking over a glass of water. "We hired you to get Allison out of here," he shouted. "Do your job!"

I shrank in my seat and expected Devin to do the same.

But she didn't. She calmly set her hands flat on the table, straightened her back, lifted her chin and spoke. "My job is to examine all the information, look at all the options and help Allison choose the best one."

"There is only one option." My father's thick, long finger shot out, stopping inches from Devin's nose. "Allison needs to come home!"

"Richard," my mother said in that unruffled, irritating way she has.

Devin didn't flinch. "If you don't remove that finger from my face, you might not get it back."

My father slowly lowered his hand, his barrel chest rising and falling rapidly.

"My job," she repeated, looking my father dead in

the eye, "is to review the evidence and choose the best defense strategy. The prosecutor is planning to move Allison from juvenile to adult court and charge her with first-degree murder. If we go to trial, she will end up in jail for the rest of her life. Guaranteed."

My father lowered his face into his hands and started crying. My mother looked down into her lap, frowning with embarrassment.

When I stood in front of the judge—a man who looked exactly like my physics teacher—even though Devin prepared me for the hearing, told me what to expect, the only words I heard were *ten years*. To me that sounded like a lifetime. I would miss my senior year of high school, miss the volleyball, basketball, swimming and soccer seasons. I would lose my scholarship to the University of Iowa, would never be a lawyer. I remember looking over my shoulder at my parents, tears pouring down my face. My sister hadn't come to the hearing.

"Mom, please," I whimpered as the bailiff began to lead me away. She stared straight ahead, no emotion on her face. My father's eyes were closed tightly. He was taking big breaths, struggling for composure. They couldn't even look at me. I would be twenty-seven years old before I was free again. At the time, I wondered if they would miss me or miss the girl they wanted me to be. Because my case initially began in juvenile court, my name couldn't be released to the press. The same day it was waived into adult court, there was massive flash flooding just to the south of Linden Falls. Hundreds of homes and businesses lost. Four dead. Due to my father's connections and a busy news day, my name never hit the papers. Needless to say, my parents were ecstatic that the good Glenn name wasn't completely tarnished.

I follow Devin as she leads me to her car, and for the first time in five years I feel the full weight of a sun that isn't blocked by a barbwire-topped fence. It is the end of August, and the air is heavy and hot. I breathe in deeply and realize jail air doesn't really smell any different than free air. "What do you want to do first?" Devin asks me. I think carefully before I answer. I don't know what to feel about leaving Cravenville. I've missed being able to drive—I'd had my license for less than a year when I was arrested. Finally, I'll have some privacy. I'll be able to go to the bathroom, take a shower, eat without dozens of people looking at me. And even though I have to stay at a halfway house, for all purposes I'll be free.

Read all about it...

MORE ABOUT THIS BOOK

MORE ABOUT THE AUTHOR

Read all about it...

QUESTIONS FOR YOUR READING GROUP

1. *One Breath Away* is set in a sudden snow storm. What role does the weather play in the story, both literally and metaphorically?

2. Stuart asks "What kind of town is this? Doesn't anyone know who their father is?" What role do fathers play in *One Breath Away*? Discuss the different relationships between fathers and children.

3. Discuss the influence of the small-town setting on the characters.

4. *One Breath Away* is told from multiple points of view. What do we learn about the characters from the perspective of their families? What do we learn about Holly from her father? About Augie from her grandfather? About Mrs Oliver from Cal?

5. The gunman in the story poses a physical threat to the children in Broken Branch and several characters are determined to protect the children—Mrs Oliver, Meg, Augie. In what other ways do characters try to protect each other? How do they succeed? How do they fail?

6. On the day the gunman arrives in the school, Will is awaiting the birth of the calves. How are the seasons and the cyclical nature of life evoked in this novel?

Read all about it...

INTERVIEW WITH
HEATHER GUDENKAUF

What was the genesis for *One Breath Away*?

The idea for *One Breath Away* has evolved
over many years. When I was a senior at the
University of Iowa a disgruntled former student
entered a classroom with a gun, killed five and
gravely injured a sixth person before turning
the gun on himself. At the time of the shooting I was with my roommate near the centre of
campus. A beautiful, gentle snow started falling,
transforming the campus into a winter wonder-
land and in the distance we heard sirens. Very
quickly we learned of the tragedy and hurried
back to our dorm where we called friends and
family to assure them that we were safe. When
an event like this happens so close to home it
can change how you see the world and has the
potential of shattering one's sense of security.
I often think of that terrible day and wonder
what I would have done, how I would have
reacted if I had been in that classroom.

There have also been many high-profile campus
and school shootings—Columbine, Virginia
Tech, West Nickels Mine—that have left us
reeling and struggling with the question of how
events like this can happen at our schools and
universities with whom we entrust our children.
One Breath Away explores this issue and how
the fallout of one such event can draw together
and wrench apart a community. That said, as
an educator of twenty years, our school systems
and law enforcement have worked tirelessly to
put into place policies and procedures that go a
long way to ensure the safety and security of all
students.

Read all about it...

In addition to your career as a writer, you have also spent many years as a teacher and a consultant within the education system. How did your background as an educator influence this novel?

I come from a long line of teachers and from a family that values education. Over the years I have also been fortunate to work with several wonderful school systems and have had the opportunity to meet some amazing educators. Mrs Oliver, the third grade teacher in *One Breath Away*, embodies many of the characteristics I have come to admire in my fellow educators: dedication, high expectations, a true desire to see the children they work with become better students and better people. The educators I know, like Mrs Oliver, work tirelessly planning lessons, spend their own money on classroom supplies and books, go to sleep worrying about other people's children, and would willingly put themselves in harm's way to keep their students safe.

You often write about children or young adolescents. What do you find appealing about this stage of life?

I think that children are so wise, much more than we often give them credit for. Time and time again, as both a mother and educator, I am reminded of this. The adolescents I've encountered are accepting of others, passionate about worthwhile causes, and want so badly to make a difference. They are caring, have a great capacity for empathy and still have to be tough and world-wise. No easy feat. We expect so much from our children and they rise to the occasion. I look around at the upcoming generation and I smile. I think we are in good hands.

Every person in town is affected by the presence of the gunman in their school. Talk about your decision to set this book in a small town.

I love small towns and to me there is something almost magical about them. By setting *One Breath Away* in the fictional town of Broken Branch, Iowa, I wanted to illustrate the familiarity and sense of camaraderie often found in small communities. This same feeling of solidarity can be shaken during catastrophic events, but more often than not, communities are brought together. I also think that there is often a perception that in small towns everyone knows the intimate details of their neighbours' lives, that there are no secrets. As the reader quickly learns, this couldn't be further from the truth. As within our own towns and communities, there are many secrets behind the shuttered windows of Broken Branch and we never really know what's going on behind closed doors.

OBA is set in the midst of a sudden snow-storm. Where did this idea come from?

This is one of the great things about living in Iowa; the weather can change in a minute. It can be sixty degrees and sunny one day and the next, a raging blizzard. In *One Breath Away*, the unexpected spring snowstorm exemplifies how quickly life can change. One moment we are carrying out our usual, often mundane, daily routines and then out of the blue comes an earth-shattering, life-changing event in the form of an accident, an illness, a natural disaster. These are the reminders for all of us to, in ordinary, quiet moments, gather our loved ones close and tell them how we love and appreciate them.

Read all about it...

OBA tells the story of a small town from five different points of view. How did you develop the individual voices for this story?

Before I even put pen to paper, I begin to develop each character as fully as possible within my mind. I imagine what the character looks like, sounds like, the way she moves, the expressions on her face. I then jot down details about each character, birthdates, favorite colours, prized possessions, the pets they had while growing up. I write down anything I think might help me as the novel progresses. I really love getting inside the minds of each of the main characters and discovering why they make the decisions they make and why they say the things they do. I also enjoy the challenge of writing in this manner—trying to make each character's voice sound unique and authentic.

OBA is like a puzzle, with each of the five narrators providing important pieces of the full picture. How did you decide upon the structure of the story?

The events that unfold in *One Breath Away* occur rapidly within approximately an eight-hour time span. Each character, through thoughts, words and actions gives his or her account of one harrowing day. Each perspective is uniquely framed by the individual character's memories and experiences. My hope was to give the reader a glimpse into how a teacher, a child, a mother, a grandfather, and a member of law enforcement might react to the same terrible incident.

This is your third novel. How has your writing process changed and developed?

I've learned so many lessons about myself and my writing over the past few years. I still begin each of my novels by buying a journal or

Read all about it...

notebook and writing the first fifty pages or so of the story in longhand. I've learned that it's possible to write just about anywhere—in the car, in a hospital waiting room, at the edge of a creek. The important thing for me is to get my thoughts and ideas down on the paper. I know that I can always revisit and revise what I've written.

While I begin a new project with a sense of knowing where I want the story to go, very often the characters will take me in new, surprising directions. I've also learned that it is so important to follow my instincts, to write the kinds of books that *I* would enjoy reading.

Sometimes, one small mistake can have life-altering consequences…

One blistering summer's day, Ellen Moore takes her eyes off her baby.

Not for very long, just for a few seconds. But this simple moment of distraction has repercussions that threaten to shatter everything Ellen holds dear.

Powerful and emotionally charged, *Little Mercies* is about motherhood, justice and the fragility of the things we love most.

'Totally gripping' —*Marie Claire*

'Her technique is faultless' —*Sunday Express*

One innocent child
A secret that could destroy his life

Imprisoned for a heinous crime when she was a just a teenager, Allison Glenn is now free.

Shunned by those who once loved her, Allison is determined to make contact with her sister. But Brynn is trapped in her own world of regret and torment.

Their legacy of secrets is focused on one little boy. And if the truth is revealed, the consequences will be unimaginable for the adoptive mother who loves him, the girl who tried to protect him and the two sisters who hold the key to all that is hidden…

HARLEQUIN®MIRA®
www.mirabooks.co.uk

**'Two little girls are missing. Both
are seven years old and have been
missing for at least sixteen hours.'**

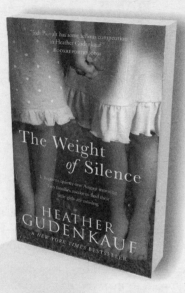

Sweet, gentle Callie suffers from selective mutism.
Petra Gregory is Callie's best friend and her voice.
And both have disappeared.

Now Callie and Petra's families are bound by the
question of what has happened to their children.
As support turns to suspicion, it seems the answers
lie in the silence of unspoken secrets.

Your future is within your grasp. How far are you willing to go?

Gina Higgins is on a desperate journey across the country to save her daughter. Armed only with an old diary, she must find the Kiss River lighthouse that holds the answers she so urgently needs.

But the lighthouse has been destroyed by a hurricane and the key to Gina's future is buried under the ocean.

Now she must uncover the secrets hidden within the diary, a Second World War love story that has the power to change her life forever…

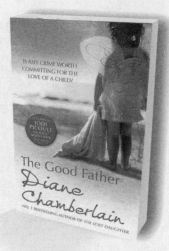